DESPERATION

Carol-Anne stood at the Lord and Taylor register listening to the blips and beeps the machine was making. Sweat trickled down her back, a fine dampness glistening on her brow.

Nadia needed a new winter coat, bad-weather boots, underwear, clothes for school. Carol-Anne didn't know if Max had canceled the Lord and Taylor charge card. So she stood there, sweating, tense.

The silence seemed infinite. She became aware of people moving around her and the etched ecru ceiling above. With a flick of the wrist, the sales clerk whisked out the receipt for Carol-Anne to sign. Her hand shook as she signed. A bead of sweat ran for freedom d

At the end state-ment. He wou ninety-three dollars dren's department. C out it now. Her miss

Her daughter had clothes.

"Margaret Johnson-Hodge brings a sassy, witty and contemporary edge to a novel that explores the ups and downs of love . . . Add Ms. Johnson-Hodge to your list of auspicious debuts."
— Romantic Times *on* The Real Deal

A NEW DAY

MARGARET JOHNSON-HODGE

St. Martin's Paperbacks

The poem "A New Day" copyright © 1988 by Darryl Holmes. Published by Meta Press. All rights reserved. Used by permission.

A NEW DAY

Copyright © 1999 by Margaret Johnson-Hodge.

ISBN: 0-312-96915-5

Printed in the United States of America

St. Martin's Paperbacks edition / April 1999

St. Martin's Paperbacks are published by St. Martin's Press, 175 Fifth Avenue, New York, NY 10010.

10 9 8 7 6 5

I dedicate this book to my all homegirls:

Brenda, I love you.

Audrey V. Lawrence, Leslie E. Lawrence, and Shannon Lawrence, who drove all over Georgia trying to find me. Words can't express how much I love you all. (Remember Mya Joy? Remember Bermuda, Head Mountain, and watching Isaac Hayes?)

Valerie Jean Jefferson Barnes Escoffery (Remember Central Park and our talks on the curb?)

Evelyn Richardson (Khalilah) (We Just Keep On Keepin' On)

Bettina Bellinger Stafford (Whatsa DOS?)

Millie Diaz Banrey (Remember Blow Pops, egg creams, and Winkie?)

Terrie Foster Russell (Remember waiting in the freezing cold for the Q65 bus after cheering our butts off?)

Cynthia Simmons (Remember watching the Earth, Wind & Fire tape and how that sax player played his horn? Did we ever stop screaming?)

Jeanette Fisher (The best maid of honor anyone could have)

Vivian Smith (From Margaret Johnson-Hodge-Evans-Cox-Pierson-Smith!)

Cynthia Rogers (My Harlem Sista by way of Queens)

Sherry Daniels Johnson (My favorite ex-teller)

Renee Wright-Hodge (Tanté Renee, you know I love you, girl)

Derrick Rhoden Stokely and Traci L. Johnson, because I promised.

And lastly to the men I love:

My hubby, Terence Anthony Hodge, who is still making my dreams come true

And my best friend, Georger Walter Xaverian Bellinger, Jr., who taught me how to laugh when I needed it most.

God bless all of you.

Acknowledgments

I want to thank Neeti Madan, who keeps my dreams going, and Glenda Howard, for her editorial skills which helped to make this book better.

A NEW DAY

this morning
on the train
i overheard an Asian woman
Sneeze
in her native tongue
and wondered
why we (Black People)
cannot even learn
to love each other

Chapter 1

Harlem on a winter night was a dismal place to be. Remnants from the last snowfall clung to curbs in mottled clumps of gray. Litter gathered in frozen heaps around trash cans and against metal sewer grates. Buildings once grand, now stripped of their cornices, crowns, and molding, loomed like dead colossi above the sidewalks.

Street lamps painted the streets in surreal strokes. Metal cans full of furnace ash looked like forgotten soldiers from some proletarian war. People moved about quick and urgent like lost souls in the darkness. There was no joy, no beauty, just disdain and hopelessness. It clung to Max like a body bag.

It was not a night for walking, but Max walked. His tall body bent, his strong shoulders withered. Despite the cashmere coat, fur-lined gloves, and wool scarf tucked around his neck, Max was cold.

The wind rushed him like a hurricane, stinging his face, nipping his ears. The bitter cold invaded his bones to the marrow. Max's regality was gone, his sense of self and purpose vanished. Everything he was had abandoned him.

Who am I? For a few minutes Max didn't know. He couldn't remember his corner office on the fifteenth floor of the Regor Building. Could not recall his title—director of mortgage, who he was—tall, handsome, and single. The color of his skin—

chocolate-brown, nor where he lived, West 158th Street.

For a few minutes Max didn't know anything but pain. It washed over him like a rough tide. He looked up, seeking answers. The universe blinked cold stars in his direction. *Why?* his heart shouted, but Max knew. His unwillingness to ask had bought him this grief and as a result four years of love had been annihilated.

Max hadn't been certain of anything. The only tangible he had was Samone's withdrawal and her announcement that she would be busy Saturday.

She had spoken of wanting to go shopping and do some real house cleaning. The stores were having a wonderful after-the-holiday sale and with New Year's Eve just around the corner, she needed to give her apartment a good cleaning.

"You know how much you hate tagging behind when I'm shopping, and when's the last time you helped me clean? I need Saturday for myself. We can get together Sunday," she'd insisted.

Not once during Samone's barrage had Max pressed her for the truth. He allowed her lies to eat at him most of the night till morning came and his conscience demanded that he stop her. That he call her and tell her not to do it. *Don't kill our baby.*

Max had suspected weeks ago. Samone's body had felt different, she was tired all the time and her pack-a-day cigarette habit had vanished overnight. He told himself that Samone was too smart to get caught. Still, a part of him braced himself for her announcement and her need to "run down to City Hall before the baby comes." A part of him had hoped Samone would do just what she'd done, but here in the cold darkness of the night, Max wanted to take it all back. Wanted the baby he could no longer have.

An hour ago Samone had stepped out of the cab, her face drawn and gray, the abortion draining her of life and color. Max had rushed to her, his tears coming quick. They had hugged outside her building. Her sorrow—"*Oh, Max*"—breaking his heart. Together they rode the elevator to her apartment. Samone went to take a shower and Max made her tea. Their conversation grew hostile quickly, accusations flying fast and furious around the room.

"*Christmas morning,*" Samone had yelled at him, "*that's when I decided. Hell of a day to choose, isn't it? I opened my gift and saw a bracelet. Knew you still didn't want to marry me and a baby would have made it worse.*"

Max swallowed. Another tear fell. He wiped his eye, studied the city night sky. A gust of wind rushed his back—move on. Max wiped his eyes one last time and quickened his pace; the cold winter night, no place to be.

The mules had been tossed so far back into the closet Max had to get down on his hands and knees and crawl to get to them. Behind him a black garbage bag sat filled with shoes, sneakers, perfume, and makeup. There were ankle socks, little lace panties, tampons, and nail polish. T-shirts, sweatpants, nightshirts, and a toothbrush. There was deodorant and body powders and glass vials of bath oils from the Body Shop; a black knit jersey dress, pantyhose, and a half-empty jar of Taster's Choice. These were Samone's possessions and Max had held on to them for too long.

It had been six months since they'd broken up and the memory of their last meeting still made Max's heart tremble. His mother had actually wept when she heard the news. She'd had such hopes for her son and Samone. Had envisioned half a dozen children with Samone's toasty brown skin and Max's Asiatic eyes. *They would have been beautiful*, Max's mother had muttered. *I would have had the prettiest little granbabies anybody ever saw*. It had been so close,

Momma, he had wanted to say. But his mother would not have understood and an explanation would have been too painful.

Max knew he needed a change and the first step was cleaning Samone's things out of his apartment. He tied the bag up tight and headed for the incinerator. Held the trapdoor open until he heard the garbage bag thump a final time. He left the tiny hot room and headed for his apartment.

The warmth of the day eased into his living room, brilliant sunlight dusting the floor like liquid gold. Max stood at the window gazing down into the world he had withdrawn from. Envy, profound and abrupt, rushed through him. Suddenly he wanted to be down there, out there, with people, going places and doing things. Samone was not coming back and Max would not ask her to return. That part of his life was over. It was time to start anew.

It was a good thing the world didn't revolve around Max because it would have stopped a long time ago. He was glad to see the pristine summer day was as potent as God could create. Was glad to see that the outside world had carried on fine without him.

He couldn't remember the last time he had ventured out with no destination in mind and pleasure on the brain. As he took in the sights of Amsterdam Avenue near 158th Street, his mind swirled with all the activity and the people.

Little children clutched mothers' hands, store owners stood outside their shops chatting in the warm breeze. Cyclists looked futuristic in shiny black spandex as they pedaled down the avenue, dodging buses and cars and pedestrians in their path. Music was in the air, a celebration of life in the making. Max lifted his face and inhaled; a warm breeze filled his lungs and gave life back into his soul. *Son, things gonna get better,* his father had told him. *There's gonna be a new day.* Max could only hope it would be soon.

Nadia McClementine, age eight, decided that the big dark man eating a rum raisin ice-cream cone in the Baskin Robbins store needed further investigation. Nadia had watched the man the whole time it took her mother to order two cones to go. A hot day, the wait was long.

Ice cream in hand, Mommy getting her change, what finally prompted Nadia to go up to him was the way he looked: kind of lost, kind of bewildered. It was a look Nadia had seen often enough.

Nadia, all of eight, had discovered Maxwell Scutter all alone on a hot Saturday afternoon. And in her discovery, Max met Carol-Anne McClementine.

"Hi, I'm Nadia, I'm eight years old."

"I'm Max."

"Is that rum raisin you eating?"

Max stared into the dark brown face, the liquid black eyes. Two pigtails pinned to the sides drew her eyebrows upward, giving her a quizzical look. He smiled cautiously, unnerved by the curious child before him. "Yes, in fact it is."

"My mom won't let me eat that. Says I'll get drunk and start acting silly."

"Nadia, leave that man alone." Neither Nadia nor Max had seen her come up. Suddenly she was there, one hand resting on her hip. Her gaze shot toward Max. She was clearly embarrassed. "I'm sorry," she said apologetically, corralling her daughter by the shoulder.

"No," Max offered, revealing much, "don't be."

They stared at each other. Mysteries unfolded in the seconds it took for Nadia to look up at her mother and back to Mr. Max.

Max extended his hand. Carol-Anne McClementine lifted her own.

"I'm Max."

"Carol-Anne," she replied, the mystery half solved.

The sun was high in the sky as they exited the ice-cream store. Amsterdam Avenue was full of activity as they strolled. The traffic island overflowed with pumpkin-yellow marigolds. It was a startling bit of beauty in otherwise dreary surroundings; a bit of brightness in a world dulled away by stone and concrete.

Despite knowing better, Max could not stop staring. Carol-Anne was not a striking woman, but there was a beauty to her. Five seven, her short hair auburn, with skin more sienna than beige, down South she'd have been called Red. Carol-Anne had wide hips and medium breasts. Max knew she'd never see size ten again but she was wearing her size twelve very well.

Carol-Anne, aware of Max's stare, looked straight ahead.

"She's your only child?" he inquired as casually as he could manage.

"Yes. Just one."

"I see . . . she's a beauty," Max went on to say, a wistfulness in his voice.

Carol-Anne risked a look at him, a quick drift of soft eyes his way. "Thanks." A small laugh escaped. "Motor mouth is what we call her."

"We?" Max asked, prepared for the worst.

"My family."

"Oh?"

"No, not like husband family. Y'know, aunts, uncles. Grandmother."

"Oh."

"How about you. Children?"

"No. No children. Single."

Carol-Anne's mouth went dry. "I see."

As far as dates went, it wasn't a date. He walked them to a bookstore near 151st and gave Carol-Anne his number. She took it, letting him know that she wasn't really looking for anything or anybody. Max said he understood but that didn't mean they had to end things. He truly enjoyed talking to her and Nadia. If ever she wanted to talk again, at least she'd have his number.

In the bookstore Nadia eagerly checked books, flipping happily through the illustrated pages. She found two that she really liked even though her mother said she could only get one. Nadia was ready to argue for getting both books when her mother spoke.

"Nadia. You were out of place today. You know that, don't you?"

"Yes, Mom."

"Well, if you know that, why'd you carry on so?"

"Because."

"Because what?

"I just saw him sitting there, eating ice cream and he had this look that reminded me of something."

Carol-Anne frowned. "Reminded you of something? What, honey?"

"You," Nadia answered, those luminous eyes piercing Carol-Anne's soul.

Sometimes, in the evening, with Nadia bathed and tucked in for the night, Carol-Anne would draw her feet up in her old wing chair and read. The view from her window only offered the building across the street, but if she craned her neck she could see the sky holding on to the peach and royal-blue colors that always arrived right before nightfall.

Sometimes she'd just sit, no book in her lap, and gaze out the window, enjoying the solitude of being alone. Enjoyed no noise, no children's questions, demanding adult answers. No need to praise every single scrap of childish artwork as if it were a Picasso, no need to tend to a scraped knee or mend a zipper.

Sometimes, late at night, Carol-Anne would put on her jazz station and have Loud Thoughts in her quiet time.

Loud Thoughts were old friends. Loud Thoughts had started nine years ago when she decided that she wanted a child, and wanting a child did not necessarily mean wanting a husband. Wanting a child simply meant: *my seed is gonna bear fruit.*

Wanting a child had meant saying goodbye to her married lover of five years. Wanting a child meant going off the pill and telling her married lover that she was leaving him but not that he was going to be a father.

These were Carol-Anne's Loud Thoughts. The kind that would pop up at the most inopportune moments. But Carol-Anne had put up with Loud Thoughts and her daughter never knowing her father because she wanted a child more than she wanted anything. Carol-Anne had been thirty and a day when Nadia was born.

There hadn't been anyone to tell her the flip side of this particular want: financial woes, change of lifestyle, and those uneasy questions: *Who's my daddy? What's a period? Why do you have breasts and I don't?* Loss of friends: *Can't you get a baby-sitter?* Loss of possible mates: *You have a daughter how old?* Not being able to just run out and buy a pair of eighty-dollar shoes, *Have to pay the baby-sitter this week.*

Rubbing pennies: *Sorry, baby. Mommy can't afford that Speak and Spell right now.* At the supermarket: *Seventy-three dollars? Oh, no. Well, take off that can of ravioli. And that pack of spareribs, too.* Rubbing pennies till they turned to gold: *Here's the twenty-five dollars for your school pictures . . . you like your new winter coat?*

Carol-Anne's fingers almost seemed green from rubbing so many pennies, and it was hard not being able to give Nadia all those things she wanted. It wasn't any fun eating that can of salmon that had been hidden behind three rows of food four weeks ago and now was the only protein in the house. Carol-Anne would take a trip to International House of Pancakes over pancakes from scratch any day of the week. But just buying a box of Aunt Jemima when her rent and utilities were due was difficult.

Carol-Anne did not enjoy washing panties and un-dershirts by hand night after night because she didn't have enough money for the Laundromat. There was no joy in turning the cushions over on her couch be-cause they had holes in them and she couldn't afford a new sofa right now. Nor did she like finding two pair of matching hose, cutting off the legs with runs, and wearing the good ones together. Or getting her next-door neighbor Tina to "touch up" her perm be-cause Carol-Anne didn't have the extra forty dollars for the beauty parlor.

She did not enjoy having men tiptoe around her place so as to not wake her daughter. Or having to rustle them awake at ungodly hours, such as four-thirty in the morning when they did stay over, before Nadia got up. There was no joy in sleeping on the old pull-out couch because she could only afford one bedroom and that was for Nadia.

The rewards? Hearing Nadia say *Momma* without ever saying *Da-Da*. The first tooth. Nadia's excellent grades and hearing her teachers rave. There were a lot of things Carol-Anne wanted, and possibly needed. But she had gotten wise when it came to needing. And by the grace of God, she was making it. Not in the style she wanted, but it was definitely a style all her own.

Carol-Anne did not believe in love at first sight, the luck of the lottery, or Guardian Angels. Carol-Anne did not believe in fate, destiny, or hope. You would never catch her tossing salt over her shoulder, avoiding the underbelly of a ladder, or fussing at anyone who opened an umbrella in her house.

Carol-Anne McClementine did not believe in miracles, fairy tales, or tall, dark, handsome men who would love her. Yet as she fingered the piece of paper with Max's number scribbled in haste, she couldn't help but consider the possibility.

Chapter 2

A date.

It had been too long, Max realized as he pulled a pair of pants from his closet and checked his cedar chest for his cotton sweater. Suddenly Max wasn't sure how much cologne to splash on, or whether to wear shoes or dress sandals. Didn't know if he should cut his toenails or leave them curled over the edge of his toes.

Suddenly Max didn't know a thing except that he couldn't wait to see Carol-Anne again. The idea excited him like nothing else had in a long time.

It took a few days for her to call, her voice unsure as she asked for him, laughter giving away her uncertainty. But if Carol-Anne was being cautious, Max was at the opposite end of the spectrum. There was a deep need to belong to someone again. Carol-Anne seemed like a good candidate.

Max felt like a teenager. Felt a giddy kind of sweet madness that rushed him through his dressing. Max knew as he locked his apartment door behind him that he was leaving too soon for their date, but nothing could keep him inside his apartment another second. He took the crosstown bus heading toward the East River and caught the bus going downtown. Then he walked the seven blocks to Carol-Anne's apartment on Pleasant Avenue and 121st. He took note of everything as he moved through Spanish Harlem, an area seemingly destined for collapse.

Drug dealing was rampant, the buildings were in ill repair. Dwellings so long ago forgotten and un-lived-in, it was a wonder no one had torn them down. Despair was everywhere Max looked.

He proceeded with caution as he navigated down the street, bypassing abandoned buildings, weed-strewn lots, and broken, misaligned sidewalks. It was so different from where he lived and he wondered about the people who called the area home.

Max checked building numbers, coming face-to-face with a tenement sandwiched between two build-ings of the same bland architecture. The lobby reeked of urine, the lock was broken, and what remained of the intercom hung from tattered exposed wires.

The hairs on the back of his neck went up.

The mailboxes had been gutted and the ceiling lights couldn't have been more than twenty-five watts. With no elevator in sight, Max began the climb up three flights of stairs. He was out of breath by the time he arrived at the dim cloistered landing. His skin prickled with a tight fear.

Max pushed the doorbell hoping it was working, wanting nothing more than to get out of the dark rank hall and safely behind Carol-Anne's apartment door. He was giving the bell a second try when her voice eased toward him.

"Who is it?"

"Max."

"Just a minute." A minute and half later, two deadbolts slid back and the door opened with a force-ful quiver. Too early, Max realized as he took in the yellow T-shirt and cut-off frazzled-end denim jeans.

"You're early," Carol-Anne stated, half annoyed, though a smile dusted her face.

Max nodded toward the space behind her which she seemed determined to conceal. "Can I come in?"

"Yeah, sure." She stepped away, pointing to her sofa. "Have a seat." Even from across the room Max knew the chocolate and off-white plaid couch was lumpy and lacked real support.

He made his way, by-stepping the bundled newspapers and a pair of sneakers. A lavender bike leaned against the TV. Two blankets and a faded comforter sat on top of a softwood wardrobe. Magazines were crammed under the belly of the TV cart. The water-stained coffee table overflowed with bric-a-brac and photo albums. Not an inch of baseboard was visible. Every bit of wall had something jammed against it.

There were cardboard boxes piled high with clothes, LPs, and encyclopedias stacked a foot tall. The wing chair near the gated window had split near the seam, revealing gray and black hair that looked uncannily human. The linoleum floor was so worn the paisley pattern had fatigued in places. An end table had a taped-up leg and its pumpkin-colored finish was mostly gone. There was a fine coat of dust on the TV, the old stereo, and the pictures on the walls.

Carol-Anne's apartment was a hovel.

As he looked at the dusty TV, the food-smeared coffee table, the curtains thick with dust, he knew he'd have to think hard about what he was getting into. It was one thing to be poor, but at least you could be neat. The living room looked as though it hadn't been cleaned in weeks.

The neat freak in him rose. Max felt the need to wipe the coffee table, tear down the drapes, throw out the newspapers, and dump every carton he could get his hands on. Max felt the need to rip up the linoleum and order a new hardwood floor. He had the urge to come in with a huge vacuum and suck everything out. He wondered if Carol-Anne's bad housekeeping extended to her personal appearance, wondered if he had made a mistake, when Carol-

Anne appeared, hair in place, makeup flawless, clothes smart and impressive.

"Da-daaah!" Carol-Anne said, offering magic.

"Oh, yeah," Max muttered, her transformation complete.

A soft warm breeze blew, carrying the sound of salsa, rap, and house music as they strolled down the congestion of Second Avenue near 122nd Street.

"Can I ask you something?" Carol-Anne began, bringing an end to the silence between them.

"Shoot."

"Are you seeing anybody else?"

He hadn't expected her to ask and it surprised him. "Mighty bold question," Max said, his footfalls measured.

Carol-Anne's voice became sharp and defensive. "There's just me and Nadia. That's all. I have certain responsibilities to both of us. You understand?"

"I think so."

"If I get involved with a man, it's going to have to be for real."

"Meaning?" Max asked, searching her face.

"My daughter is the center of my life. What affects me, affects her. If a man can't deal with both of us, then I can't use him."

"You always come off this strong?"

"Let's just say I earned my knocks the hard way . . . I don't like outside people disrupting my life in a way that could be bad for my daughter."

"I get your drift."

"Do you?"

"Yes. I do."

"And?"

Max could feel her stare, knew she was holding her breath awaiting his answer. He shrugged. "Guess we just have to see."

It wasn't the right answer. By the time they left the movie theater, they were hardly speaking.

At her door.

The key was in the lock and turning before Max could open his mouth.

Carol-Anne looked briefly over her shoulder. "Well, goodbye," and pushed the door to a shuddering open. She had one foot inside when she felt Max's hand on her arm.

"You just going to leave it like this?" Max asked, surprised at her coldness.

"Just like what, Max?" she asked, her back to him.

He turned her around, leaning in to make sure she could see his eyes. "You know what, Carol-Anne? You've had this serious attitude since we had that little talk."

He was crowding her and Carol-Anne resisted the urge to push him away.

"Max, I just told you how it has to be for me."

"Okay, I'll grant you that. But you really don't know me and you're already condemning me."

"Look, Max. Every time I meet a man, he's around a few weeks or a few months and then he's gone. It's not just me who gets hurt, Nadia gets hurt, too. I'm just not having it."

"But you don't even know me yet. How can you judge me?"

She raised her brow. "You're a man. That's all I need to know."

"Oh, I guess you're just about perfect, huh?" He saw the hurt flash in her eyes. Cooled his heels as his eyes softened, his voice lowered. "Look, I don't want this to be the end of something that just might be wonderful. I understand what you're saying about Nadia and I respect that. All I'm asking is, don't judge me without knowing what I'm capable of."

He had a point, but all men did. Carol-Anne sized

him up, gave an off-center smile. "You want to come on in for a little while?"

"Love to."

With the wine bottle empty and the night moving into early morning, Carol-Anne yawned so loudly her jaws cracked. "Oh, I'm sorry. Please forgive my manners."

Max looked at his watch. "It is getting late."

"Time flies," Carol-Anne offered, moving toward the turntable.

Max watched as she relieved the needle from the record. "You have a wonderful jazz collection. I tell you, I have CDs up to my elbows, but there's something about a vinyl record that's special, you know? I mean, I know with a CD you can program to hear any song in any order, but there's something to be said about going to a stack of albums, thumbing through them, and then sliding out that big old round piece of plastic and laying it on a turntable." Max paused, realized he was rambling. Shook his head.

"God, I know I must be tired."

"No, go ahead. I love a man who shares."

"I better quit now . . . got to be heading home."

Carol-Anne nodded. He could not stay the night.

"Want me to call you a cab?"

"A cab? No. I'll just walk over to Fifth and catch the bus."

"This time of night?"

"I was born and raised in the Bronx. Moved to Harlem when I was twenty-five. I'm a native. I know how to take care of myself."

"Obviously. Your mother raised you well."

Max's smile was quick. "What a nice thing to say."

"I say it as I see it."

"Yes, I noticed. But I like that."

Carol-Anne looked away from him, her mind

churning full speed with what could and couldn't be.
She didn't want him to go, but he could not stay. She
took up the empty bottle and the two glasses and
headed for her kitchen.

Max looked around him and rubbed his eyes as a
sweet weariness settled in his spine. Patting his pock-
ets for his keys and wallet, he slipped a token in his
jacket and headed toward the spill of light from the
kitchen. Carol-Anne was rinsing glasses when he got
there.

"I'm going to get ready to go."

The kitchen window was open, a soft breeze made
its way inside. Max listened for the roar of a bus or
the scream of a siren, but the air was hushed and
respectful of his mood.

He moved toward Carol-Anne, needing to be
closer to her. She accepted the arms that found her
and allowed herself to be held in his embrace. Their
bodies drifted in search of a good fit, drifted lazily in
a side-to-side motion. A longing, a soft heat, surrounded them. Seconds from crossing the fine line
Max released her. "I'm going," he said, putting her
at arm's length.

"Yes, you are," Carol-Anne responded, her eyes
full of caution.

An idea came to him. "The Black Cowboys are
going to be at Mount Morris Park. You think you
and Nadia would like to go?"

"Oh, Nadia would love that."

"Well, okay, then. I'll call you."

She nodded. "Come on, let me walk you to the
door."

"Do I get a kiss good-night?"

"I'll let you know when we get there."

With care Carol-Anne swung the door open, her
bright eyes looking away from him. *How I would
love to take you back to the living room and unfold
my raggedy-ass pull-out. How I would love to see*

*your face as I undress you, button by button, zip by
zip. See you naked, hard and wanting me as much as
I want you this second.*

*But I can't do that, Max. Can't even risk a kiss
because there's a burning fire inside of me that's too
hard to control.*

Carol-Anne kissed his cheek. "Thank you for a
wonderful evening, Max."

He smiled, carrying all her secrets. "I'm letting you
off easy this time."

She urged him through her door. "Go. Be safe."

"I will." And then he was gone.

As promised, Max took Carol-Anne and Nadia to see
the Black Cowboys. Then it was off to Sylvia's for
supper. Later they went across town to Nadia's
mother's place, where Nadia would stay the night.

Their last stop, Max's place.

Carol-Anne's mouth fell open the moment Max
opened his apartment door. Gilt-framed lithographs,
terra-cotta walls. Adobe pottery, mud-cloth tapestry.
Rich black leather seating, Persian rugs, sculptured
works of art. Everything was shiny, sparkling, and
looking all too new.

Carol-Anne had known he was in banking, had
known he worked in the mortgage department. That
his clothes appeared expensive and he had a wallet
full of credit cards, but that was all.

"Did you do this?" all she could ask as she slipped
out of her muddy sneakers and padded barefoot toward the sofa that looked butter soft.

"Yeah, I went out and picked out the furniture and
the artwork and stuff."

She touched a smooth metal sculpture that was
about four feet tall and must have weighed as much
as she did.

"Max, this is fabulous."

"Like it?" he asked.

"Oh, God, yes. How much did this cost?"

"A pretty penny, but it's insured."

Carol-Anne knew he worked at Chase in the mortgage department but that was all she knew. As her eyes danced around the smartly furnished apartment, she could not hold back her curiosity. "What do you do again?"

"I told you, I work in mortgage for Chase."

"No, I mean what is your title?"

He looked at her, his eyebrow rising. "Director of mortgage."

Carol-Anne blinked twice. "Did you say director?"

"Yeah. Sounds a whole lot sweeter than what it really is."

"Like you make over a hundred thousand dollars a year director?"

"Something like that."

Carol-Anne could only stare.

Max's bedroom . . .

Carol-Anne stood in the doorway, studying the arms opened wide toward her. It had been a while since she'd played this game, the moment of "will I or won't I?" even though the answer had been decided from the minute they left Nadia with her mother.

"Won't bite."

But somehow Carol-Anne sensed Max would. That he would dig his claws into her so deeply and so completely that she'd be forever changed when this night was through.

He was, in a word, everything she had wanted.

And the idea that she could have him was scaring her. The idea that this wealthy, fine, tall, dark, handsome, built, sweet, considerate, gentle, warm, princely black man two years her junior could be hers made her falter.

She had entered other men's beds and they in turn

had entered her own on a gauntlet that offered nothing to lose. Those other men had never been as perfect as Max. Had not moved her soul like the sight of him standing there in Calvin Klein jeans and a white cotton oxford shirt did.

The others did not have the chocolate Hershey Bar skin, the slinky Chinese eyes, or the mustache that brought tremors to her belly from just the thought of it grazing the insides of her thighs.

She did not know how she knew Max was a "downtown" man, but something about him told her that he had no fears or qualms about going south of her Mississippi, which was now flowing warm and wet as the river itself.

Carol-Anne knew Max wouldn't stand there forever with his arms out, would no doubt take her pausing as a sign that she did not want this, even if she did. With every beat of her quick heart Carol-Anne wanted to feel Max inside of her all hot, and heavy, and hard. She wanted all nine inches or whatever he measured so far inside of her that her uterus contracted twice in sweet anticipation.

Carol-Anne had no qualms about desired penis size. She liked her men big and thick and round and black, and even as she stood in the door, still pausing, her feet glued to the spot; she could see the rise in Max's pants that no doubt was contemplating her arrival.

As if to entice her, Max began undoing the buttons on his shirt, his fingers deft and fluid as each tiny white translucent button slid past the minutely stitched hole. She watched, her mouth dry, fascinated as Max slid the ends of his shirt out of the waist of his pants, as his arms ejected themselves from the sleeves of the oxford cloth, thick muscular biceps flexing, veins hard for her benefit.

He was seducing her.

Max tossed the white cotton shirt onto the black

leather easy chair. Grabbed the edges of his white
T-shirt and eased it slowly up his chest, revealing a
narrow waist, tight belly, and blackberry nipples
against rich chocolate skin.

Max stood there, his left leg supporting his weight,
his hips to the right, posing much like a model right
before the camera flashes.

Sexy.

His chest was well developed, two half-moons of
hardened mounds with nipples that pointed in her direction. Max unbelted his belt, unzipped his jeans, let
them fall to his feet, showing long muscled thighs
and, to her surprise, slightly bowed legs.

Very sexy.

His white briefs were cut low, hiding nothing, especially the thick slab of penis laid across his groin.

"Come here."

Carol-Anne went, feeling foolish and old and so
far from Max's world that it seemed ridiculous that
she was even there. Her body had flab and cellulite.
Her belly wasn't flat and smooth, but soft and spongy
to the touch. Her breasts did not sit high, but hung
down, nipples pointing toward her feet. Even her underwear was not sexy. Her bra was beige cotton, and
her panties were big old bloomers.

Carol-Anne longed for darkness.

She stood six inches from him, her eyes level with
his chest. The fine down of black hair called out to
her tongue to taste it and she did. Salty and warm.

She teased his nipple with prickly teeth, the smell
of Grey Flannel pitching her arousal level a touch
higher. With care Max relieved her of her sleeveless
mock turtleneck shirt, unsnapped the button of her
jeans, lowered the metal zipper. Carol-Anne found
herself standing in her cotton undies, jeans around
her feet.

She stepped out of them and Max took her hand.

Their destination, his king-sized navy blue satin-comfortered bed.

He eased her panties past her knees, a snail's trail of stickiness slicking her thigh. She wondered if he noticed the stretched-out elastic, Max's invitation catching her off guard.

He leaned over, blew warm breath against her pubic hair, which parted her thighs as if a button had been pushed. He edged his nose across the crinkly down and it was all Carol-Anne could do to keep her hands off the top of his head.

More breaths, but that was all. No hot wet rough tongue drawing nectar from her peach. No furry mustache grazing the soft insides of the thighs.

No downtown.

He turned his attention to her breasts, slipping the bra straps off her shoulders while Carol-Anne reached around and unhooked the back. They shook free like raisin-topped Jell-O and drew upward, begging for Max's lips.

There was something to be said about a man sucking her breast, something familiar about his head lowered to her chest, his mouth over the nipple. It was instinctive the way Carol-Anne's hand found Max's head and held it.

There was something to be said too about the way Max's fingers delved between her thighs, giving up just the right strokes—not too hard, not too easy, just right, against her clitoris.

Carol-Anne was reaching meltdown.

She grabbed Max and pulled him on top of her, her groin quick and agitated against the hardness in his underwear. Like a river unstoppable, Carol-Anne knew her juices were flowing, knew that if she touched herself she would be wet and creamy slick. Dimly she wondered about the soaking Max's underwear was no doubt getting, and if he cared.

Through her hot passion, Carol-Anne wondered

about condoms and when she should mention it, because she was getting that crazy sensation of wanting Max inside her, *now*. She knew how she could get carried away and just take him into her body without any precautions.

As if reading her thoughts, Max pulled away and reached into his nightstand drawer. Carol-Anne watched out of the corner of her eye as he slipped off his underwear and his penis was set free.

It hovered above his belly, a good nine inches from its base. Her nether lips throbbed twice. She looked away as he slipped the condom on, her hips moving of their own accord, like a snake charmer enticing the head of a cobra. They rolled and arched, hungry and maddened with desire. Max took her by her shoulders and pulled her toward him until she was straddling his crotch.

She was to do the riding.

Instinctively Carol-Anne edged up, grabbing Max's penis with her hand. She brought it to her lips and eased down gently.

Tight.

She was like a forgotten cave; there had been no entry into her in nearly eight months. Carol-Anne gritted her teeth and lowered her hips. Pain rushed up her spine like hot cleats, but it was a good pain and, despite her discomfort, she wanted all of him.

Slowly she opened, slowly she descended, a lazy delicious hurting journey well worth the ache. She leaned against him, catching her breath, feeling minute contractions from both of them. Moved her hips painfully slow, each motion culling an *ahhh* from her parted lips.

Dying and going to heaven was how Max felt inside of her. And when she couldn't stand it another second, Carol-Anne let go, taking him all the way inside of her until they were crotch-to-crotch. Her orgasm came swiftly, overwhelming in its intensity and release. She clung to him, drawing in the pleasure, the sweetness of the man warm beneath her.

Carol-Anne came out of the bathroom, showered and dressed. She came out of the bathroom unsure of Max's mood or what his expectations were. It was a little after ten in the evening and she was hungry, ravenous and uncertain if a meal was included in this evening about to come to an end. She was in between paychecks, with only three dollars to her name, she found herself wondering what she could pick up on the way home.

She became aware of Nancy Wilson's voice coming from the living room. Was surprised that such tender, sweet music was filling the air. About this time the man would be waiting at the front door ready to escort her out.

Max was in the kitchen, a T-shirt hanging loose off his broad shoulders, basketball shorts showing the fine rise of his behind. He turned at the sound of her and smiled, a head of lettuce in his hand.

He's smiling . . . oh, thank God, she thought, letting go of the stony face she presented.

"Figured I'd fix us up something to eat . . . got steaks under the broiler, potatoes in the microwave. I'm getting ready to make salad." If she was unsure of what this moment would bring, it was obvious from Max's uncertainty that he was just as unsure.

Carol-Anne made her way over to him and reached for the lettuce. "I'll make the salad." She bumped him out of the way with her hip. "Better check those steaks," she said, commandeering the space over the stainless-steel double sink. "I smell something burning."

She watched him out of the corner of her eye as he opened the oven door and pulled out the metal tray, two glistening, nearly done T-bones for her view.

T-bone steaks. Carol-Anne hadn't been able to afford those in years.

"I forgot to ask you. How do you like your meat?"

"Well done," Carol-Anne said with a seductive smile. She found herself laughing, head back and mouth open. Could not remember the last time she had felt so free and certain with a man. She knew that Max had given her that.

After dinner Carol-Anne wiped countertops and the table while Max loaded the dishwasher. She didn't mind because Max had a dream kitchen with all the amenities she could think of. Coffee machine, microwave, a refrigerator with a water and ice dispenser. He could grill inside his oven, had a Cuisinart, a blender, and a basket full of those things Carol-Anne always wanted but never could find money to buy—hand whisk, potato masher, garlic press, pasta server, ginger grater.

His kitchen cabinet doors were huge panes of clear glass, showing everything on the inside from the outside. There was a view of the Hudson right outside his window and the kitchen was a real eat-in affair.

Every single dish he owned matched.

Carol-Anne grabbed a sheet of paper towel and dried her hands. Felt Max watching her.

"What?" she asked, enamored with the look in his eye.

"Hate to see you go."

Carol-Anne shrugged. "Got to. Work tomorrow."

"You can stay the night. Nadia's with your mom, you don't have to pick her up. We can set the clock early and I'll send you home in a cab."

"A cab, Max? You can't get no cabs in the early morning in Harlem."

"I contract out with Black Diamond. They come anytime I call."

Carol-Anne took in the man before her, her head shaking back and forth. "God, Max, what can't you do?"

Chapter 3

Tina took the glass of iced tea from Carol-Anne's hand. Sighed and wiped sweat from her brow. "Lord, Carol-Anne, how long you been hoarding this stuff?" she asked, staring at the pair of powder-blue gauchos she'd pulled out of a box.

"Too long, now come on, we still have a lot to do."

They had been working on Carol-Anne's living room since morning.

"Well, I must say I'm glad you clearing this place out."

"Long overdue," was all Carol-Anne would admit to. She had left Max's apartment feeling embarrassed and ashamed. She could only wonder what he thought about her apartment. She was determined to get her place in order and had enlisted her neighbor's aid. But two hours later the place looked hardly touched. Everywhere she looked there was a pile of something. Her head hurt.

"I'm surprised you never had rats. This place is perfect for nesting."

"No rats. Mice like everybody else."

"Yeah, and I see where they come in at." Tina pointed to the hole in the base of the wall. "Lord knows how long that hole been there."

Carol-Anne looked around, seeing her apartment through Max's eyes. It was a wonder he hadn't run screaming the first time he came here. "This place is just too damn small," she said, resigned.

"Work with what you got, Carol-Anne. Just work with what you got," Tina said as she started on another box.

The newspapers were gone. The boxes, vanished. Nadia's bike was out of sight and the end table with the broken leg and bad paint job had been trashed. Carol-Anne had stacked the books and records in the hall closet, and with money that was supposed to pay her phone bill, she'd purchased an area rug for the worn floor.

Tina had an old comforter that fitted over Carol-Anne's couch, and with a five-dollar rod and three bucks' worth of remnant, she designed Carol-Anne a drape for the window.

It was late evening by the time they finished.

"A hundred percent better," Tina piped from the sofa.

"It's a start," Carol-Anne muttered, her mind on the can of rust remover she'd purchased, hopeful that her old claw-foot bathtub would give up its rust stains willingly.

The area rug was a good choice, Carol-Anne thought as she brought the glass of ice water to her lips, her hips and elbow resting against the soft weave. She watched Max and Nadia arguing over the price of Park Place, their haggling intense.

"Two thousand," Nadia insisted, her small toffee palm extended Max's way.

"Two! It only cost you three-fifty," Max said in disbelief.

"Yeah, but you gonna put hotels there and when I pass I'm gonna have to have money to pay you," Nadia shot back.

Carol-Anne turned her head toward the open window. She studied the drape, watching for the slightest quiver, but the pressed cotton was as still as midnight. An upright fan moved in a lazy half-circle in the corner but the most it offered was the occasional drift of warm air. Eighty-eight degrees outdoors, it was just as hot inside.

"Right, Mom?" Nadia asked, halting Carol-Anne's breeze watch. "Right?" Nadia insisted again, her eyes wide and demanding.

"What, babe?"

"Mr. Max, he's gonna build hotels and then I'm gonna hafta pay him lots of money."

Carol-Anne smiled, looked at Max, her heart filling at the sight of him smiling back. Had there ever been a moment like this for her and her daughter? Had any man ever taken so much time and care to include Nadia the way Max did? Something as simple as playing a game of Monopoly on a Sunday afternoon had never brought her this much joy.

"She's right, Max," Carol-Anne decided with a smirk.

"Two against one. Guess I have to pay." Max picked up his gold stack of paper money. Carefully laid out three five-hundred-dollar bills. Handed them to Nadia. She laid them one at a time onto the rug, counting along as she went. Laying the final bill down, she looked up at him quickly. Her was face stern and full of suspicion.

"You owe me another one."

"Why?" Max asked shrewdly.

" 'Cause there's only fifteen hundred here and you owe me one more to make it two thousand."

Max reached out a hand and waggled her scalp. "Good girl," he said. "Don't let nobody cheat you out your money." And with that he gave her the final five hundred dollars.

Carol-Anne stood in the bedroom doorway, Max next to her. "Good night, baby."

"Night, Mommy."

"Good night, Nadia."

"Good night, Mr. Max."

Carol-Anne clicked off the ceiling light, drew back and closed the door. She moved down the hall quickly, in need of reprieve. She needed space, a moment of solitude to settle all that she was feeling.

She made her way to her kitchen, flipping on the light. Attempted to squash a roach with her sneakered foot, but the bug was too quick.

She heard Max in the living room fiddling with the radio and was glad he had not followed. She went to the sink, rested her palms against the cool porcelain edge. Hung her head.

Her eyes drifted heavenward as if seeking answers, but eventually she gave up the quest. She turned on the hot water, put the stopper in the sink, and gave a good squirt of dish detergent. Grabbing the dirty plates, she carefully lowered them into the rising suds.

"Hey."

She turned and saw Max in the doorway, his face carrying her emotions like a billboard on an empty highway. She looked away, unwilling to share or confirm all that was inside of her.

With gentle hands he touched her shoulders, turning her slowly toward him. "You okay?"

It was all she could do to hold it in, all she could do not to wrap her arms around him tight and never let go. With a quick hand Carol-Anne swiped at the wetness in the corners of her eyes, nodded.

His arms moved around her, drawing her in close. "It's okay," he murmured, lifting her face toward his. "Had a good time today. Had a real good time and we're going to have a lot more days like this, okay?"

Her mouth started to open in protest, but he shushed her with the edge of his finger. "Nothing to be afraid of, Carol-Anne. I'm here and there's no other place I'd rather be. Now come on, walk me to the door." He turned and made his way, Carol-Anne taking measured steps behind him.

"Quite a kid you got there."

"Yeah, she's my heart."

"I was really impressed that she knew how much two thousand was."

"Nadia's a very bright child."

"That's because she has a very bright mother."

Carol-Anne's eyes danced around his. "Nobody's ever done the things you've done for us Max . . . Guess I just got a little overwhelmed."

"I haven't done nothing I didn't want to do, Carol-Anne."

"Thank you," she said softly.

"For what?"

"For being the person you are."

"I'm just plain old Max," he countered. He studied her for a moment, his mind moving full throttle with future plans. "You think you can get some time off from work?"

"Time? Like when?"

"Was thinking about going down to Virginia for a weekend. Leave on a Thursday night, come back on Sunday, what do you say?"

"What about Nadia?"

"Think your mother can watch her?"

"Are we talking Virginia Beach?" she wanted to know.

"A few days of sun and fun, what do you say?"

She looked at him, seeing the hope she'd never dreamt, the countenance that never held real probability; the man before her a cornucopia of goodness she'd never felt entitled to.

Time, she needed time to swallow, digest, absorb it all. Her eyes shimmered. Too much too soon, they implored.

"Just an idea, Carol-Anne. It's okay if you don't want to."

"Can I let you know?"

"Sure. Take a few days, think it over." But even as Max spoke those words Carol-Anne could see the soft hurt in his dark brown eyes. The last thing she wanted to do was hurt him. And what was the harm? What would be so wrong about going away with him for a few days?

Didn't she deserve a break, time away from work and her daughter? When was the last time she'd had time off—nine, ten years ago? When was the last time she'd done for herself or someone else had done for her? Nadia could be without her for a couple of days.

Carol-Anne's head shook, an off-center smile finding her. "I don't have to think it over, Max. I'd love to go."

Carol-Anne sat on the edge of the tub, toothbrush and one leather sneaker in hand. She scrubbed at the heel, scrubbed the ridged rubber along the bottom, wiping away the dirt with a wet rag.

She set it next to the other one and saw how the toes of the sneakers turned up and away from the floor.

It was two days until her trip.

Tina, the good neighbor/friend that she was, had given Carol-Anne a cross-back summer dress, a maillot bathing suit, a denim jumper, and a couple of T-shirts in pastel colors. She had loaned out costume jewelry, a black linen shell dress, and a purse to match. Carol-Anne had polished her black leather pumps and had found a few dollars for some new white socks. But she didn't have a decent nightgown or even an overnight bag.

She was sitting there staring at her run-over too-old-to-ever-look-new-again sneakers when the phone rang. She leaned toward the bathroom door and called out to Nadia to please get the phone.

Nadia appeared sometime later telling her it was Mr. Max.

"Hi. What you doing?" he began.

She'd never tell. "Nothing."

"Got to pick up a few things for the trip, was wondering if you wanted to come along."

"Not really in the mood, Max."

"Oh, come on now. You can help me pick out stuff. Keep me from mixing checks with plaids."

"You're definitely not the checks-and-plaids kind," which plunged the knife in her gut a little deeper.

"Look. I know how things are going for you. Just wanted to take you shopping. You gonna let me do that? You gonna let me take you shopping, pick up a few things?"

There it was, the best and worst of her fears laid bare. The night before she had lain in bed trying to find a way to get what she needed. The idea that Max could buy her things had come but Carol-Anne pushed the thought way. He was already paying for the trip, how could she ask for anything more?

"Just a few things for you. Would that be okay?" he went on to say.

"I got clothes, Max."

" 'Course you do. But I know when I go somewhere it's always nice to get something new."

Carol-Anne couldn't even remember the last time she had gone shopping for herself and she definitely needed some things. But she was stuck on the fact that she was in no position to get them for herself.

"You like steak?" Max said quickly. "We could go down to Thirty-fourth Street, shop, and then pop into Tad's Steaks. Bring Nadia along if you'd like."

Tad's Steaks, the home of the cheapest, best steak your money could buy. A New York strip grilled on an open flame, it came with baked potato, salad, and garlic bread. Carol-Anne hadn't had a Tad's steak in years. The idea made her mouth water.

"A nice juicy Tad's steak with all the trimmings. I know my belly's ready for one," Max added. "We can take the subway, a cab, or even the bus, any way you want to go, we can do it."

Nadia loved riding the bus. Carol-Anne loved Tad's Steaks. She did need things. No more debating. "Okay."

She shook out the last bag over her couch and added the receipt to the pile. Carol-Anne got her calculator and began adding up figures. Could not believe the final tally—five hundred thirty-seven dollars and twenty-nine cents, not including the shorts sets and sandals Nadia had gotten, too.

Around her lay two pairs of Keds sneakers, one in leather, the other in open-back canvas. There were the leather sandals, three cotton nightgowns, a silky bathrobe, and a bathing suit. Her favorite chair held a black linen jacket, three lacy bras and matching panties, and her coffee table supported a pair of white Levi's denim shorts and a pair of Levi's relaxed-fit jeans.

For me, she thought, removing price tags and fitting the clothes into the suitcase Max had loaned her. *He did this for me,* she realized as she carefully folded her new jacket and found space for her shoes, as she moved the silky bathrobe over her cheek, imagining the feel of it against her naked skin.

Her eyes closed, snapped open. A smile found her and Carol-Anne whirled around in a fast circle. Three days in the sun with Max. Life had never been so good.

The sunglasses hid his eyes but not the direction of his gaze. Max watched as Carol-Anne stood at the shore, testing the water temperature with her toe. She turned slightly. "Not too cold," she shouted as Max nodded and continue to watch her.

He studied Carol-Anne in this unguarded moment, being at Virginia Beach stripping away her armor, allowing her to enjoy all the trip had to offer. Here there were no tenements or broken streets. Here there was no tiny, cramped one-bedroom apartment or hot surly nights where she was victim to the heat. Here she did not have to look after her daughter, prepare meals, or worry about making a safe trip to the corner store and back. Here there was no worry.

Max felt good about bringing her here. Felt good about Carol-Anne, period. After so many months of being alone, he enjoyed spending time with her and Nadia. Carol-Anne made him feel like a man again and he was in desperate need of that affirmation.

She did not possess the classy sophistication that Samone had but that wasn't what Max needed. He needed Carol-Anne's simplicity and reveled in it.

Now as he watched her wade into the ocean, he took in all of her beauty. He loved the way the shiny black Lycra hugged the slope of her shoulders and the soft roundness of her breasts. He loved the way her skin glowed under the hot Virginia sky, and the movement of her hands through the gentle waves.

He loved the way she whispered his name late at night as though he were the best thing and the beauty of her smile when she was happy. He admired her determination to make a good life for her daughter and their close bond that was as real and potent as the sky above him. He loved Carol-Anne's fierceness and her take-no-prisoners attitude.

Yes, Max loved it all and more.

Chapter 4

"Mom?"

"Yeah, Nadia?"

"You and Mr. Max gonna get married?"

Carol-Anne turned around, surprised. Nadia was giving her that wide-eyed stare, brimming with a mixture of hope and awe.

"Married?"

"Yeah, you know, married."

She hadn't thought about it. Told Nadia the same thing.

"I wish you could."

"You like Mr. Max, don't you?"

"Yeah. I was wondering if I could call him Uncle Max 'stead of Mr. Max. 'Mister' sound like he a stranger or something and 'uncle' sounds better."

Carol-Anne knew that Nadia liked Max and that they got along very well, but it wasn't until now that she realized the extent of her daughter's feelings. She was grateful for it.

"Well, Nadia, you have to ask him if it would be okay."

"Think he'll say yes?" Nadia asked brightly.

She looked down at her daughter, a tiny slice of faith finding her as a knock on the front door came.

"Who?"

"Home Depot. Got a delivery for a Carol-Anne McClementine," a voice shouted through the door.

"I didn't order anything," she insisted, looking out her peephole and seeing two sweaty men, both black.

"Are you Carol-Anne McClementine?" the man said, annoyance in his voice. "I got two Whirlpool portable air conditioners for a Carol-Anne Mc-Clementine purchased yesterday by a Mr. Scutter."

"Oh," all she could say as she fumbled with locks and opened the door, seeing two boxes on a red lacquered dolly and two men who did not appreciate the fact she lived on the third floor with no elevator.

"Yes, please come in. I'm sorry."

The men entered and made their way into her living room. "Where do they go, ma'am?" *Go?* She didn't have a clue. She studied the boxes, trying to figure it out.

"Got two," the man said impatiently. "One unit's for a window, the other is a free-standing model." The man eyed her gated window. "Guess the freestander goes in here."

"The other is for the bedroom," Carol-Anne decided. She watched them unload the boxes, waited while they installed them. Only half listened as they gave operating instructions while Nadia bounced joyfully on her bed.

She thanked them, unable to offer anything more than two glasses of ice water, and waited until they were gone. She got on the phone and called Max. "You're spoiling me," were her first words to him, these gifts unrefusable.

They were as they often found themselves whenever Max came to visit, hugged up on her couch, television going and Nadia asleep in her room.

"You don't mind, do you?" Carol-Anne asked for the third time that evening. "I mean because if you do, it's okay, you can change your mind?"

"How many times I have to tell you that I don't

mind? I like the fact that she wants to call me Uncle Max. Makes me sound like family."

Carol-Anne didn't mention the other question. Did not trust Max to be as compliant as he was about being called uncle. The idea of marrying anyone had left Carol-Anne long ago. She saw single motherhood as the only path she'd go.

"Max?"

"Yeah?"

"What do you think about Nadia?"

He looked surprised that she was even asking. "I think she's wonderful."

"No, that's not what I mean."

It took Max a second to fully understand. "Oh. You mean how do I feel about her?" His eyes drifted. A crooked smile came into play. "I tell you, some days she just looks at me and my heart is all hers." His eyes danced with memory. "Some days it's like she's mine, too y'know? I mean, I know she's not, but there are times"—he shook his head—"when I feel like she is."

"Yours?"

Max shifted. "I mean, I know she's not and I've only known her what, a couple of weeks, but she just does my heart good."

Carol-Anne looked at him carefully. "You sure?"

"Never lie about something like that, Carol-Anne."

It was like the sky had opened and the whole world was shot through with a burst of color. Carol-Anne's heart ran over and she could not hold it back this time.

"You crying?"

She shook her head, turned away.

"You crying. What are you crying about?"

Carol-Anne could not get her mouth to work. The most she could do was shake her head.

"After all this time you still don't know me?" Max asked.

She risked a look his way, fresh tears spilling down her cheeks. "Just never thought."

"What? That I cared about her?"

"Yeah and other things."

"How could anyone not love her?"

But others had, men coming and going through her life without so much as a real nod in her daughter's direction. Nadia, standing on the fringes of Carol-Anne's social life, waiting to be noticed, to be considered . . . and now?

"Nobody else ever did," Carol-Anne said after a while.

"I'm not nobody else, don't you know that by now?"

Yes, she did and she loved him for it. Loved him for things he'd done, the man he was, for bringing her real joy. Carol-Anne shifted on the sofa. "New to me, Max, that's all. Everything about you is so new and different."

"Nothing to be afraid of."

She laughed bitterly. "Easy for you to say."

"You think so?" There was an edge to his voice Carol-Anne had never heard before. She'd touched raw nerve.

"Think it's easy going around with your eyes wide open all the time? I wasn't born this way, Carol-Anne, and for a long time I shut my eyes to a whole lot of things. Refused to see so much that when I finally got a good glimpse it was too late." Max paused, looked away. "Lost lots in my lifetime, Carol-Anne. Good things, important things. Don't want to do that anymore. Don't want to lose another good thing."

Her question came, her eyes showing all her fears. Her voice was fragile and barely audible. "Am I a good thing, Max?"

"The best." He kissed her then, a deep, soul-stirring brew of his lips and tongue. He held her in a powerful embrace and she grew dizzy with the strength of him. His love poured into every pore she owned, filling her.

They shifted along the pillows of the couch, Max upon her, she beneath. Her shirt was off, her shorts gone before she realized where they were headed. She eased from beneath him. Stood. With a careful smile she pointed toward her sofa.

Together they removed the cushions, unfolded the bed and retrieved pillows from the closet. Together they turned off lights, undressed, and got in, drawn like moths to a flame.

They lay side by side, soft light spilling into the living-room window. The clock alarm had gone off two minutes before and it was time for Max to go.

Carol-Anne did not want him to leave, especially not at five in the morning, but she had little choice.

"Hate to see you go."

"Hate to be going, but I understand." Max sat up, swung his legs over the side.

The touch on his back surprised him. "Max?"

"Yeah?"

"When you said you lost something . . . were you talking about a someone?"

He sighed, lowered his head, broad back to her. "Yeah, I was. Her name was Samone. Loved her. Being blind to so much, I lost her."

Carol-Anne rolled the name around in her head, forced it off her tongue. "Simone? Was she French?"

Max twisted, peered over his shoulder. Laughed softly in the early morning darkness. "No. Harlem gal. Born and raised."

"Oh, just that the name sounded French."

"French name with a black kind of spelling. S-A-M-O-N-E, not S-I-M-O-N-E, you see."

"How long?" Carol-Anne said after a while.

"How long what?"

"That you were together and have been apart?"

"Four years together, six months apart." Max stood. "No more questions. You want to help me find my underwear?"

Carol-Anne hadn't thought much about accepting Max's invitation to his goddaughter Shamika's birthday party. She thought it was sweet that he wanted her to meet his friends, knew Nadia would have a good time.

Carol-Anne came to the apartment on Riverside Drive expecting only to meet new people and her daughter to enjoy the party. Carol-Anne never expected to come face-to-face with the woman who used to occupy her space.

Carol-Anne and Nadia had just arrived when Max came up to them, giving them quick kisses. "Want you to meet somebody," he said, giddy as anything, ferrying them toward a pretty, slim woman arranging snacks on the table.

"Carol-Anne, Nadia, this is Samone."

This was Samone. This beautiful, sexy creature was Max's ex-girlfriend.

"Nice to meet you," Samone uttered, lifting her hand.

Even as Carol-Anne raised her own she could not stop staring. Look at that hair, past her shoulders and not a weave track in sight. What size was she, a five? Those eyes were like drops of caramel, her teeth were Pepsodent-bright. How do you stand before perfection?

Carol-Anne smiled, took back her hand. Sensed Samone could see every flaw she'd ever owned. "Nice to meet you, too," she managed, her smile still bright as she turned and found a seat in the corner.

Her smile stayed when Max brought over Patricia

and Ray, introducing them as two of his oldest, dearest friends. "Shamika's their daughter," he added before going off again.

She sat watching Max help Samone lay out treats. Watched them thick as thieves as they arranged presents and redraped a fallen swirl of crepe paper. Carol-Anne watched as they handed over gifts to Max's godchild and served plates of strawberry cake and vanilla ice cream.

Their eyes, their body language, suggested more than two people who were no longer involved. Together they moved through the party looking more like an old married couple than former lovers.

Samone. Sexy, smart, gorgeous. How could Max want her after being with that woman? What did Carol-Anne have to offer that Samone didn't?

Carol-Anne tried to conjure up Virginia Beach, tried to convince herself that she was the one. She looked across the room in need of Max's smile, but as his eyes drifted past hers without any acknowledgment, she knew.

Samone had wiped away her existence.

"Mom?" Carol-Anne jumped, ambushed by Nadia. "You having fun?"

"Fun?"

"Yeah, fun," Nadia insisted.

"Yes, I'm having fun."

"You don't look like it."

How could she tell her daughter the truth? Carol-Anne smiled. "I'm just fine, baby."

"You want me to get Uncle Max?"

Her answer came like a sigh. "Yes."

She watched Nadia make her way across the room. Watched her daughter's hand find Max's arm. Saw the little pink lips move, the seriousness of her daughter's face. Looked away a split second before Max headed toward her.

"You wanted me?"

She glared at him, angry at her feelings of abandonment and the vagueness with which he posed his question. She swallowed, looked away. "Just wanted to know what time we were leaving."

He laughed, relieved. Smiled at her, his hand settling on her thigh. "Not too much longer," he answered, turning and walking away.

At her door.

"Not coming in?" Carol-Anne asked.

"No, not tonight." Seeing Samone had done things to his heart, and Max needed some thinking time alone.

"Nadia's going to wonder why."

"Tell her that everybody had a big day and we all need our rest. I'll call you tomorrow. Promised to take Nadia to that new Disney movie."

So that was his plan. Just proceed as if the afternoon had never happened. As if he hadn't been all up his ex-girlfriend's butt. Carol-Anne knew her tone was sharp but she could do nothing to calm it.

"Oh, I'm not invited to the movies?" She didn't want to go but wanted the option of saying yes or no.

"Thought you were going to spend Sunday filling out your college application and financial-aid forms?"

He had a point. She had promised to get the ball rolling toward her undergrad degree. "You're right," she said, her anger subsiding, the necessity of it fading as the day drew to a close.

Max leaned in and kissed her cheek. "Good night, babe." Carol-Anne's fear mixing with his own doubt.

But as Max turned away, disappearing down the stairs, Carol-Anne couldn't help but wonder if she was really his babe or was it the pretty woman way across town.

* * *

As promised, the next day Max took Nadia to the movies. He bought her popcorn, a hot dog, and Bon-Bons. Stayed awake in the darkened theater, even though the movie bored the shit out of him. God forbid he'd fall asleep and wake up to find Nadia gone.

After the movie, Max took Nadia to the card shop, where she bought Disney character stickers, still in the Disney groove. By the time they got back home, Carol-Anne had not only finished filling out all her forms, she had made dinner, too.

But Max wasn't hungry. Carol-Anne, feelings hurt, did not press him into staying; she took the man before her with a grain of salt, suggesting to Nadia that she go and wash up, because dinner was ready and she could eat now.

"So, how was the movie?" Carol-Anne asked, drying her hands on a dish towel as she moved toward the kitchen.

"Fine if you like Disney," Max said, peeved.

Carol-Anne looked surprised. "Thought you loved Disney."

"Yeah, when I was seven."

"If it's gonna be like this, Max, then maybe you should leave now."

"Maybe I should."

Carol-Anne tossed the towel onto the table, her hands easily finding her hips. "You want her? She's on the other side of town. She's the one with nice clothes and no kids. I'm not her, Max."

"Carol-Anne, what are you talking about?"

"I'm talking about yesterday and how you've changed since then."

"Nothing's changed."

She gave him a look full of daring. "Nothing but your mind." The fire had her and wouldn't let her go. "Should have seen yourself yesterday, Max, all up Samone's ass. Acting like I wasn't even there. Don't know why the hell you invited me in the first place."

Yes, he was guilty, and Max had been expecting

her anger since yesterday, but he knew now was not the time to discuss it. "Can we talk about this another time, when Nadia's not around?"

"Yeah, we could, but do we really want to?" Carol-Anne tossed back.

"I don't know," Max offered, moving one step closer to the truth.

"Well, if you don't, I sure as hell don't." They were at an impasse with no place to go. Max shook his head, unwilling to utter another word about it. "I got to go."

Carol-Anne turned her back to him. "Say good-bye to Nadia."

"Okay."

That night, long after the clock had struck midnight and Nadia was deep into her sleep, Carol-Anne got into her old wing chair, brought her knobby knees to her chest, and cried. She didn't ask herself why as she held in the moans that wanted to escape and let loose the tears needing release.

She knew why. And he was on the other side of town.

For a moment, Carol-Anne considered picking up the phone and calling him. Considered letting her sorrows travel through the wires quickly, urgently, in need of Max's rescue. But her tears were her own, personal and direct, and she would not share them with anybody.

Max closed the book and put it on his nightstand. He looked at the clock and saw that the hour was late. Realized even if he got up the courage to call her, most likely Carol-Anne'd be asleep.

Yesterday, for a few moments, Max had taken a quick plunge. His emotions got loose and headed straight for Samone. Before he could check them, they were seeking out old love and moot possibilities. He knew he had hurt Carol-Anne and he needed to speak to her.

Max picked up the phone. Dialed. "We have to talk," he began.

"Yeah, I know."

"Not on the phone."

"Okay."

"Tomorrow after work?"

"Yeah. I'll send Nadia to her friend's house." The conversation would be full of things that Carol-Anne did not want Nadia to hear.

Nadia barely spoke to him, drifting by like a ghost, dashing off to Tina's apartment across the hall. This did not surprise Carol-Anne one bit but Max was heartbroken.

"She's perceptive, Max," Carol-Anne explained, a calmness surrounding her. "She knows when things aren't going right."

Carol-Anne had thought long and hard about her relationship with Max. Max made too much money, was too handsome, too hot a property to ever stay with her. Carol-Anne was a struggling single mother living in Spanish Harlem in a dilapidated antiquated apartment. Max was a rich, single, handsome black man with no kids, the flyest apartment this side of the Hudson River, and money to burn.

He was Stacy Adams. She was Payless. He was *Porgy and Bess* on Broadway and she was pirated cable TV. Max was the man with the masters in finance and Carol-Anne was simply a graduate of the school of hard knocks. He was weekly trips to the barber shop and accounts at Barneys. She was do-it-yourself perm kits and sales at John's Bargain World on 125th.

Max was T-bone steak, Carol-Anne was ground beef with more fat than meat. They were ambushed from the start.

She knew this. It was his turn to realize it, too.

"Look, Max. Maybe it's time to let it go."

"You want to do that?"

"I have to look after my own interests."

Max studied her. Hair un-neatly pinned to the back, dark hollows beneath cinnamon eyes. He saw her weariness and recognized her need to protect what was ultimately hers. But that wasn't how he wanted it to go.

"You're not answering the question. Do you, as you put it, want to 'let it go'?"

She shifted in her chair, her eyes on fire with the need to know his heart. "You still love Samone?"

"Yes. But that has nothing to do with me and you."

She laughed in awe and disbelief. How could he even say that? His feelings toward Samone had everything to do with them.

"It's obvious that you love her. So why are you here, Max? What happened between you and her? How come you're not together?" Carol-Anne was hungry for his answer. Needed to know from A to Z what had happened that had made her and Max possible.

He took his time responding, reluctance in every breath he took. And when his answer came, the impact was devastating.

"A baby."

"A baby?" Carol-Anne could not believe what she heard.

"Yeah. One I never knew. Was never given the chance to know. Samone had an abortion before I could even think about changing her mind. That's what broke us up." He looked at Carol-Anne. "Saw you and Nadia in the ice-cream store that day"—he shrugged, sorting out his feelings—"something clicked. Something about Nadia being yours."

"But if there had been no Nadia, you never would've bothered. Is that it?"

His heart hammered but he had to tell her. "Probably not."

" 'Cause I had a child, that's why you wanted to talk to me."

"Yes, but only in the beginning. As I got to know you better, it stopped mattering."

"You sure about that? You sure I'm still not some damn surrogate because Samone had an abortion? You have a hell of a nerve to even sit here and tell me that."

"You wanted the truth. I wanted the truth."

"So what am I supposed to say now? That it's okay? That that was then and this is now and you don't feel that way anymore? How do I know that, Max?"

"Didn't you hear what I said? It's different."

But Carol-Anne wasn't hearing anything. Anger had her, which she'd survive. What would take her by surprise would be the hurt. A hurt that was forming even as she jumped up from her chair, one arm extended.

"Get the hell out."

When Max made no move to stand, Carol-Anne flew down the hall. Her fingers fiddled with the locks and she was about to swing the door open when Max grabbed her. Grabbed her and held on as she raged against him. When the hurt arrived, draining her of all resistance, he held her, knowing she was in need of support.

"You bastard," she hissed, tears staining his shirt.

"I know."

She pulled back. Her eyes dismal and forsaken. "How could you do this to me?"

"I'm sorry. It's not how I meant it to go. You wanted the truth. But that's only part of it. Carol-Anne, I really want to be with you. That's why I'm here. Forget yesterday and what I've lost. I see what I have now and I don't want to lose it."

Her moment of weakness was quick in passing. "Let me go."

He released her, accepting the shove as she pushed past him and went to settle in her chair.

Max stood there for a long time, accepting her silence and her body turned away from him. He watched, waiting patiently for her verdict. It came quick and swift.

"Do you care about us?"

"Lord knows I do, Carol-Anne."

"You better mean it, Max."

She was offering up a second chance and Max snatched it before she took it back. "More than the air I breathe."

"You hurt me. You won't get a chance to do it again."

"I know."

"I want to be alone." There were new additions to her Loud Thoughts and Carol-Anne needed time to settle them.

"All right. I'll call you later."

Carol-Anne didn't move, didn't turn around. Max let himself out.

She would be in the chair for a while.

Chapter 5

Max picked up the phone. Buzzed his secretary. "Angela?"

"Yeah, Max."

"You didn't get Ms. McClementine yet?"

"I got her voice mail . . . I left two messages."

Max breathed into the phone. *Now what?*

"Max?"

"Yeah?"

"Want me to try again?"

"No, that's fine." Max hung up and looked around his office. Stared at his in-box for a long time. Four different reports to be finished by week's end and he hadn't so much as lifted the first from the stack.

For the first time Max could ever recall, work was taking a back seat. He had spent a lifetime of putting his nose to the grindstone but now it all seemed insignificant.

Carol-Anne had taken center stage in his life and she was all that he cared about. *Just want to make it right between us,* he thought, picking up the phone to call her, but he changed his mind at the last minute. He'd caught sight of his in-box.

Work was the least of his worries.

* * *

Carol-Anne closed her apartment door, sliding in the deadbolts as Nadia headed to the kitchen for cherry Kool-Aid.

It was miserable outside. All she wanted was a cool shower and her air conditioner. Max . . . Carol-Anne turned away from his name for the hundredth time that day. The sound of that white woman leaving *his* name and *his* number still irked her hours afterward. The least he could do was pick up the phone and call himself. But no, he gets his secretary to do it for him. The nerve of him.

"Mom?"

"Yeah, Nadia."

"Can I go over Celia's?"

"Over Celia's? You just got home."

Nadia looked up at her with those eyes of hers and Carol-Anne knew better than to press for a reason. Deep inside she knew why. The whole apartment was filled with ghosts from last night, overrun with her rage, fears, and the battle she had fought.

"Well, first you got to wash your face and your hands. Then you have to brush your edges, they're sticking out of your head like a brushfire. Then change your clothes. After that, you can go to Celia's." *Too rough,* she realized after the fact. *Last thing she needs is me giving her a whole list of things to do before she could escape.*

Carol-Anne started devising an apology. Something quick, not too heavy. But before she could open her mouth, Nadia turned around and marched off to the bathroom. She shut the door so hard a picture shook. Carol-Anne's first instinct was to go after her, snatch her up and pop her, but she wasn't up to it and it wasn't Nadia's fault.

Just what she didn't want. From the beginning Carol-Anne had told Max that she didn't want this. But did that make a damn bit of difference? He came in spewing his truth, knowing full well what the consequences were going to be. Now Nadia didn't even want to stay here. *Damn him . . .*

The phone began to ring. Carol-Anne listened to it ring two times before deciding to answer. By the time she picked up there was no one there.

Dinner. Had to make dinner. But there was nothing in Carol-Anne's refrigerator she wanted. What did she want? She stood there a minute doing a mental check. Some fish sticks in the freezer. Kraft macaroni and cheese. A can of peas. Dinner.

Carol-Anne started for the kitchen but glanced down at her work clothes and decided to change into something else. She was in the wardrobe searching through the hangers, still trying to figure out what she really wanted, *to make it better . . . like before last night, but that ain't in my kitchen,* when the sound of the bathroom door opening made her turn her head.

Nadia stood there, naked as the day she was born. Not a stitch of anything, just brown skin from face to feet. She hadn't done that since the age of four, appearing like magic without clothes.

This was deep. It wasn't anything a trip to the ice-cream store could fix. But Carol-Anne couldn't move. The sight of her daughter like that numbed her. *She's doing this for my benefit,* Carol-Anne realized. *She can't tell me, so she's got to show me . . .*

Carol-Anne searched Nadia's glistening eyes and read the message "help me" clear across the room. But for the first time in a long time Carol-Anne didn't know how. She could not move, couldn't lift her arms, force her feet, or simply say she was sorry.

It took all the strength Carol-Anne had not to cry, all her effort to mutter, "Go put something on."

"Look like your dog died," Tina said, holding open her front door as Nadia flew by without so much as a hello. Despite her sarcasm, Carol-Anne was glad that Tina was home.

"You know I don't have a dog." A reluctant smile curled the left side of Carol-Anne's mouth.

"I know." Tina took Carol-Anne's arm, and closed the door behind them. "Well, you just in time. I was snapping string beans and you know how much I hate snapping string beans."

"That's 'cause you ain't figured out the rhythm. Now you take my mother . . ." They moved down the hall, and entered the kitchen through the first door on the right. "Girl, you talk about rhythm. My mother makes those beans sing when she snaps them."

"I bet she does. Here, you snap and I'll wash my potatoes."

It never ceased to amaze Carol-Anne what a little paint, a good imagination, and a course on home improvement could do. She and Tina had the same exact place, down to the living-room window looking onto nothing but the buildings across the street, but Tina's place always seemed full of light and air.

Her kitchen was Dutch-blue and white. She had painstakingly removed the layers of paint from the glass panes of her cabinets, revealing a stylish array of china, crystal, and midnight-blue coffee mugs. Tina was the only one Carol-Anne knew with custom-made blinds in a one-bedroom walk-up.

"Just 'cause it ain't a big place don't mean I can't act like it is," she'd say. Tina may have been a single mom just like Carol-Anne, making the same money she did, but it was hard telling.

Carol-Anne picked up a green bean. Ran her thumb along its bumpy edge. Got a good hold on the tip and flexed both wrists. *Snap.*

"So, what's going on, Carol-Anne?"

"What ain't?" *Snap. Snap.*

Tina sized her up from the kitchen sink.

"You tell me . . . Last night Nadia was over here with Celia and I saw Max ringing your bell."

"Yeah, well, looks can be deceiving."

"Now, really?" Tina asked, moving the paring knife over the potato.

Snap. "Really," Carol-Anne answered, full of spite.

Tina turned on the tap and held the potato under. She rinsed it for an incredibly long time before the question Carol-Anne waited for arrived.

"What happened?"

Carol-Anne held the green bean between two fingers, and when she realized what her answer would be, she looked away.

"I don't know."

Tina chuckled, her shoulders moving easily beneath the sleeveless cotton blouse. "Oh, don't go tell that lie. You do know. So I'm gonna ask you again. What happened?"

"A party."

"I see."

"Nothing really."

Tina picked up another potato. Eyed a green spot and took to it with her paring knife. "Must've been something."

Carol tossed the bean aside, pushing the whole bowl away as an afterthought. She didn't snap her own damn beans, why should she snap somebody else's?

"Max's friend's daughter had a birthday party. Thought it'd be fun if me and Nadia came. But the real reason was he wanted me to meet *her*."

"Ooh, a *her*."

"Oh, yes, sweetheart. Miz Samone something or other. Tall, thin, sexy. Got long hair all hers. Dresses like she only buys at expensive stores. I mean, the child had on a pair of shorts and a damn T-shirt, but she was like the sexiest, smartest-dressed woman there." Carol-Anne took a breath. This first speaking of her anger, her jealousy, throwing her for a loop.

"He still with her?"

"No."

Tina waved a potato in her direction.

"He with you, then?"

"Who the hell knows?"

"Well, up till this party, was he?"

"He never came out and said it, but you know." She pulled the bowl back toward her. Picked up a green bean and held the end between two fingers. *Snap.* "Took me to Virginia Beach. Bought me and Nadia clothes, two air conditioners." Carol-Anne's voice faded.

"*Two* air conditioners?"

Carol-Anne looked up, surprised at Tina's reaction. "Yeah. One for the living room, one for Nadia's room."

"Let me get this straight. A single black man takes you on vacation, buys you and your child clothes and tosses in two air conditioners for the hell of it and you don't know if he's with you or not?"

"Yeah."

Tina shook her head. "Honey, he's definitely with you."

"Was."

"How so?"

"The party," Carol-Anne implored.

"What happened at this party?"

"Nothing more than him looking, but you know how a man sees something he wants real bad and can't have? That was Max. And then he drops me off and makes some excuse about why he couldn't stay."

"He stay over?"

Carol-Anne shook her head. "No. You know the routine. Leaves about three hours after Nadia goes to sleep."

"Well, so far, all I'm hearing is he looked a little hard at his ex and didn't stay the night."

Carol-Anne looked up at her. Her voice was more sigh than words.

"You would."

"Well, if there's suppose to be more, you ain't telling, so I haven't heard it."

Carol-Anne hadn't told her the real nitty-gritty. The in-your-face part.

"It's nothing you can touch," Carol-Anne said, moving past it.

"But strong enough to make you believe anyway?"

"Yeah."

Tina studied her friend. "If it's that deep you don't have to tell it," she said carefully. "But whatever it is you got to make sure you're seeing the whole picture. Weigh the pros and cons. Decide what's best for you." And with that Tina went back to the business of cleaning potatoes.

Do you care about us?
More than the air I breathe.

Carol-Anne left Nadia over at Tina's. A cool breeze sprang up from nowhere so she opened windows and turned off the air conditioner, willing the ghosts of last night away. Then she called Max.

"Still breathing?" she asked when he picked up.

"Carol-Anne?"

"It's me."

"I been trying to reach you all day."

"I know. I got the messages."

"How's Nadia?"

Carol-Anne blinked back a tear. "Funny you should ask."

"That bad?"

She nodded. "That bad."

"I'm sorry."

"Yeah, so I heard. But that ain't doing a thing for my daughter, now is it? . . . I told you. I warned you, Max."

"Look, you wanted the truth. I gave it to you.

Now if Nadia's hurting over something I told you, well, whose fault is that?" Max asked adamantly.

"That's easy for you to say. You didn't see her like I saw her today."

"What happened?"

"It doesn't matter what, just that it did."

"You gonna tell me what happened, Carol-Anne?"

"Let's just say that she's really upset."

"She okay? Physically, I mean?"

"Physically, yes."

"I never wanted anything bad for her."

"Too late now, isn't it?"

"She there?"

"No."

Max was silent for a long time and Carol-Anne knew he was spinning his wheels seeking out solutions. She wanted to save him time, because there were none.

"When she comes home, will you tell her how sorry I am?"

I'm sorry . . . Had Carol-Anne told Nadia that herself? In her anger and her fear, had she even hugged her or told Nadia that she loved her?

She sighed. "It's getting late, I better go and get her."

"About being with you and Nadia, I meant that."

"I don't know, Max. I need a little more time. To think. To clear things up."

"I was hoping we could go and see the Garth Fagan Bucket Dancers this weekend. They're going to be at City Center."

"Can I call you Thursday and let you know?" Carol-Anne asked wearily.

"Sure. Thursday would be fine."

"Okay. Talk to you then." Carol-Anne hung up. Looked around her. Dinner. She had forgotten about dinner. It wasn't dark yet. She had a few dollars. She'd take Nadia to McDonald's.

Nadia loved their Happy Meals.

* * *

Carol-Anne watched as Nadia dipped the Chicken McNugget into the sweet-and-sour sauce. Watched as she brought it to her mouth and took a bite. Watched the little mouth chew the fried morsel.

"Good?" Carol-Anne asked.

"Um-hum." Nadia replied, not looking at her.

"Nadia, look at me, please."

Eyes so big, so wet and shiny, they looked like pure liquid. And scared, so scared. On the verge of tears.

"Yes, Mom?"

"I just wanted to say I'm sorry about today. I didn't mean to sound so mad. It's not you. It was me. Just mad at myself, that's all."

"I was scared, Mommy." Finally, there it was. The need to reach across the table and pull Nadia to her was fierce. And who would care if she did?

"Come here, baby."

Nadia scooted out of the hard plastic seat, her pink denim jumper easing the way.

Carol-Anne hugged her hard. Maybe too hard. She resisted the urge to cry. Spoke what should have been spoken hours earlier.

"I love you, Nadia, and I'm sorry."

With the last barrette in Nadia's hair, Carol-Anne held her at arm's length.

"You look marvelous."

Nadia giggled.

Carol-Anne shook her head and finger and spoke in her best Billy Crystal/Fernando Lamas voice. "No, I mean you look marvelous!"

"Are they gonna do 'Rebelations'?" Nadia wanted to know, her knowledge of dance limited to Alvin Ailey and the Dance Theatre of Harlem.

"No, honey, this is a different dance company."

"Not the bird dance?"

"No, honey, this is going to be the Garth Fagan Bucket Dancers."

"They gonna dance in buckets?"

"No, honey, that's just their name."

"When is Mr. Max coming?" she wanted to know and Carol-Anne was glad to hear her ask.

"In a little while."

"We gonna take the bus?"

"I don't know, Nadia. We have to see."

"Are they gonna do the dance with the red balls on their head?"

"No, baby, that's Dance Theatre of Harlem."

"Where I went to once?"

Carol-Anne nodded, remembering.

While Nadia fussed impatiently for Max to arrive, Carol-Anne worried her brain over tuition money for more dance classes. She knew that after today, Nadia would ask if she could take dance classes again. But there was no extra money. And Nadia was no closer to getting a scholarship now than she had been two years ago.

When Carol-Anne had decided her daughter was going to dance she took Nadia down to Dance Theatre of Harlem for scholarship auditions. Nadia hadn't known a pointed foot from a flex, where to set her arms, or even how to do a simple side-to-side motion.

Determined to give her daughter the gift of dance, Carol-Anne had robbed Peter, Paul, and the phone company to pay for lessons until she found herself with nobody to rob and a handful of shut-off notices. That was the end of Nadia's dance classes.

Good things just don't last, her last thought as she heard her doorbell ring.

It didn't take much coaxing for Max to buy the Garth Fagan Bucket Dancers' poster and T-shirt for Nadia, all of which she insisted on carrying herself as they headed out into the waning sun toward the bus. The train would have been much quicker but Carol-Anne knew that this was Nadia's day and Nadia wanted to stay aboveground.

"Mommy, I want to dance."

Nadia's announcement had been expected from the moment Max said they were going. Carol-Anne had been bracing herself ever since.

"I know you do, Nadia."

"Can I?"

"We'll have to see." Which was a whole lot more optimistic than the answer Carol-Anne didn't give.

"You want to dance, Nadia?" Max asked. Carol-Anne could feel it coming as certain as the bus headed their way.

"Uh-huh. I used to dance. I took ballet and tap. Then Mommy said I couldn't go anymore."

Carol-Anne looked at Max, annoyed that she'd have to be a part of this. "Money," was all she said.

Max touched Nadia's cheek. "Well, we'll have to see about you dancing again."

Carol-Anne looked away.

Chapter 6

Carol-Anne stood, arms folded, face pensive, watching her sofa bed exit the front door. Behind her the smell of rubber cement permeated the air. *Making it nice,* Max had told her. Most women would have been grateful, would have dropped to the floor and rolled over in gratitude. "Honey, are you crazy? The man want to fix up your place, let him," Tina had insisted when Carol-Anne shared Max's grand designs for her one-bedroom walk-up.

Carol-Anne wasn't most women. All her life she had gotten everything for herself and by herself. She wasn't used to other people having twenty-five-dollar-a-yard carpeting laid in her living room and buying her a couch and getting her daughter a new bedroom set. Carol-Anne felt put-upon.

Yes, she loved the new flooring, and her body was buzzing from the idea of sleeping on a new sofa bed. Yes, the floor lamp was a nice touch and she would have picked the same green-stained armoire Max had had delivered that morning so she could take her things out of boxes and have a real place for storage. But Max had been doing so much lately and Carol-Anne wanted to do it for herself.

"Coming through!" The voice, deep, rough, and unfamiliar, startled her. Carol-Anne turned in time to see her new sofa bed coming her way. She gave the delivery men a few minutes to settle the couch against the wall before she entered her living room. *Pinch me,* she thought, her body drawn to the rich midnight-blue sofa like a moth who knew better but could not resist the flame.

Making it nice.

A new set of dishes. A coffee maker. Shower curtains for the bathroom, bath mats in matching cranberry. Making it better.

Taking her downtown to shop. Max giving in when Carol-Anne refused to even consider Lord and Taylor. "Macy's is just as fine." Moving through the stores, bags upon bags in their hands. A new two-hundred-dollar pocketbook, seventy-five-dollar Calvin Klein jeans. Panties and bras and silky nighties. A new pantsuit, a new pair of Nine West shoes.

Clothes for Nadia. Shoes for Nadia. The three of them moved through Macy's like Max owned it. So many packages, so many bags, they had to take a cab back uptown.

They dropped off the packages and went out to a Chinese restaurant, with paper lanterns, real linen tablecloths, and waiters in black pants, white shirts, and red vests. They shared fortunes, ate almond cookies. Enjoyed the delectable flavors of a well-prepared meal.

For the first time in all the years since Nadia was born, Carol-Anne knew what it felt like to be a two-parent family.

On a brisk end-of-October day, dusk was descending as Carol-Anne and Nadia headed up the subway steps to walk the four blocks to her mother's West Side apartment. Near the park, the sounds of touch football brought a humane touch to the cacophony of city traffic.

A profusion of oak leaves in burgundy, yellow, and brown crunched pleasantly under their feet, and the sunlight, though fading, was brilliant. It was the type of day that made you think of harvests, pumpkins, and Thanksgiving just weeks away.

Carol-Anne visited her mother at least once a month. The two of them talked a whole lot about nothing. The old picture albums would be pulled out for the hundredth time and they would look at the snapshots as if it were the first time. There was always some tale behind a picture or two; Carol-Anne and her mother would take turns telling them.

Her mother's apartment was one of few things in Carol-Anne's life that hadn't changed. The carpet was still the same one that Carol-Anne had shampooed as a teenager back in the days when a super Afro'ed Don Cornelius hosted *Soul Train*.

"You got a letter," her mother said, taking off Nadia's new teal stadium jacket.

"A letter? From who?"

"I don't know."

Carol-Anne had been gone from the apartment for years, and only creditors knew her at her mother's address. "Must be a bill collector."

"It's there on the console." They didn't make them like that anymore: stereo consoles four feet long and two feet wide. The middle panel lifted and inside was a turntable, a radio, and an eight-track. It was as much a part of a time gone by as the red brocade drapes and the plastic slipcovers.

Miss McClementine ushered Nadia toward the kitchen. "Granny got some hot chocolate. How about a cup?" Nadia smiled. Granny always had things just for her.

The plastic squawked as Carol-Anne sat on the sofa. The white legal-sized envelope was postmarked five days ago. She tore off a small corner and used her good nail to slit it open. Neat script greeted her and her heart began beating fast.

Dear Carol,

I'm writing this to you with no idea if you will get it or will even want to get it. It's been a long time coming.

So much has happened since I saw you last. Lately you've been on my mind. You and the baby.

I only ask that if you want to, to give me a call. If not, I understand. It's funny, but after all this time, the way you laugh stays with me the most. Well, I had promised to keep it brief. I just hope you find it in yourself to call. Like I said, everything has changed now.

Love,
Jeff

Carol-Anne saw the ten-digit number and recognized the New York exchange. She tried to find herself, lost in what it all meant. The sound of Nadia telling her mother about school and her dance classes at Dance Theatre of Harlem brought her back.

He knows. Things have changed. How much, Jeff? Are you and Adrienne together or apart? Will the changes in your life matter now that so many have occurred in mine?

"Carol-Anne?" her mother yelled from the kitchen.

"Yeah?"

"Who was it from?"

"Jeff," Carol-Anne yelled back, heading toward the kitchen. The condemnation on her mother's face did not surprise her.

"What he want?" her mother asked, indignant.

With good reason, you never liked him, Momma. And I see time hasn't changed your heart. It wouldn't matter what Carol-Anne said.

"I don't know."

"Who's Jeff, Momma?"

Carol-Anne sought guidance but her mother looked away. Dirty dead secrets should stay buried as far as her mother was concerned.

Her mother had pulled out crayons and a coloring book. Nadia was coloring the stem of a rose green. The cup of hot chocolate sat to her side; steam rose like fine mist from its center.

This is the world I've made for my daughter. A world of hot chocolate in her grandma's kitchen and the simple act of coloring pretty pictures. This is the world I've struggled to maintain for her. Not a world full of married men and babies with no daddies... So do I tell her and shatter all that she's known? Or do I lie and keep dirty dead secrets buried, like I'm sure my mother thinks I ought to?

Carol-Anne paused; her life on another brink. Then she smiled to her daughter born eight years ago out of love. Smiled at the daughter wanted, and looking so much like father.

"Jeff? Why, Jeff is your daddy." Something snuck loose about then. Something that had never really been there, but had never really gone away. Carol-Anne did not deny the need to hold her child; did not deny the need to soothe her against changes coming. Did not deny the tear spilling unnoticed on Nadia's ribboned braid.

Nadia craned her neck in her mother's sudden tight embrace.

"My daddy?"

Look at her ... like she never owned one, or was never due one; her eyes wider than a harvest moon. The world being made perfect for her even if the odds had her beat.

"Your daddy, honey. The letter is from your father."

"Where's he been?"

"Away . . ."

Despite her better judgment, she went to the

phone. With Nadia itchy and anxious beside her, Carol-Anne sat on the plastic-covered couch and made the call. The words poised on her tongue quickly vanished as she heard the answering machine.

"Hi. I'm not in at the moment, but would love to hear from you. So please leave a message at the beep and I'll return your call as soon as possible." It was strange hearing his voice again. Carol-Anne swallowed, left a message.

"Jeff, it's Carol. I just got your letter and am giving you a call. I'm not home now, but you can call me later. My number is . . ."

Carol-Anne clicked on lights as she moved through the apartment. She was weary from Nadia's nonstop questions that demanded answers Carol-Anne wasn't ready to address.

"Can we call him?" Nadia insisted, going to the phone.

"Who?" Carol-Anne chided.

"My father," Nadia insisted.

"Yes, we will call your father in a little while but first you have to take a bath and get into some pajamas."

"Aw, Mom."

"Aw, Mom, my foot. It's way past your bedtime. And there's school tomorrow. Go!" And Nadia, basically a good child, went.

She dialed while Nadia sang TV commercials, nursery rhymes, and Queen Latifah songs in the bathtub.

"Hello?"

"Jeff?"

"Carol?"

"Yeah."

"Oh, baby, it's so good to hear your voice again." Straight to her heart. "Same here."

"How have you been? What about the baby?"

"Well, first off, I've been okay and the 'baby' is eight."

"What's her name?"

"Nadia. Nadia Clarice McClementine."

"Nadia?"

"After the gymnast," Carol-Anne admitted.

"Okay. Let's see. Clarice, that's your mother's name."

And McClementine, that's mine, Carol-Anne thought bitterly. "You remembered?" she said, moving away from the thought.

"A lot of things I never forgot."

"So, why after all this time?"

"I never stopped wanting you in my life. Even when you disappeared, I wanted you."

"Where's Adrienne?"

"Long Island."

"Without you?"

"Yeah, we divorced about three years ago."

"Can't say I'm sorry."

"I wouldn't expect you to. What I want is to see you and the ba . . . Nadia."

"I guess that can be arranged."

"What are you doing tomorrow?"

"I have classes."

"You went back?"

"Yes." *Thanks to Max, who stayed on my butt till I cried uncle. Max . . .*

"Good for you."

"Yeah," Carol-Anne said, thinking of the person who had been responsible for so much of late. "Good for me. Listen, if I don't let Nadia talk to you, she'll die."

"Well, put her on."

"She's in the tub. You have time?"

"Sure . . . is she pretty?"

"Looks a lot like her father."

"Then she must be a darl."

"That she is." And then the present, a fleeting thing, vanished. The past, vague and empty, offered little for discussion. While Carol-Anne knew that she could put the phone down now and go get Nadia, she was reluctant to do it just yet.

"Still there?" he asked.

"Yeah."

"Quiet."

"I think I have the right."

"But it's different now."

"Oh, that makes it okay?"

"It wasn't my fault. You disappeared. Never told me. If I hadn't run into Howard, I probably still wouldn't have known."

"How long have you known?"

"A while."

"How long is a while, Jeff?"

" 'Bout three years."

"So why suddenly now?" *Like you could smell me and Max trying to make a real life together.*

"Because."

"Good answer, Jeff."

"Don't start, Carol. It's different this time."

"Different don't make it better."

"Do I get a second chance?"

"For what?"

"To be a father. To be with you?"

"I don't know, Jeff. I really don't know."

"Won't know till you try."

"There are other things involved. It's not just me and Nadia."

"I gathered as much."

"So what would you have me do? Just tell my friend that he has to go 'cause you're back?"

"No."

"Then what do you suppose I do?"

"I just want the chance to see you and Nadia. Beyond that, it's your call."

But that didn't make her choices easier.

"Let me go and get Nadia. Hold on." She put the phone down without ceremony. Took care with drying Nadia off and slipping on her nightgown. Carol-Anne gave her daughter a long look before she released her to the phone and the father she had never known.

Chapter 7

Carol-Anne had never expected to have this conversation. Not with Nadia. Not with Max. Not with anybody ever. Jeff had never really loved her and she had been so long gone from him that talking about him didn't seem necessary.

But here she was sitting in Max's living room, fear keeping her tongue from telling it all at once; her life with Jeff coming out in dribs and drabs; bits and pieces released slow and painful. She could feel Max's apprehension and fear, and his mixed emotions made it clear to her what she meant to him.

It was all she could do not to weep.

No tears, she told herself for the fifth time since she had arrived.

And Max, *oh Max*, so good about it. He was as concerned and considerate as ever, not forcing anything from her, letting her tell it the best way she could.

Far too late to wonder what he thought of her now, as this tale of a secretary having an affair with her married boss spilled cautiously from her lips. She told of her need to have a child and the choice, condemned from the start.

Carol-Anne found herself remembering how she went off the pill and had unprotected sex anytime and anywhere Jeff wanted; how she'd hurried the business of getting pregnant so that she could leave him. How finally, she had felt in control of something. Something powerful and full of change. How she had anticipated the moment when she could disappear. "Because then he'd feel the pain I always felt when he left me to go home to his wife. It would be his turn to suffer . . ."

"Makes sense?" she asked, as if Max could tell her yes.

Max, wounded, looked away. Said he didn't know.

No tears. She shook her head. "No, it doesn't. But it did to me. It made all the sense in the world. I could never have him the way I wanted him, he had a wife and a kid at home, but I could have his baby . . . You don't know what I went through. Getting pregnant like that and not being able to tell a soul." Her eyes wandered, drifted. Floated in the space above his head.

"Of course, I had to find another job. He was my boss, after all. Couldn't stay. The plan was to escape."

She reached for the glass of wine Max had supplied. Took a long sip. Cool, crisp, and lightly sweet.

"When I hit my third month, I quit. Went on welfare for the first time in my life. Stayed on it till Nadia was a year old. Found another job . . . less money, but I took it. Hard life back then. And my family. They hated me. Of course, they knew he was married, even though I told them he wasn't.

"I thought I'd never see him again. As the years went by I put it out my mind. When Nadia started asking about her father, I told her he had to go away . . . She's a good kid"—a quick smile—"never pressed for the truth. Now he's back and he wants to make like he never been gone." Carol-Anne looked at Max for the first time in a while. "Nadia is thrilled, of course. They been talking on the phone for the past two days. Tomorrow he's supposed to come by." She shook her head.

"You still love him," Max decided, his heart burdened. She would never admit it but Max knew. Had known from the moment she had told him that Nadia's father called.

She shook her head. "Shouldn't . . . have enough reason not to."

It was important to Max that she admitted it. "But you do?"

"I *did*."

Max nodded. Stood. Wouldn't look at her. "We better get going." He headed to the door.

It was dark. A chill hung in the air. Carol-Anne huddled inside her trench coat, thinking it was time to put in the lining. Max, beside her, was silent. His eyes looked straight ahead, as if he were searching for something.

She reached for his hand. Gave it a squeeze. He looked at her, a little shaken.

"Max?"

"Yeah."

She longed to take his arm and hold on to for dear life.

"Doesn't mean much, you know."

"You can't say that, Carol-Anne. Means everything."

"Only if we let it."

Max looked away.

Carol-Anne started cleaning the night before. Washing floors, scrubbing fingerprints from around doorknobs and light switches. Carol-Anne dusted, vacuumed, disinfected. She hot-pressed Nadia's hair for the first time ever.

Made meatloaf and mashed potatoes. She set her tiny kitchen table and put her work clothes back on.

She put on makeup and tuned the radio to the jazz station. Her eye never strayed far from the clock.

Seven-thirty was what he told her. It was now twenty after seven and the wait seemed too long to bear.

As she stood in her living room, spot-checking for loose game pieces and bits of paper, straightening pictures and sipping her second glass of wine, it dawned on her that no matter what she did to the place, Jeff would never be impressed. He hadn't been impressed when she gave him her address. *"Spanish Harlem, why Spanish Harlem?"* He certainly wouldn't be impressed once he saw it.

Someone had broken the lock on the lobby door for the seventh time this year. The super hadn't mopped the halls in weeks and the second-floor landing was awash in old pee. The mouse problem had gotten extremely bad and Carol-Anne had poison and glue traps in every hidden corner she could find.

No, Jeff would never be impressed. After all, he lived in a fashionable brownstone on South Elliot Street in Fort Greene in Brooklyn. Not ritzy, but nice enough.

Carol-Anne had been there once when Adrienne and Jeff Junior had gone to Florida for a week's vacation. The front entry door was solid mahogany with stained-glass borders. The huge living room had a working fireplace, Persian rugs, brass planters, ferns, and white batik-covered furniture.

A black baby grand sat in one corner.

Upstairs the master bedroom had had its own private bath, a four-poster bed, and everything was done in peach and mint. Little Jeff's room had Batman sheets, comforter, and drapes. He had a student desk with its own desk lamp; the toy chest overflowed.

The memory stung her.

Everything in the guest room had been white.

White walls, white rug, white down comforter, white chaise lounge.

Jeff had had sex with Carol-Anne on the living room floor, letting her clean up in the downstairs bath before sending her home in the cab. He wouldn't let her spend the night, and refused to let her even sit on his bed.

Wasn't anything good about those times.

"Mom?"

"Yeah?"

"He coming?"

"Said he was."

"He was a nice man?"

Carol-Anne looked away. Lie or truth? "Yeah, honey, he was."

The doorbell rang. Carol-Anne looked at her daughter. Prettier than two pictures. She reached out and took Nadia's hand. Together they went to answer the door.

His eyes hadn't changed; those instruments that had snared her so long ago still had the same power. Carol-Anne blinked once, twice, opened her mouth to speak.

"Hello, Jeffrey."

He reached out and embraced her before she had time to think. His cologne was the same, nauseating now, unlike then. Carol-Anne pulled away, reached for Nadia's hand. Too many bad times were mixed up in that smell.

"This is Nadia." Who had been looking up, waiting to be noticed the whole time.

"God, she does look like me. Like looking in a mirror." They stood there a minute, door open, not talking. Nadia waited, her eyes wider than a beacon. Waiting for her daddy to do the daddy things. To swoop down, scoop her up, spin her. Tell her how much he missed her. Loved her.

But when the pause became stagnant, Nadia

looked away and the moment was lost forever. Carol-Anne closed the door.

He bent to get a closer look. Carol-Anne, off to the side, waited for him to touch his daughter. To say how pretty she looked. To say hello.

But Jeff stood, brushed imaginary wrinkles from his pants, and smiled at Carol-Anne. "She's beautiful."

"Tell *her*, not me," Carol-Anne suggested, fighting off annoyance.

"You're beautiful, kid."

"Thank you," Nadia managed, pulling her eyes away from him.

Don't he know that she's been waiting for this moment forever? And he's giving nothing. Nothing at all. Anger found Carol-Anne easily. So much preparation for this moment, which was fizzling and dying right before her eyes.

Without being asked, Jeff started toward the living room, his eyes busy on everything.

"Some place," he offered.

"It's not that bad."

He sat on her couch, disregarding one of Nadia's books that became wedged beneath his thigh. "Not bad? You're kidding, right?"

Carol-Anne took a deep breath. "Yeah . . . look, I made dinner in case you're hungry."

"No, thanks. I ate before I came."

Just like you use to. My kitchen always offended you in a way my open thighs never could.

"Well, if you will excuse us, me and Nadia are going to."

"Sure, go right ahead." He picked up the remote. "You get ESPN?" he asked, clicking on the TV and easing back against her sofa bed.

"I don't know. I'm not into sports."

He laughed and the sound was an insult. "Oh,

yeah, that's right . . . Got any beer?" he wanted to know.

"No." She had wine, but damn if she would offer him any.

In the kitchen while Nadia sat at the table solemn and quiet, Carol-Anne removed the third setting and asked Nadia to get ice for the glasses. She began making plates for her and her daughter, the first thing that felt right since Jeff arrived.

"Mom?"

"Yeah, baby."

"He my daddy?"

She wanted to tell her no, that it was a mistake. That the man now sitting in her living room watching her TV, refusing to eat her food, was not her daddy. That her daddy would never be so inconsiderate and so lacking. That her daddy would have come with chocolates, a teddy bear, and a big hug, not been empty-handed and absentminded.

"Yeah, baby. That's him."

"He don't seem like it."

Carol-Anne convinced him to play a game of Monopoly with them. A hard feat pulling him away from the football game, but Carol-Anne would not take no for an answer.

Nadia loved Monopoly and if Jeff was ever going to be a father to her, he'd have to learn to love it, too. At the last minute Carol-Anne backed out of the game and left them alone to play.

She went to the kitchen with the excuse she had to do dishes, but in fact she wanted Nadia and Jeff to be alone. That would be the extent of his involvement. He'd be in Nadia's life, but not hers. Not ever.

From bad to worse? Seemed nine years had done just that. While Jeff had had little or no patience before, he was running on empty now. He had gained a few pounds and hadn't stayed current. His suit was at least five years old and his shoes were in need of a shine and a lift. His hair was half an inch too thick and he had a little pot belly. He was four years older than Max, but it might as well be ten. *Max . . .*

My tall, handsome, hard and lean, money-making banker man. Who hugs Nadia every time he sees her and pays for dancing lessons. Who always says something nice to her and doesn't mind kiddy chatting . . . They say everything happens for a reason and Jeff coming back now is as clear as my reflection in a mirror. Lord knew that if he had come sooner I might have wimped out and tried to get with Jeff's program again just because he's Nadia's father . . . Don't even know why he bothered to come, 'cause he sure hasn't shown any interest in his daughter.

Nadia got sleepy around nine. As Carol-Anne put her to bed, Jeff lingered in the doorway, watching. Her offer to come and tuck in his daughter was refused.

He didn't go into the room. Didn't read her a bedtime story. Didn't even kiss her good-night. He hadn't kissed Nadia at all.

"How she doing in school?" he asked her as she closed the bedroom door.

"Fine." Carol-Anne bent down and began packing away the Monopoly game.

"She's so cute."

"Yeah." She stood, game box in hand. She was tired and was ready to call it a night. She slipped it under the couch.

"Getting late." She hinted.

He smiled at her and nothing in her wanted him.

"Not that late," he decided for them both.

"Yeah, Jeff, it is. I have to get up in the morning."

"Bet you still get to work on time."

"Yeah. You ready?"

He was a little annoyed, but Carol-Anne moved past it.

"Was hoping to spend a little time with you."

She shook her head. "No."

"Came all this way just to see you."

"I thought you came to see your daughter."

He shrugged. "Yeah, her, too."

"Look, Jeff, let's get something straight. You want to be in Nadia's life, then be in it. If it's something else you fishing around here for, then you better be on your way now."

He moved past her advice. "Talked to my mother. She invited you and Nadia to our Thanksgiving dinner. Family's dying to meet her."

Carol-Anne shook her head. "I'll have to let you know."

He looked at her. Hard. "You still look good, you know that?"

"Whatever. Come on, let me get your coat." When he didn't make a move, Carol-Anne got his coat out of her closet and opened the front door.

Reluctantly, he headed her way. Looked at her and shook his head. "You were always a tough cookie, that's what I liked about you most."

Jeff slipped on his coat, something heavy, limpish, and gray. Her guard down, Carol-Anne looked away. His tongue, wet and pungent landed against her mouth, startled her. She shoved him so hard he hit the wall. For a long time she glared at him, surprised by her show of strength, by the sheer will she used to move him away.

He look more hurt than wounded. "Just a kiss, Carol."

She didn't speak. Held her breath till he was in the hall. Did not say good night but shut the door and slid in the deadbolts. Waited with her ear pressed against the door until she could no longer hear the sound of his shoes on the stairs. Slid down to the floor. Held her head and cried without noise. She didn't want to wake Nadia.

Chapter 8

Naiveness is granted anyone who doesn't know the whole truth. For this reason Carol-Anne, against her intuition, accepted Jeff's invitation to Thanksgiving dinner at his mother's home even though it was painfully obvious that he was a stranger and a father to Nadia in name only.

Nevertheless, for Nadia's sake, Carol-Anne dressed her in her Sunday finest and donned a gray angora dress, matching gray shoes, and faux pearls for herself. It was with great optimism that Carol-Anne stood at the bottom of the brownstone steps, waiting for someone to answer the door.

"Don't worry," Jeff intoned, his hand fidgety against the knot in his tie.

Carol-Anne glanced up at him and saw the changes time had wrought. *More than his looks have changed. I don't know him anymore. He's so different and unyielding. Stiff. Selfish. My God, that man is selfish. Whatever I thought I saw in him nine years ago is gone.*

"I still think it's too soon, Jeff." The only reason Carol-Anne was there at all was because of Nadia. She wanted to meet her other "grandma." But meeting his family on Thanksgiving was pushing it. Carol-Anne wished she had listened to her instincts.

"Everybody knows about you and Nadia, so it won't be a big deal," Jeff told her.

But it was.

Everyone treated her as if she were glass and Nadia a freak in a sideshow. They touched Nadia, and talked about her as if she weren't there. They marveled at how well she carried on a conversation and the manner in which she spoke, as if illegitimacy were a disease that affected the brain. By the time the bird had been put on the table, Jeff's other children, two boys aged eight and eleven, had pulled out all of Nadia's hair ribbons and called her names that no little child should ever speak.

Still, there was another part to the equation. A part so small and so scary that Carol-Anne kept it buried deep down inside and would never share it with anybody.

Jeff's family didn't know her for who she was today, only for what she had been a long time ago. Some secretary that Jeff had slept with and gotten knocked up was how Carol-Anne was certain they saw her. She was certain they considered her some sleazy impoverished illiterate from *Spanish Harlem of all places,* who no doubt was responsible for the breakup of Jeff's marriage and had brought Jeff to his ruin.

This tiny part of her, so small you'd need a microscope to find it, wanted to show them who she was today. She wanted to be all that they thought she wasn't. Poised, beautiful. A wonderful mother to a wonderful child. She wanted to show that in Jeff's absence, she and Nadia had wanted for nothing. That she could live perfectly and happily without ever having to see him again.

If there was anyone she needed to prove herself to, it was Jeff's mother. She was delighted when Mrs. Gadson asked her to help her to set the table.

Mrs. Gadson, a slim, trim sixty-seven-year-old, glanced at Carol-Anne with severe eyes. "So, Carol, what do you do?"

"I'm an administrative assistant with General Services, but I'm working on my B.A."

"Oh. Well, that's nice. Jeff has his masters."

"Yes," Carol-Anne said cautiously, "I know."

"Of course"—a tight smile—"your daughter is a doll. She looks a lot like Jeffrey's sister Rosetta did at her age." But the remark was full of surprise and suspicion. Carol-Anne shrugged, her eyes noticing the crystal chandelier in the formal dining room, the freshly polished wood trim around the tall windows and the baseboards.

She took note of the fancy tablecloth and the cut-crystal vase full of roses. Must have been three dozen around the house in all.

"You know, Jeff's children are doing quite well in school. How is Nadia doing?"

"Well, she's only in the third grade, but she's doing pretty well."

"Yes, I see. I better check on the rolls. Maybe you should see what Nadia is up to."

Dismissed.

That part of Carol-Anne bent on proving them wrong vanished. She realized that she could have had a Ph.D. pinned to her chest and it wouldn't have made a damn bit of difference.

But that was fine with her. All she really wanted was to make this day a thing of the past. Because after today, she'd never have to be here again.

"It's getting late, Jeff. I have work tomorrow."

Jeffrey, sprawled on the carpet between his two sons, was engaged in a video game. Off to the side, Nadia sat, watching both her father and the video game alternately.

Look at my baby. She wants to play. She wants to be down there with her father enjoying a round of Super Mario Brothers. But he doesn't even realize, or care.

*He's down there with his sons and that's all he
knows. His sons called his daughter a bastard and he
didn't even correct them. Just said that it wasn't a
nice name to call anybody. Like she really was and
he wasn't her father.*

*They picked over my daughter like she was some
animal in the zoo. Jeff hasn't pay her a bit of attention
since we got here. Don't he realize that she's been
wanting this forever . . . ?*

"Jeff!"

"Yeah, okay. Just one more game."

*What made me think he had changed? Look at
him down there with his ugly-ass boys. He hasn't
even thought about asking Nadia to play.*

"Daddy, you leaving?" Jeff junior asked.

"Yeah, Daddy has to go soon."

"Mommy said maybe we would spend the weekend with you," Alex stated, in need of verification of
his father's time.

"Well, I have to check with her."

"Is she living with you?" Jeff junior asked, indignant. Jeff looked over his shoulder in surprise,
laughed. "No. Ms. McClementine is not living with
me."

"No," Alex interjected, he and his brother on the
same wavelength. "Not her. That girl."

Carol-Anne's face burned. She stole a look at Nadia and knew her daughter's bowed head meant that
tears were on their way.

Enough of this shit . . .

Her was voice full of fire. "No, Nadia lives with
me." She stared Alex down until he was forced to
look away.

"Well, she better not," Jeff junior decided, as if his
opinion were law.

Jeff senior laughed again.

He's enjoying this shit. He's tickled pink. His

daughter is over there hurt as all get out, and he thinks it's fucking funny?

"And why can't Nadia live with me?" Jeff asked, riding the wave of bitter sibling rivalry.

" 'Cause we was yours first," Alex said, proud and sullen.

That's it. I'm out of here, even if I have to walk.

"I'm getting our coats. Come on, Nadia. Come help Mommy." Nadia stood, the crinoline springing her dress to life as she rose. *Pretty as two pictures,* Carol-Anne thought. *And Jeff, you don't have the slightest clue. Your daughter that you obviously want for show-and-tell and little else, will grow up to be the one who'll make you proud, not those other shits. But by then, it'll be too late. I can't wait. I just can't fucking wait. Get back together with you? You must be crazy. The only way you'll see Nadia again is if she wants to.*

She took Nadia into an empty bedroom. Sat her daughter on the handmade quilt and gently lifted her chin. The tears were real now. It wasn't where Carol-Anne wanted to have this conversation, but it could not wait until they got home. She had to apologize for that idiot. Carol-Anne had to sit there and tell her daughter lies.

"Nadia . . . your father isn't too smart sometimes. Sometimes it takes him time to see how precious something is. He doesn't mean to be unkind, but sometimes he is. You know that you have a whole bunch of people who love you. You are loved, you are pretty and precious. You understand?"

"Mommy, why they call me that name? Why Daddy let them?"

Don't call him that. "Oh, baby." Carol-Anne wiped tears from her daughter's cheek. "Because they're stupid and jealous. Them boys looked at you and realized that you have something they would never have. They saw you were smarter, prettier, and better, and so they're jealous. When people get jealous, sometimes they can be very mean."

"Let me see if I can find it."

The door swung open and Mrs. Gadson walked in. For a second she stared, her hand moving to her throat as if Carol-Anne were about to snatch her gold.

"Oh. You scared me," she said, bewildered.

Carol-Anne didn't speak, keeping her gaze steady. She wanted Mrs. Gadson to see the pain she and her daughter had suffered this day.

"What's wrong? Something's wrong?" She moved into the room, carefully closing the door behind her.

Carol-Anne looked down at Nadia and back up at Jeffrey's mother. It's all about how you raise your children, she decided.

"The boys, Jeff Junior and Alex. They called Nadia a bastard. Jeff didn't tell them different. That's part of it. Shall I go on?"

Mrs. Gadson paled beneath her Vera Moore makeup. *Good.*

"They did what?"

"Called her a bastard." The word was hard pressed coming off Carol-Anne's tongue. But Carol-Anne would soon be gone and never return and she wanted the story told right in her absence.

"You must be mistaken."

"Why would I make such a thing up? And besides being call an awful untruthful name, and Jeff not saying she wasn't, he has ignored my daughter the whole time we've been here. That's what's wrong, Mrs. Gadson. So if you'll excuse me, I'd like a few words with Nadia and then we'll be going."

"Where is he?" Mrs. Gadson wanted to know. From her tone of voice, Jeff could have been all of ten. Like she was about to send him to his room without supper. But he was grown now. It was way too late.

"Playing video games."

"I'll be back."

Carol-Anne wanted to tell her not to bother. But she figured she'd be gone soon enough.

"Mommy, I want to go home."

"We're going."

"Is my father coming with us?"

"He has to drop us."

"I don't want him to. He doesn't like me."

"He doesn't really know you, Nadia." Which had always been the bottom line.

Like a paramedic rushing to a hit-and-run victim, Jeff burst into the room.

"What's going on?"

"Nothing, Jeff. Can we go?"

"What do you mean, nothing? My mother comes in, raving about the boys calling Nadia awful things and how I've been ignoring her."

"That's the story. Can we go?"

"Is she upset?"

"Wouldn't you be if your brothers called you a bastard and your mother stood by and let them?" The word was getting harder on her tongue, but she wanted Jeff to feel the hurt it had caused.

"I told them about that."

"Yeah? What did you say, Jeff? All you said was that was not a nice name to call somebody. Never said she *wasn't.* Not once. She was sitting in a corner almost in tears and you never once looked up from your boys or that stupid-ass game. She's sitting in tears now, but have you thought about going to her? Thought about asking her what's wrong? No. You ask me, like she don't even matter. I just want to go home."

Finally he looked at Nadia. But she had her head down. He walked over to her and got on his knees.

Too late for the cavalry now . . .

"Nadia?" he asked, his voice full of concern.

"Yes?"

"Can you look at Daddy?"

She looked up. Her eyes were red and puffy.

Carol-Anne batted back tears.

"I'm sorry about this, baby," Jeff went on to say.

Carol-Anne watched closely as Nadia nodded.

She doesn't believe him. Good. Don't believe another thing he has to say about anything, especially about you, Nadia. Mommy's got his number and I swear nothing like this will ever, ever happen to you again. He broke my heart years ago and won't get a second chance to break yours.

The scene was going nowhere. It was time to go.

"Let me get our coats and then we'll go, okay?" Carol-Anne decided.

Nadia nodded, flying past Jeff. It was her mother's arms she sought. Carol-Anne was ready, bent down low, receiving her with open arms.

"This will never happen again, Nadia. You hear Mommy saying? Never. Again."

Jeff gave Carol-Anne the car keys and stayed behind to say good night. It took him ten minutes.

Probably making nice with his sons, now that Grandma done put them on punishment for the week they're staying with her. What she tell them? No video games, like that's an eye for an eye.

Lord, just get me home. Please. Let us just get home.

She was blowing hard on the car horn when Jeff appeared. It would have been best if she had just let dirty dead secrets remain buried.

For once, Mommy, you were right on the money . . .

It was all about fear, Max realized in the aftermath of Thanksgiving and the careful, painful telephone call he received that night from Carol-Anne. Max was too afraid not to let Carol-Anne go with Jeff, and Jeff had been too afraid to keep her. But in the end, Carol-Anne and Max were both still there.

"So, what happens next? With Nadia, I mean?"

Carol-Anne didn't even pause, the words came out of her mouth fast and furious. "If it were up to me, she'd never see that bastard again . . . but it's not. If and when Nadia wants to see him, then she will. Until then, he better not come nowhere near her."

"He is her father."

"Yeah, but you and I know, sperm don't make you one. Any idiot can do that."

"Beyond all that, my point remains. He is her father."

"He hasn't been since the day she was conceived. Okay, so I didn't tell him straight up, but he has known for three years now. Three whole years. It took him three years to decide that he wanted us in his life? Bullshit, Max. That's fucking bull."

"So what do you think it was?"

"I think that he's making some money and getting old and thought Nadia was a good investment. His other kids are total assholes, you hear me? Spoiled, selfish, and ugly to boot. Hell, I wouldn't want to be their daddy, either. So I figure Jeff looked around and said, 'well, I sort of screwed up with my children, let me see how Nadia's doing.' You know, play that weekend-daddy crap. Be her father Friday night through Sunday, and the rest of the week, he wouldn't have to be bothered.

"Nadia's beyond Pampers and formulas, so he probably decided he'd look her up, and take her around to his friends to brag about his little girl, like she was some great acquisition. That's what I think. And every time I think it"—*it's a knife in my heart going around and around*—"I just want to scream . . . or kill him. It hurts that bad. Nadia didn't deserve none of that, Max. None of it."

"Where is she now?"

"Sleeping. In my bed."

"I'm sorry, Carol-Anne. I had no idea."

"You couldn't. You don't know him. Hell, I don't even know him anymore. He's like this awful, self-centered conceited fuck, y'know? And all I can ask myself is how in the world did I ever get involved with him? I mean, if he's like that now, he must've been like that then."

"Love makes you do strange things."

"Don't I know it. Anyway, listen. I'm going to bed."

"I'll call you tomorrow."

"From home, you lucky dog."

"Is it my fault that I'm the mortgage director and was able to swing the day after Thanksgiving?"

"Yes." But Carol-Anne was laughing now, the day fading away. The present more important.

"We staying in tomorrow night?" Max asked.

"After what Nadia went through, I think it's best."

"I'll order Chinese, we'll play a couple rounds of Monopoly, and then wait for Nadia to fall off to sleep."

"Then what?"

"You know what."

"Don't I ever, Mr. Scutter. Don't I ever."

Carol-Anne hung up and got into bed, pulling her sleeping daughter close. Her eyes danced over the shadows, the day's events settling like dust around her heart. She kissed Nadia's forehead, studied the beatific wonder of her slumbering daughter's face.

Never again, baby. Never, ever again . . .

Chapter 9

Carol-Anne closed her eyes and sighed. *Another year nearly gone. Tomorrow when I wake up, the past will be history. A whole lot of changes have come, for the better, thank God. For the better.*

Her eyes settled on the Christmas tree. Eight feet tall. Scottish pine. A cascade of white organza bows and golden trumpeting angels. Gifts, too many to count, lay arranged beneath the spreading branches. Max wanted this to be the best Christmas Nadia ever had, and it was. An Easy Bake Oven, an easel, paint and brushes. Roller skates, Disney movie videos. Books, puzzles. A new Monopoly game. And the clothes. Max had spent four hundred dollars on Nadia, easy.

More than her father ever thought to do.

Carol-Anne pulled away from the thought. Nothing was going to spoil her holiday. She looked around her. She loved Max's place. It was her home away from home and Carol-Anne came here often.

Christmas Day having come and gone, December 31 found her dressed save for a little more perfume and a retouching of her lipstick. But even as she considered last-minute things yet to be done, Carol-Anne languished. She was in no hurry to move from the leather sofa.

It was New Year's Eve and they were going to Pat's. If it was up to her, they would stay home. The last person she wanted to see five minutes before the New Year was Samone.

Her choice would have been to go to the early church service with her mother, Nadia, and Max, and then come back here, minus Nadia. She and Max would have crawled into the big old king-sized bed, eaten lobster salad on wheat crackers, and drunk chilled expensive champagne. Watched the ball drop in the comfort of his bed, not at a crowded party way across town.

Nadia, dressed, hair combed and face greased, sat on the edge of the couch eager to get going. And while Carol-Anne knew that she should get up, that she still had things to do, the peace was too complete.

Max came in from the kitchen with a tray of eggnog. He handed one to Nadia and watched while she took a sip.

"Good?" Max asked.

"Yeah, it tastes like rum raisin ice cream."

Nadia had not asked about her father since Thanksgiving, and when he called asking for her, Nadia refused to take the call. *Her choice,* she had told Jeff.

Jeff had threatened her with a custody battle. He had talked of dragging her into court for the right to see Nadia. It had got Carol-Anne's blood boiling, but she finally realized that no court in the world would give him Nadia. If Nadia did not want to see the man who gave her life, no court could make it so.

Carol-Anne took her cup of eggnog and leaned back against the couch. One minute Max was there and the next he was gone. He reappeared with a small gift box. Handed it to Carol-Anne as if it were the most natural thing in the world.

"What's this for?" Carol-Anne asked, not trusting the size, nor the weight, light as air.

"For you," was all Max would say.

"Max, Christmas has come and gone. What's going on?"

"Will you just open it?"

"Not till you tell me what's going on."

"Can I open it, Mommy?"

"No . . . Max?"

"Will you just open it?"

"Go ahead, Mommy."

"It better not be what I think it is." Carol-Anne's heart was beating faster than she could think. *I'm not ready for this, Max.*

"Will you open the box?" he implored.

Carol-Anne slid a finger into the fold and paused. Undid a flap. Undid another. When the small gray velvet jewelry box lay unopened in her palm, her eyes sought his.

Max nodded and Carol-Anne opened the box.

"Oh," was all she could say. Even as she reached inside, bringing the platinum band with the small diamond up to the light, then slipping it on her finger, she could not speak.

"Now before you go and bawl me out, this is not an engagement ring, okay? This is just something I wanted you to have so when the world gets a little funky you'll know that somewhere out there, I'm waiting for you."

"Oh, Max."

Damn if she didn't cry.

Carol-Anne's dress was black satin, off the shoulder, and skimmed just above her knees. Her stockings were sheer, her pumps black velvet with rhinestones.

Her hair had been layered and strands swirled around her head like ripples on a pond. Her nails, fake and ruby-red, matched her fiery moist lip color. There were glittery stones dripping from her ears and a matching choker around her neck. But Carol-Anne felt as if she were wearing a potato sack when Samone arrived at the party.

The Christmas-red tight-fitting sateen dress with the extremely low back and the plunging neckline was about a size seven. Every curve Samone owned was visible from across the room. Her hair had been gathered up, with tendrils falling seductively over one eye, along the sides of her face, and down her bare back.

By far she was the most stunning creature in the room. Even Carol-Anne wanted to reach out and touch her beauty.

Samone came to them, her white boyfriend behind her. Carol-Anne didn't know his name, but she had seen his type before. Handsome, smart, and intelligent. He would have to be all those things in order for Samone to date him, much less bring him to the Upper West Side to a party full of black faces.

It wasn't hard to hate her.

"Hi, guys," Samone offered, her eyes focused on Carol-Anne, then Max.

"Hi," Carol-Anne forced herself to say. "Happy New Year."

So animated, so pretty, so sexy and assured. Samone was in her glory as she took her boyfriend's arm. "Jon, this is Max and his friend Carol-Anne."

"Nice to finally meet you." But there was tension in Max's voice that Carol-Anne did not miss.

"Nice to meet you, too," Jon answered, his cat eyes twinkling like diamonds. "Heard so much about you, feels like I've known you for years."

"Be nice, guys," was all Samone said, obviously luxuriating in this moment at every one's expense. Carol-Anne smiled so hard her face ached.

"Well, if you will excuse us," Samone said, taking Jon's arm.

"Good to see you again, Samone," Carol-Anne intoned, wishing her gone, knowing Max's mind now and his every thought. Knowing that inside his fine suit his heart was breaking, and the longer Samone stood there being sexy and cute and unattainable, the more Max's heart shattered.

Carol-Anne gave his hand a squeeze. A little nudge that said *Yes, but I'm here . . . right here. Right next to you, loving you.* But if Max felt it, he didn't show any sign. His eyes were searching Samone's face like a beacon. Carol-Anne wanted to turn his head, smack him. She wanted to throw her arms around him. Kiss him. Be a magician and make Samone vanish, but she didn't possess that kind of power. As the music was turned down and the TV up, Carol-Anne knew her worst fear was going to be realized. They would be spending the final seconds of the old year in Samone's presence.

Carol-Anne saw Samone returning Max's stare as if no one else existed, as if they were alone in the crowded room. Her palms sweated.

Max could feel Carol-Anne's stare but could not tear his eyes away from Samone until people started shouting *"Happy New Year!"* Until Jon took Samone into his arms and kissed her with all the passion he possessed. Only then could Max look away. Only then did he remember Carol-Anne beside him. She accepted Max's arms around her, a desperate meeting that drove his lips hungry against her own.

As they broke apart Carol-Anne found herself watching Jon. She wondered if he knew what had just occurred. If he did, he hid it well.

"To you, babe," she heard Max say, turning and seeing his glass raised, his eyes soft with joy and pain. Carol-Anne forced a smile, raised her own glass and drank deeply.

It must be bad news, Carol-Anne decided, as she watched Max drop down onto the sofa, the phone cradled tight against his ear. The collar of his leather bomber touched his chin, the keys to the rental car lay on the carpet where they had fallen from his fingers.

They had been on their way to pick up Carol-Anne's daughter from her mother's when the phone rang.

"No, Samone. No . . . when? . . . Where are you? . . . He is? . . . Okay . . . Yeah . . . Don't cry, babe, please don't cry . . . I have to see . . . yeah, later . . . all right."

Max hung up and brought both palms to his eyes. Rubbed them for a long time before he looked up and saw Carol-Anne leaning anxiously against the wall. Max's eyes pulled away from her slowly, Samone's pain still with him.

"Samone's uncle just died," was all Max offered, taking a few more seconds to regroup, to press back the need to mourn. He stood, sensing Carol-Anne's questions. Later, when he had time to really think, he'd tell her.

"Come on. Let's go get Nadia. Then I'll drop you. I have to go across town."

Carol-Anne, into day one of their new year, knew she had been pushed aside in the wake of this news. Beyond being Samone's uncle, he must have been a friend to Max as well, she told herself.

But then she kept on hearing her man on the phone with his ex-lover. Kept on hearing him calling her *babe*, something he called Carol-Anne only occasionally. It had sounded so natural, you'd thought it really was Samone's name.

Carol-Anne's life with Max would always be filled with such moments, she decided, a new hurt appearing in her eyes.

"He was a good friend?"

Carol-Anne surprised him. Max had not expected her to ask now. "Let's go downstairs, I'll tell you on the way."

"No, Max. No. Here and now. Let's talk now.

This instant." She paused, took a breath. "You didn't hear yourself on the phone . . . You have any idea how I'm feeling? Listening to you talk to her like that?"

"Carol-Anne, don't do this. Not now. I got to get going."

"Get to where, Max? To pick up Nadia? That can wait."

"I have to get to Uncle Chicken's."

"Why? To do what?"

Max moved to answer, but he realized he didn't know. To do what? Console Aunti? No, Samone.

"They're like family to me. Can you understand that? Uncle Chicken was like my uncle. It's like my uncle died."

Carol-Anne's hand waved in front of her. "That's all you had to say, Max. Not just spew out instructions like I know where you're going and why. A little consideration, that's all I'm asking. Don't assume I know your life like you know it . . . I'm ready. You can drop me at my mother's. Me and Nadia will take the train home."

Her stinging words brought everything to a screaming halt. They made him stop. Think. Max slipped his keys into his jacket pocket. Extended his arms, and gave Carol-Anne a humbled look.

"I'm sorry," he said.

But it wasn't enough for her.

Max continued. "You were right, again. There's no need for me to rush over there. What can I do there anyway? There'll probably be enough people there already. I won't be missed."

She gave him a questioning look. "I thought you said he was like an uncle to you. Like it was your uncle who died."

"He was, in a lot of ways, but that was all tied up in me and Samone being together."

"Well, at least you admitted it." She took a cleansing breath. "Samone calls and your immediate instinct is to go running? You have to get past that, Max. You're my man now, not hers."

Carol-Anne brushed by him, his arms, still extended. Were pushed aside in her wake.

Chapter 10

Tina pressed the steamer to the wallpaper. With her other hand she steadied the putty knife. Forced the edge at the seam and pushed.

"So, you thought about it?"

Carol-Anne eyed her. "Thought about what?"

"Max's offer to move you out of this hellhole. Move out the 'hood."

"Not lately," Carol-Anne said, not wanting to talk about it.

"You're gonna have to, you know. Sooner or later he's gonna insist that you do."

"Why do I have to move? I like my place. I've been here damn near ten years. Waterside Apartments? That's on the other side of the Hudson."

"Why? Because it's not just about you anymore. It's about the two of you."

"I just can't see moving out and moving in with him. What happens if it don't work? Then where will I be?"

"Seems to me that Max would never ask you to move in with him unless it was serious. That ring on your finger speaks for itself."

"This?" Carol-Anne held out her finger. Looked at the platinum band with the diamond center. "Oh, this is just a friendship ring."

The ring. The last thing Carol-Anne had expected.

Max swore it wasn't an engagement ring, but everyone who saw it swore it was.

Carol-Anne fingered it. "It's not."

"Yeah, and my name ain't Tina." She worked on the paper with her knife. Carol-Anne watched her from the sofa.

"How long you been at that?"

"Since morning."

Carol-Anne looked around her. At the paneled ceilings, at the Levolor blinds. She looked at the leather ottoman and the brass curios in the corner. Carol-Anne studied the lithographs on Tina's walls and the area rug beneath her feet.

It was beautiful inside Tina's apartment. But outside it was still Spanish Harlem. Still the ghetto. Tina would go to her grave living inside this one-bedroom. Carol-Anne wondered if she was willing to do the same.

Carol-Anne didn't want to leave this side of Manhattan. Didn't want to leave her 'hood. She knew Max hated it here. Didn't know of anyone else in her tenement who stayed because they wanted to. Didn't know anyone else who had the choices she had.

Carol-Anne had put in some overtime and it was dark by the time she got off the bus. She moved swiftly down 119th Street, her pocketbook over her shoulder and across her back. She moved quickly because today was payday and on payday Carol-Anne made it a rule to go straight home. But there was no milk for her morning coffee and there was no bread for Nadia's lunch.

Carol-Anne broke her rule. She stopped at the corner store.

Before she left work, she had put her set-aside money, a new five-dollar bill, in the outside zipper of her pocketbook. More than enough for whatever she needed. But once Carol-Anne got into the crowded bodega she realized there were other things she needed. Like toilet paper and deodorant. Realized that the five dollars would not be enough. That she would have to go into her stash.

Four hundred and sixty dollars in twenties, slipped down so low and deep into her bag that it would take a real good thief to find it. Carol-Anne looked around her. Didn't see anyone near. Opened her bag quickly and dug deep. Handed Pedro the money, took her change, and headed out of the brightly lit store, darkness greeting her.

Carol-Anne noticed the man leaning against the pay phone, a lit cigarette in his hand. She looked up her block and saw two other people coming her way. Carol-Anne clutched the groceries with one hand, her pocketbook with the other, and started walking, instinct pushing her toward the curb.

Carol-Anne crossed the street. She heard footfalls behind her. On red alert now, Carol-Anne went another yard then slipped between two parked cars. Stepped out into the street again, she resisted the urge to run.

Three doors from home now.

Carol-Anne had just stepped up on the curb when she sensed a motion behind her. Turned and came face-to-face with the man who had been smoking the cigarette, except now his hands were empty and his eyes were hooded; they stared into her soul.

Two feet away Carol-Anne stared back.

Adrenaline shot through her, but she continued her stare, her eyes fierce and protective. *Mine,* her eyes shouted. *Mine,* not yours.

They stood there, Carol-Anne on the curb, the unknown assailant in the street. They were so close Carol-Anne could smell his fetid breath.

Mine, her eyes shouted once again. The young man sucked his teeth, lifted his head with slight disgust, and turned, walking away.

Carol-Anne stood there, watching his retreating form. Numb, scared, faint. She felt a coolness on her legs, gathering around her ankles, and realized that she had wet her pants. She didn't know how long she stood there, breathing hard in the chill night air.

But the feel of her tears got her feet moving. Fear held her steady until she was inside the building. That's when it came, the mixed brew of relief and terror.

She couldn't tell anyone.

Not Tina and certainly not Max. They would point fingers. Say, *See, I told you . . . it's time to leave this place*. Tina would cluck her teeth, shake her head, and tell her it was a sign. Max would demand she pack her things and move in with him.

Yes, she had been scared tonight. Scared of losing her life over two weeks' pay. Scared that something she worked so hard for could so easily be taken away. Scared but still here.

Pleasant Avenue had been her home for a long time. She did not want to turn the reins of her life over to any man. She had done that once with Nadia's father. Had let him lead her down a wayward path.

She would just have to be more careful, that's all. Be more careful.

Max walked down Pleasant Avenue, the sound of his Benito Italian loafers muffled against the pocked, uneven pavement. He held his briefcase tightly, looked straight ahead, but noticed everything around him. He passed the graffiti-strewn window of the Laundromat, eyed the bricked-up X-marked abandoned buildings.

He entered Carol-Anne's building, key ready, but found it wasn't necessary. Someone had broken the lock and with an easy push he was inside the foyer. The low-watt bulb overhead offered little illumination and plenty of shadows. As his foot hit the first step of the black-and-white chipped-tile staircase, his eyes drifted to the darkness looming above him. The bulb had blown again.

Senses open, everything working overtime, eyes, nose, ears, Max took measured steps, mindful of the laptop inside his briefcase and the Rolex on his wrist. Max had grown up near the Grand Concourse in the Bronx and had lived most of his adult life in Harlem. Max had fought many fistfights, but not even the swiftest right-hand punch could stop a bullet.

Max knew that he was ill-prepared if someone with a gun decided they wanted the contents of his briefcase, the monetary holdings in his wallet. If they decided his Rolex would look much better on their wrist. These were the thoughts that consumed him every Friday evening as he made his way to Carol-Anne's apartment, sweating beneath his London Fog trench, heart racing as he moved through the shadows of the landings.

Only his love of her brought him here.

As he rounded the second landing, darkness around him, the steel-threaded windowpane offering muted light but no illumination, he heard two distinct pops up above him. Max stopped, breathing lightly in the fetid air of cooking smells, ammonia, and a quick drift of gunpowder. Max held his breath, waiting, listening for more popping noises, the sound of running feet. But the air above him was hushed now.

Firecrackers.

Long past the summer holiday, firecrackers were still a mainstay in the area. That and M-80s. Max hurried up to the third landing, his key aiming for Carol-Anne's front door. With a shudder the door swung open, sepia light spilling from the kitchen.

Max closed the door, set the two locks, the dead-bolt and the link chain. Still, it gave him no sense of security.

"Hey," Carol-Anne called from the kitchen.

"Hey," Max called back, easing out of his trench, sweat trickling down his spine as he drifted toward the sepia light of the kitchen.

✕

Chapter 11

There were certain things that Carol-Anne had learned to live with; the roaches that filled her kitchen at night, the poor heat, gunshots outside her windows. Mice.

She bombed her kitchen every other month, tossed Raid roach bait in corners, got flannels for herself and Nadia, and placed glue traps with peanut butter along the walls.

But this was different.

Carol-Anne walked into her kitchen one morning, her mind on coffee. Dragging herself, half asleep, she had her mind on getting a quick fire beneath the kettle and making a nice cup of instant that would shrug the weariness from her body and kick-start her brain.

She eyed the chipped porcelain kettle like an old friend. Reached for its brass handle when something caught her eye.

Beans, on her stove.

Carol-Anne looked at the beans a long time, trying to figure out how they had got there. She started to gather them up with a paper towel when she realized they weren't beans. Her mind flashed back to pet stores. Flashed back to black pellets on yellowed newspaper; furry animals scampering in cages, their tiny claws like clicks of a castanet against the mesh.

Droppings, she realized, still half asleep, reaching for the spigot to dampen the paper towel, her mind still foggy as she turned on the tap. The cold water snapped her awake. The hows and whys of the droppings hit her full force.

Rats.

She had seen plenty of dead ones in the gutter and had witnessed the final death throes of a particularly large one on the second-floor landing. She knew people in her building had seen them, too, but this was her first experience with them inside *her* apartment.

Her eyes did a fast sweep of the floor. She noticed her pantry door was open and corn meal scattered on the shelf. Her heart raced. Afraid to move, afraid to breathe, Carol-Anne willed her feet forward anyway, easing up to the pantry and carefully pulling the door all the way back.

The box of farina she had stored in a freezer bag was gnawed through at the bottom. More droppings were scattered in the mix.

"Morning, Mommy."

She looked up and saw her daughter, realized they were both barefooted. "Nadia," she said carefully, "go in the room and get your sneakers, put them on, okay?"

"But I haven't even had a bath yet."

Carol-Anne moved toward her, her eyes sweeping the floors like a beacon. She sensed something was watching her. "I know, honey, but the floor got stuff on it and I don't want you to get any on your feet."

Nadia looked down. "I don't see nothing."

"It's kinda invisible," Carol-Anne said, forgiving herself the lie. "Now go ahead." She watched her daughter retreat and thought about the space beneath Nadia's bed where her sneakers were kept. Do rats hide under beds?

Carol-Anne hurried down the hall, grabbing her daughter by the shoulder. "You know what?" she said quickly. "Go get in the shower and I'll bring you your clothes, okay?"

No, it wasn't okay. Nadia didn't know what was wrong but whatever it was, it must have been really scary. She had never seen her mother look so afraid.

She stood, hand on her hip, glaring down at her super, who was taking his time having his morning coffee.

"You got to do something, Mr. Matthews. There's droppings all over my kitchen. I got a child up there."

"Well, now, Miz Clementine, I'm gonna do something but I don't do nothing until I've had my morning coffee. If you got rats you don't have to worry about them now. They like darkness, rarely come out in the day. If you got any food out, just put it in the fridge. Dump all that meal and stuff from your cupboards. Make sure you empty your garbage at night. They just looking for food, and if you keep food locked up, they go off and find another place to eat."

"Oh, so I'm supposed to just march upstairs, empty my cabinets, and throw away my garbage, and that'll take care of the problem? What about traps and bait? Sealing holes?"

Mr. Matthews looked up at her over the rim of his bifocals. "Now, I told you, Miz Clementine—"

"*Mc*-Clementine," Carol-Anne said impatiently.

"McClementine, I'm gonna take care of it. Now, you can stand there and watch me finish my coffee or you can go on upstairs and get doing what I said."

Only his age—seventy—prevented Carol-Anne from telling Mr. Matthews to go fuck himself.

Carol-Anne stood outside her door for a good five minutes. She did not want to enter, did not want to clear her cabinets of food. Where would she put it? Her refrigerator was only so big and nothing else was secure, certainly not her shelves.

She had walked Nadia to school, then had come

back and gone straight to Mr. Matthews's apartment on the first floor. Now she had to go inside her apartment and the idea of rats lurking there in her absence made her stomach churn.

She had yet to call her job and let them know she wouldn't be in, and she had to—soon. Carol-Anne was still standing there when Mr. Matthews arrived, flashlight and a paper bag in his hand. Was that all he had to work with? What was he going to do, club them to death?

"You first," she insisted, stepping back and letting Mr. Matthews go ahead of her. He headed toward her kitchen without pause. He grabbed her stove and worked it from the wall, flashed his light behind. "Uh-huh," he said.

"Uh-huh what?" Carol-Anne wanted to know, but Mr. Matthews ignored her. He dropped down to one knee, pulled back the curtain beneath her sink. Shined his light in there. Rose.

"Back of the stove and sink."

"What about it?"

"That's where they coming in at."

How many nights had she stood over both washing dishes and making meals, unaware of what lurked in the walls?

He reached in his paper bag, removed a small packet. Tore it with callused hands and sprinkled a little under the sink and the rest he dropped behind her stove. He stood, wiped his hands on his coveralls. Nodded.

"Poison," he said to her curious stare.

"Is that enough?" she wanted to know.

"For now. Got to get some more."

"When?"

"Well, I got to get a work order, take it down to the hardware store."

"When?"

"Let's see, today's Tuesday. No later than Friday."

"Friday?" Carol-Anne's voice was as high as it could go.

"Now, don't go worry your head, Miz Clementine. I put down enough to start. They eat those, get thirsty. Go off in search of water. Now you make sure your taps are tight and maybe put something heavy on your toilet."

Mr. Matthews headed toward her front door. Carol-Anne flew behind him. "That's it?" She was screaming now. "That's all you gonna do? No steel wool, no traps?"

"I ain't got no more traps and same for the steel wool. If you can't wait, there's Miguel's Hardware on Second and One Hundred Eighteenth. They got plenty of stuff there." With that, Mr. Matthews left her apartment.

Heart pounding, halfway to a stroke, Carol-Anne put on rubber gloves and slowly and carefully began to clear out her pantry closet. With every box moved, every can lifted, she felt her nerves shatter a little more. Lord, please don't let me see a rat. Lord, please don't let me see a rat. She said this to herself until the bottom of the pantry was empty and the spillage was swept away.

She decided to do what Mr. Matthews wouldn't do until Friday. She decided to go to the hardware store and stock up on poison, steel wool, and traps. She had a little daughter, there was no choice.

She didn't shower, just slipped into clothes and hurried out. She didn't have a lot of money on her— twelve dollars—but she would get what she could. She walked the brisk, chilly Manhattan street, her blood pressure elevating. She was walking so fast that a few times spots appeared before her eyes. With relief she entered the hardware store, the smell of sawdust thick in the air.

She found the rat traps and was dismayed to see

they were charging three dollars apiece. The poison was two dollars a pack and the store clerk told her she needed at least four. She only had enough left over for a little steel wool, which she knew would not be enough to plug the hole beneath her sink, nor the one behind her stove.

With pennies left in her pocket, Carol-Anne headed home. She ripped open the poison and dropped two packs behind her stove. Heart racing, she lifted back the curtain beneath the sink and tossed the final two packs against the wall.

She would have to warn Nadia about the green pellets, that they weren't candy but rat poison. Carol-Anne would have to tell her child there were rats in their apartment.

Next she took the steel wool and a butter knife and attempted to fill the hole beneath her sink, but it was too large and she lost her precious deterrent down in the hole.

She stood and looked around. *Where are you, motherfuckers?* Anger overrode her fear. *Where the fuck are you, you big, nasty sons of bitches?*

She moved through her apartment, her eyes quick along the floors. She saw nothing. Tired now, exhausted and still light-headed, Carol-Anne sat on the edge of her unmade sofa bed. She moaned, falling back, the mattress firm beneath her. She rolled until she was on her belly and closed her eyes with a weary sigh.

She heard *tweek-tweek,* sat straight up. Listened, heart racing. Waited an eternity before she decided it was just her imagination. She was about to give in to her weariness when she heard it again, louder, closer.

Trembling, she listened for the noise again. It did not disappoint her. *Tweek-tweek* to her right. Her comforter was trembling, how could that be? How could her gorgeous burgundy Dan River comforter that Max had picked out himself be trembling?

Carol-Anne swallowed, reached one hand toward the edge, grabbed the soft material, and pulled it back. Her scream could have woken the dead as she spotted the six newborn pink baby rats struggling blindly against her matching burgundy Dan River sheets.

In her absence, Momma Rat had given birth.

"It's a local, ain't it?" Mr. Matthews wanted to know as Carol-Anne placed a call on the black rotary phone. She ignored him, receiver pressed to her ear, a foul smell rising to her nose from the mouthpiece.

"Yes, hello. This is Carol-Anne. I need to speak to Max right away . . . In a meeting? Well, can you disturb him? This is an emergency."

Max. Yes, he would fix it. He would rescue her, make everything better.

Carol-Anne listened to dead air, a hundred things rushing through her head. She waited, impatient, willing Max to the phone.

"Carol-Anne?"

"Oh, God, Max. Oh, God." She was hyperventilating. Her lungs labored for one good intake of air.

"Carol-Anne, what's wrong? What happened?"

"Oh, God, Max. Rats in my kitchen. Baby rats in my bed. My bed!" She was screaming now.

"Calm down. Nadia okay?"

"Yes."

"Where are you? You still in the apartment?"

"No. In the super's place."

"Okay. Just calm down. Now, listen. You go back and get some things for you and Nadia."

"I can't go back there, Max. I can't."

"You got to, Carol-Anne. Take somebody with you. Get a few things for you and Nadia. I'll call a cab and you take it to my place. I'll call my super and he'll let you in. You stay there until I get home."

"What about Nadia? She's in school."

"Can you pick her up on the way? Get her out early?"

Yes. That much she could do. She could not get rats out of her apartment but she could pick up her child and take her to a safe place. "Yes."

"Okay . . . my meeting's gonna last another hour or so. I'll call a moving company, find a storage place, and put your things in storage. Don't leave any valuables behind."

What valuables? She didn't own any.

"Okay?" Max went on to say.

Carol-Anne took a deep breath, then another. She began to calm down; Max was rescuing her, making it better. "Okay." She hung up the phone, looked around Mr. Matthews's dim apartment, and knew she would never call Pleasant Avenue home again.

An apartment building in Harlem like Carol-Anne had never seen before: 121 West 158th Street.

Clean. Bright. Modern. Twenty-four-hour doormen. Entry doors that locked, elevators that worked. Well-lit halls with floors that always shined. Central heating and cooling. A laundry room in the basement.

Lots of windows.

A spacious living room, a dream kitchen. Groceries that were delivered from Gristede's on Seventy-second Street. Filtered water.

Carol-Anne slept on a twelve-hundred-dollar mattress every night. Frozen meat was no longer a problem at dinnertime; just pop them into the microwave and zap, then bleeding steaks were ready for the broiler.

With the exception of her VCR, all her furnishings went into storage. She'd given Tina, with Max's okay, her two air-conditioning units. It was Max's TV that Carol-Anne watched. His towels she dried herself with. His leather lounge she sat in. Her favorite wing chair had been refused. "Don't go with the decor,

Carol-Anne," Max told her, being firm but kind about the beat-up chair that had seen Carol-Anne through bad times.

With the new address came other changes. Carol-Anne got up extra early to get Nadia to school on time. After class Nadia went to the after-school program and then the car service picked her up. Max's idea. Max's money.

Life was different, better even, but there were still things that Carol-Anne missed about her old place.

Neat freak.

Carol-Anne used to be one back in the days when she was just a single woman with no child underfoot. Carol-Anne had been meticulous with her apartment. Then Nadia was born and all that changed. Carol-Anne became a just-enougher. Doing just enough to keep the place looking halfway straight.

Her furniture would go for weeks on end without benefit of dusting. The kitchen floor would go for days without seeing a broom, without feeling a wet mop across its surface.

The dust bunnies lived a good life under Nadia's bed and the space beneath Carol-Anne's sofa. Now that she was living with Max, Carol-Anne's old habit was forced out of retirement. Beds were made every morning, the sink was cleared of any dirty dishes, and the vacuum cleaner was pulled out every night.

Saturday afternoon was the worst day for Carol-Anne. She'd return from classes, change her clothes, and start cleaning. The duties were split in half. Max did his bedroom, the kitchen, and the master bath, and Carol-Anne had the living room and the guest bath. Nadia was responsible for her own room.

Then there was the laundry.

Max wore nothing twice. Not jeans, not shirts, nothing. When he came in from work, he put on a fresh shirt, sweat pants or jeans, and dumped them into the hamper every night.

By week's end, the hamper had filled to capacity three times. Carol-Anne and Nadia would be in the laundry room until it closed.

Saturdays were no longer a joy for Carol-Anne. By the time all the cleaning, washing, scrubbing, and polishing was done, Carol-Anne was exhausted. Too exhausted to watch TV, to think about going out. Too exhausted to start her homework or attempt to read.

Weekdays were no better.

Carol-Anne would wait for Nadia in the lobby, come upstairs and start dinner, go over homework, prepare plates, clean the kitchen, ready clothes for the next day, while Max busied himself with work he brought home.

Before she went to bed, Carol-Anne had to sweep the kitchen floor, vacuum everywhere, and put away anything left out. Life with Max was hard and Carol-Anne often found herself longing for the old days.

"What's going on?"

Max stood in her closet, one arm laden with her clothes, the other busy pushing hangers.

"Going to the cleaners tomorrow. Figured I'd take your stuff, too."

Carol-Anne looked at her collection of dress wear. She saw her white rayon blouse with the pearl buttons, her black knit stirrup slacks, her taupe cotton blazer, and her black jeans.

"Those go in the wash," she said, already sensing the direction the conversation was taking.

"Better to take them to the cleaners," Max replied, deep inside the closet.

"Why waste money like that?" Carol-Anne said, keeping her hands at her side, forcing herself not to snatch her things from his arms.

"It's not wasting money. I get clothes cleaned by the pound."

Carol-Anne looked in the corner. Saw three pairs of her shoes. Her low leather flats, her favorite pair, among them.

"What are my shoes doing out?"

"Those things?" Max asked, as if they were diseased.

"Yeah." She gathered them into her hands.

Max laughed and Carol-Anne hated the sound of it. "Babe, they really are past due."

"Past due what?"

"Past due their life span," Max said, retrieving the one dress suit she owned.

"Nothing wrong with these shoes."

Max dumped the bundle on the bed. Grabbed one black leather loafer from her hand. Turned the heel so they both could see it.

"Look at this . . . run over. So worn at the heel it's turned gray." He held the shoe flat. "And they turn up on the side. We'll go shopping this weekend."

Carol-Anne snatched her shoe, turned toward the closet and tossed it inside. It hit the wall hard. She was enraged. "There's nothing wrong with my shoes, Max."

Carol-Anne's clothes, Part Two.

It had started with her underwear. Carol-Anne had good underwear and not-so-good. The good was what she wore to work, social functions. The not-so-good was for schlepping around the house. Bras so stretched they would never support her breasts again and panties so worn the elastic had died and gone to rubber heaven.

Carol-Anne had caught Max staring at her one night as she got undressed for bed. He never said a word but Carol-Anne knew what he was thinking.

Then there had been that first morning when she was getting dressed for work. Carol-Anne had slipped on her pants pantyhose, the ones with the runs above the calf. Beneath pants, who knew?

Max did.

"You wearing those to work?" he had asked, incredulous.

"Yeah. Nobody can see the runs," Carol-Anne had explained, not missing the look of loathing on his face.

Now he was throwing out her shoes and going through her wardrobe.

Carol-Anne stood in the doorway, her mind filled with all the chores still left before she went to bed. Her mind filled with Max's latest invasion of privacy.

"You gonna keep those shoes?" he asked, hurt. Carol-Anne was seething and was trying hard not to curse him. She looked at him, determined to win the round, but the bruised expression on his face was too tender to ignore. She sighed, releasing her rage. It wasn't about shoes or underwear or any of those things. It was about who she was and who Max wanted her to be.

"We can go shopping this weekend," she said.

That night as they lay in bed not touching or talking, Carol-Anne tossed and turned, trying to find solutions, an even playing field to Max's expectations and her own personal desires.

Chapter 12

Maurice.

Max's friend. His ace, his buddy, the big brother Max never had. Maurice had taught Max about girls as a preteen, defended Max against a gang of boys from the Grand Concourse in the Bronx, and had pushed Max to get into finance.

An investment broker on Wall Street, Maurice was as buppie as any one brother with a little money could be. They both made money by moving money and had been friends since childhood.

Carol-Anne did not like Maurice. The feeling was mutual.

She suffered Maurice because he was Max's best friend. Maurice in turn had done the same because Carol-Anne was Max's woman. There had been a civility between them, until she moved in with Max. Maurice was appalled and did everything he could to show it.

He called her Carol, an insult for certain. No matter how many times Carol-Anne told him that was not her name, Maurice called her that. *Hey! Carol!* he'd yell, as if she were the maid or live-in help. Fed up one night, Carol-Anne refused to answer him and the feud was on.

Maurice was always staring. At her shoes, the way she wore her hair. At her nails that hardly ever saw fingernail polish. The way he looked at Nadia was no better.

Max, the diplomat, trying to bring the two important people in his life together, would correct Maurice when he was out of line but the slights kept coming.

It was no surprise that Maurice and his wife Babette had purchased a quarter-million-dollar home in Addesleigh Park, St. Albans, Queens. It went with his 1970 MG Midget and her Porsche. They were having a get-together. Carol-Anne did not want to go. She tried to talk Max out of making her, but he told her she was being silly. "Maurice likes you," he told her, but Carol-Anne knew a lie when she saw one.

By the time the cab pulled up to the two-and-a-half-story stone Tudor, with the rolling lawn, pruned hedges, and spotlights highlighting all the grace and comfort of the house, by the time all this met their eyes, Carol-Anne hadn't changed her mind.

She watched as Maurice greeted Max, bear-hugging, back-slapping. Exuberant. She waited patiently for Maurice to acknowledge her, did not expect the same reception and was not disappointed.

Graciously, Carol-Anne accepted the hand held her way. She shook it loose-fingered and allowed his name to fall faintly from her tongue.

"So, buddy, whatcha think?" Maurice asked, addressing Max.

"The house is slamming, brother. Really slamming." Max was impressed, Carol-Anne saw. *Money always does,* she realized, a bitterness in her mouth.

Maurice turned his back to them, gazed up toward his roof. A rude gesture of dismissal. "My wife got damn good taste," he said after a while. Only Carol-Anne flinched.

House Beautiful. A sunken living room. Thick off-white carpeting. An eight-piece sectional couch. A green marble fireplace. A thirty-seven-inch color television. A cherrywood dining room set large enough to seat ten easily.

Class.

It was in the fragile brandy snifters from which Carol-Anne drank and the track lights highlighting various works of art on the wall. It was in the pipe that Maurice smoked and the Donna Karan pantsuit Babette wore. Class was the French provincial windows, solid brass heating vents, and the feeling of openness and space.

Class met roughness in the hand-hewn wooden beams running the length of the living room ceiling and the gold-trimmed china gleaming softly beneath the flickering dinner tapers. It was the kind of place Carol-Anne would never kick back in.

The thirteen guests sat around sipping brandy, chatting amicably in groups of twos and threes. Carol-Anne had given up participations in anyone's conversation and sat stiffly next to Max studying the paintings on the walls.

She had hoped for more. She had hoped Maurice's wife would have been a little more receptive to her than Maurice, but that hope was lost when Max introduced them. Carol-Anne had been ready to open her arms and hug her, to become a part of the closeness Max and Maurice shared. But Babette was cool, shaking her hand, giving her a Mona Lisa smile, and instructing her to make herself at home.

Make yourself at home? How could she? With everyone talking finance and the latest luminary in the African-American art world, she was lost.

She could talk all day about how the cost of a box of cereal was highway robbery and get downright scientific about stretching a dollar. She did not know art, wine, or mutual funds. She didn't know a T-bill from a zero coupon bond. Couldn't quote the Nasdaq or distinguish a Charles Bibb from a Romare Bearden.

She really just wanted to get the evening over with and return back to Harlem. Carol-Anne was wondering how much longer she would have to stay when she felt eyes on her. She turned her head in time to see a woman staring. Recognized the face.

What was her name? Something with an *M.* Something French-sounding. Monique? Maison? Ma Bell? Carol-Anne stared back, waiting for the woman to drop her gaze. When she finally did, it became just another notch on her discomfort level.

Carol-Anne downed the last of her brandy.

"Another?"

She looked up. Saw Babette standing before her. Sweet relief at being noticed was still making its way through her when Carol-Anne caught something in Babette's eyes.

Carol-Anne looked down at her glass seeking answers. Of course. As a poor black woman, the bottle was supposed to be her best friend and Carol-Anne was expected to drink up, finish off half that bottle of Courvoisier sitting across the room, and still be in need of more.

Carol-Anne gave her hundred-watt smile. Shook her head no. "Water will be fine." She handed her snifter over, sat back and looked away. Watched out of the corner of her eye as Babette headed off toward the kitchen. *Yeah, that's right. Go fetch me a glass of water, you stuck-up little bitch.*

The cut-crystal tumbler was heavy and Carol-Anne grabbed it with both hands as Babette extended it her way. She sipped, hoping Babette hadn't spit in it, and rolled it around her tongue. After a few more sips, she placed the glass on the coaster, wishing Max would stop his dialogue with some man named Ken and speak a few words with her.

She shifted on the couch, antsy and bored. Glanced at her watch and wondered what time dinner was. Babette handed a refreshed drink to her husband, his third since Carol-Anne had arrived, and addressed her guests.

"I'm going to check on dinner. We'll be eating soon."

The woman who had stared at Carol-Anne got up. "I'll help."

Babette leaned on her, exaggerating her need of support. "Michele, you are a lifesaver."

Michele, yes, that was it. Michele. She had looked at Max as if she wanted to jump his bones the moment they entered the house. She'd rushed up to him, giving him a big hug, ignoring Carol-Anne beside him. When Max pulled away and said, "This is my lady, Carol-Anne," the shock on Michele's face had been delicious. But that had been forty-five minutes ago and Carol-Anne was in need of new gratification.

She touched Max's arm, interrupting his conversation. "Honey, where's the ladies' room?" She hoped he'd get up and show her, wanting a few minutes of his time.

"Guest bath is through the dining room. Make a left. Right past the kitchen." Maurice. Carol-Anne looked up, eyeing him with hot eyes. He had just robbed her of a few seconds of Max's time.

She stood quickly, moving past half a dozen feet. She passed through the dining room and was about to turn the corner when from up the hall she heard "Where did Max get her from?" Carol-Anne paused, holding her breath.

"Oh, Michele. She ain't bad-looking."

"Did you get a good look? Chick must be near forty any day now. And those earrings? Don't she know those plastic things are played out?"

"Michele, you're just mad 'cause he wouldn't give you none. That's no reason to talk about his date."

"Date? She looks more like his mother."

Laughter, mean and hateful, cut into Carol-Anne's heart.

"I know the chick is a single mother, but didn't Max say she had a job? You see her clothes? She dresses like she's on welfare. And that hair? My God, ain't she ever heard of a cut-and-style?"

Who the fuck was this woman talking about her life like that?

"Well she'd ain't no Samone, that's for sure," someone—Babette?—said decidedly. "Samone had it going on and then some."

"How did Max stoop so damn low, that's what I want to know. What he do, pick her up off One Hundred Twenty-fifth Street?"

She could wait no longer. Carol-Anne took off, her feet hitting the wood floor of the hallway hard. She rounded the kitchen door and stood on fire in the doorway. Babette saw her first, her mouth opening, her eyes blossoming wide.

"Carol-Anne?" Babette said, stammering for more words, drawing Michele's attention to Carol-Anne's presence.

Carol-Anne said nothing, glaring at them both.

"I, er, Michele—" Babette could not finish, the rage in Carol-Anne's face scaring her. Did poor black women from Harlem carry guns?

"I didn't mean nothing by it," Michele managed. "I mean, I was just, y'know . . ."

"No, Michele, I don't know. Why don't you tell me?" Carol-Anne insisted, standing in the doorway, cutting off any chance of their retreat.

"You have to excuse Michele. She doesn't have any class," Babette said, coming to her friend's defense.

"Yeah, what about you? You got any fucking class?"

Carol-Anne took a step forward, one foot flat upon the Mexican-tiled kitchen floor. "You got something to say about me, you say it to my fucking face, you hear? You don't like how I look, where the fuck

I'm from? Until you're putting goddamn money in my pocket and fucking clothes on my back, you better keep your comments to yourself.

"Who the fuck are you to judge me? Who the fuck are you to judge *me*!" she said loudly. "You don't know me. You don't know who the fuck I am or what I'm about. Who the fuck are you?" she was saying when she felt hands on her shoulders and turned and saw Max. Realized too late that she was yelling.

Max searched her face. "Carol-Anne? What's going on?"

She looked at him, still angry, still steaming. "These phony-ass bitches standing in here talking about me, that's what's going on." Carol-Anne shook her head. "Talking about my clothes and my hair . . . Just get me the fuck out of here. I've had enough of these so-called Negroes." And with that, she made a beeline for the front door.

Hurt. She did not expect it. Thought her anger would hold her until she got home, but it arrived nonetheless. She tried to break up all that had happened moment by moment, piece by piece: Tried to find justification for the scene she'd just caused, but couldn't, not now. A part of Carol-Anne believed Michele was right; a part of her agreed that she was not in their class.

She was not like them, did not move in their circle, Max was just tethering her along. Maurice knew it. Babette knew it. Everyone at the gathering knew it.

Now, as Carol-Anne and Max sat on the stoop waiting for a cab, Murdock Avenue dark and hushed, Carol-Anne told Max what had been said and the viciousness with which it was spoken. When she was finished and Max said nothing, it became crystal-clear. Carol-Anne didn't need a road map. No, she didn't belong.

* * *

Max had listened to Carol-Anne, mute and bewildered, ashamed and silent. He gave her that much because he loved her, but in his heart he knew where Michele was coming from.

Michele was coming from the same place Max was. Full of nouveau rich ideas. If you didn't have money, at least dress like you do. Act like you do. Act upper middle class. Pay twenty dollars for a tube of lipstick. Not less than ninety for a pair of shoes. Better to have a two-thousand-dollar sofa and nothing else, than an apartment full of cheap furniture and secondhand pieces.

Worse, Carol-Anne had showed her worst colors tonight, cursing and screaming and proving them all right. Proving that you could take the girl out of Spanish Harlem but you couldn't take Spanish Harlem out of the girl.

Mortified, embarrassed, and disgraced, Max had gone around saying good night to everyone nonetheless. He saw the sympathy and pity in their eyes, their silent question: *Who was that woman?*

Max couldn't tell Carol-Anne these things as they waited in front of the house for a cab to arrive. He could not open his mouth and speak as the silence of the night grew and swelled around them both. The pain and embarrassment were too deep.

When the cab pulled up they got in silently, each clinging to their side of the backseat. There was no noise save for the sound of the two-way radio as the cab hurried down Linden Boulevard and got on the Van Wyck Expressway. Silence, thick and cloying, remained as they passed the softly lit lake of Flushing Meadow Park. It wasn't until they were drifting past LaGuardia Airport that Carol-Anne found the courage to speak.

"Max?"

"Yeah?"

She sought his eyes in the darkness of the cab.

"Regardless of who I am, or what I wear, she had no right saying that."

Max did not respond.

"Max?" Carol-Anne called again.

He turned slowly, raising one finger. Uttered one word. "No." He would not speak about it now. And Carol-Anne sensed a danger in pressuring him; let him be.

Max closed the apartment door, Carol-Anne clicked on lights. She moved down the hall toward the bedroom and was stepping out of her shoes when his voice caught her totally by surprise.

"You want to know the thing that pissed me off about tonight?" he shouted as he flung his jacket on the bed. "You gave them everything they expected from you and more. Cursing and screaming like some low-class Harlem wench . . . Look atcha!" He grabbed her by her shoulders and whirled her toward the double mirrors on the closet door, her imitation-linen skirt and her too-big scoop-neck blouse coming into view. "Just look at you," he went on to say. Carol-Anne glanced down at her nylons, then at the shoes Max had specifically asked her not to wear.

Why do you have to wear that? he had asked earlier that evening. *Why not put on that nice black dress and your new pumps?* he had inquired as carefully as he could. But Carol-Anne had refused to change. She thought she looked fine, until now as Max held her toward the mirror.

"Blouse too damn big, skirt too damn small. Damn shoes run-over. Wearing this old shit. Looking like everything Michele said you were. Welfare and old enough to be my mother."

He released her shoulders and Carol-Anne whirled around, stunned for the second time that night. "What you say?"

"I said your shit is old and tired and don't even fit. I said you look like you're on welfare." His voice was venomous. "You scared and stuck and determined to stay fucking poor the rest of your goddamn life, and you embarrassed the hell out of me tonight." He unbelted his pants, pulling it sharply out of the belt loops. Tossed it on the bed.

"What is it with you?" he began. "Just what the fuck is it with you? I've been bending over the fuck backward for you and what do you do?" He shook his head at her, steaming. "Do you know what being with you has been like? How much I hated going to Pleasant Avenue? Do you?" His voice roared. "I hated your fucking apartment with its roaches . . . sleeping in the goddamn living room.

"Do you know how I hated Fridays because I had my laptop and liked to wear my Rolex and was never sure if I would get killed over the shit? Did you have any idea how much I hated taking a shower in your stained tub or eating in that nasty-ass kitchen?

"Any idea? No, 'course not. 'Cause I never told. Never said a freaking word about it, trying to give you time. Trying to respect who you were and *your struggle to get there*. And what the fuck do you do?" He turned away, started unbuttoning his shirt.

He sat on the bed, head down, laboring for breath, sweaty. "And tonight, Jesus! You just showed your ass all over the place." His head shook in weary disgust. Looked up at her, anger fading to a pain that Carol-Anne knew all too well. "When I first started seeing you, that shit didn't matter. I didn't give two flying fucks about where you lived and how much you made. You were just a woman I liked. One I didn't love, had no immediate plans about a future with. But that changed. My feelings changed. I loved you, Carol-Anne, with all my heart. Trying to do for you, trying to make it better. But no, you couldn't see that. Couldn't see what I was trying to do. Stubborn as a fucking mule, you were. Resisting me every damn step of the damn way . . . Michele talked about you tonight?" He laughed embittered. "Well, she was right on it, you hear? Right on it."

"Oh, yeah, Max?" Carol-Anne shouted back. "Oh, yeah? Well, guess the fuck what? I never asked you for one goddamn thing. Not one. All that shit you did, you did because you wanted to." Her finger jabbed her own chest. "Carol-Anne didn't ask you for nothing, you hearing me?" She took off her flats. "Not these fucking Calico shoes!" She tossed them across the room, reached beneath her blouse, unhooked her bra, and slid it off her arms. "Not this fucking Victoria's Secret bra!" She flung it at his head. She headed for the closet door, opening it so hard it banged against the wall.

She reached in and grabbed three pairs of jeans from their hangers, pitching them on the floor. "Not these fucking jeans. Nothing, you hear me? Not a goddamn thing. You the one that wanted me to change. I like me just fine."

The moment of anger left Max as he looked up at her with sad wet eyes. He glanced around his bedroom, seeing his gifts tossed about. Max shrugged, clasped his hands together, lips pulling tight. His voice came to her, too deep and too calm to belong to the moment. "You know what? I'm gonna make this simple, Carol-Anne. Real simple. You want to be in my life? Then you got to come up to speed . . . with me."

These words, expected forever, held a sweet relief. *A long time coming,* she thought silently, applauding Max for finally saying it to her face. She gave him credit for being quiet about it for so long.

"Come up to speed with you?" she asked angrily. "Well, guess what, Max, I like my speed just fine. So if that's what it's gonna take to be in your life, then I guess it's time for me and Nadia to move on."

"Do what you want, Carol-Anne. You do whatever you want."

Carol-Anne headed for the guest bedroom, undressed in the dark, and got into bed, a sweet bitter sorrow arriving as she realized come morning, when she went to retrieve her daughter from Tina's house, she would have to tell Nadia that once again, they'd be moving.

Chapter 13

Max had done everything he was supposed to do. He ordered boxes, hired a van and talked to Nadia for twenty minutes, explaining why she would not be living with him anymore.

He didn't fight Carol-Anne about it. He kept his feelings quiet and stayed out of her way as she gathered her and Nadia's things. He didn't ask where she was moving to, what her phone number was going to be, or if she was sure she wanted to do this.

Carol-Anne had her mind made up, and Max was determined to respect that. So he did his share, what he could, tying up all the loose ends, but he had forgot to do one more thing. And he did not realize it until he got a call from Black Diamond Car Service asking about Nadia.

"Our driver's been waiting twenty minutes and she hasn't shown up yet."

"I forgot to call and tell you . . . I'm canceling the contract."

"Effective when?" the Southern-born been-in-Harlem-too-long female operator asked him.

"Today," Max said, a dull ache moving through his chest.

"We have to charge for the day."

"That's fine."

There was a brief pause. "Will you be renewing

this contract in the future?" the operator wanted to know.

"I really can't say at this time," Max offered.

"Well, if you ever need us . . ."

"Yes, I have your number on file."

"Well, on behalf of Black Diamond Car Service, I'd like to take this time and thank you for your patronage."

"Thank you." Max hung up. As soon as he did, his intercom beeped. "Yeah, Angela?"

"Miss McClementine on line four."

Max didn't miss a beat. "Tell her I'm in a meeting."

"Third time she's called today."

"Tell her, Angela." Max hung up. Closed his eyes. If Carol-Anne wanted her old life back, he'd make sure she'd keep it. For as long as she felt she had to.

Carol-Anne stared at the phone. It was all in Angela's voice. He wasn't taking her calls. "I just want to get Nadia's dance bag. Will you tell him that?" she ended up saying.

Her daughter had been uprooted twice in as many months; Carol-Anne could not let her miss her dance classes. She still hadn't figured out how she was going to pay for the lessons. Max had paid until the end of April. After that it would be on her.

Carol-Anne did not get paid that week, and she had no money saved because she had used it for one month's deposit and one month's rent. She contacted Tina about the rodent problem at her old Pleasant Avenue address.

"He ain't did much about the rats, Carol-Anne. Gave everybody bait, some steel wool, but that was about it. I went to the hardware and loaded up on chicken wire and steel wool. Plugged the holes beneath the sink and the radiators. Haven't had any in my apartment, thank God, but I spotted one in the hall one night, and Jesus, he was big."

Carol-Anne found herself living in another tenement two blocks from Pleasant. She knew no one and every night after work she returned to Pleasant to pick up Nadia from her old neighbor Selma.

Carol-Anne didn't even have a one-bedroom this time. A studio was all she could afford. For all the discomfort and fear she felt living on Pleasant, there had been rewards. Like paying only four hundred dollars a month. All too soon she had discovered that would barely get her a room.

She got a studio for six hundred dollars; she and Nadia shared the pull-out couch.

Nadia cried all the time. "I want to go back to Uncle Max's. I like having my own room. I liked it when we was living there."

"We can't," was all Carol-Anne said.

She found herself doing something she hadn't done in a while—budgeting. Going to the Bronx to shop at PathMark, spending ten dollars in cab fare to lug her groceries home. She couldn't make ice or keep ice cream because her tiny freezer did not get cold enough. If Max didn't return her call, she'd find herself telling Nadia she couldn't go to dance class this weekend.

He gonna talk to me, she decided when her phone rang.

"Services. Ms. McClementine speaking."

"I'll Fed-Ex Nadia's bag to your job tomorrow. You should have it by Friday."

"Thank you," Carol-Anne said just as curtly, but Max had already hung up.

It was three weeks before Carol-Anne came to the conclusion that she had been terribly wrong. The realization would have come sooner but she was too busy being proud; too full of ego to accept the fact that Max had been right.

One day at lunch, Carol-Anne passed a mirrored store window. She caught her reflection mid-stride. Did not recognize the woman. Realized with some dismay that it was her own body she was seeing. Those little run-over dusty black shoes were hers. The hair hastily gathered back into a scrungy with the edges sticking out like a black Statue of Liberty was her hair. Those plastic earrings she still wore out of defiance looked plastic. And cheap.

Her trench coat, her one good piece of clothing, should have been sent to the cleaners weeks ago. Even in the fuzzy reflection she could see the wrinkles and the stains.

The lipstick she had put on fresh that morning had all but disappeared and her lips not only felt ashy, they *looked ashy*.

Her eyes were hollow and she had bags underneath them—she hadn't had a full night's sleep since she left Max's place. Nadia took up a lot of space.

Nadia. Withdrawn. Quiet. Not happy. Looking at her with condemning eyes. *You did this to me, Mommy. You took away my fairy tale*, her eyes told her more times than once.

They were living in a strange, cramped, dingy place. Carol-Anne didn't even know what her next-door neighbor looked like. There was no one to borrow a cup of sugar from, or stop in for a late afternoon chat.

She had been getting the evil eye from Selma, her old neighbor who took care of Nadia after school. Selma didn't have any children, and that was not an accident.

Carol-Anne's Saturday classes stopped because she had to leave to early to drop Nadia anywhere and the few times she dragged Nadia with her, she had been hyper and antsy the whole time. The more Carol-

Anne told Nadia to sit still, to be quiet, the more active Nadia became.

The raise she expected never materialized. The city was stuck in negotiations with the union. There were days she went without lunch because it came down to subway fare or a little something to eat.

Carol-Anne hadn't lived like this in a long time. Not since she met Max. *But Max ain't here, now is he? So what you gonna do?* As Carol-Anne walked home from the subway, she realized she had two choices. Go crawling back to Max or try to make a way.

Her whole life had been about trying to make a way. From the time she left Nadia's father Carol-Anne had been making a way.

There were resources out there. She just had to find them.

Carol-Anne didn't think she'd ever step through that foyer again; would never marvel at the stained-glass windows framing the thick mahogany door or step onto the Persian runner in the hall.

Carol-Anne thought she would never again see the all-white living room with the black baby grand or sit upon the pristine white sofa, never thought she'd be having a another face-to-face with Jeff. But that's where she and Nadia found themselves one Saturday. At Jeff's brownstone in Fort Greene, Brooklyn. Spike Lee was a hometown boy and his retail store, Spike's Joint, was a few blocks away.

Going there, asking Jeff for child support, had never crossed Carol-Anne's mind. But if Jeff had acted unconcerned the last time he saw his daughter, he was making up for it now. It was Nadia he greeted first, opening his arms and hugging her. Kissing her head, telling her how pretty she looked.

He presented her with a black Barbie, complete with a carry case and three outfits. He asked her if she was hungry, if she was thirsty. How she was do-ing in school.

He had lost weight since that last time, and seemed less tense. A certain eagerness came through in every-thing he said and did.

Receptive. Good.

"I never asked you for anything, Jeff, and believe me, if times were better, I wouldn't ask you now. But times are kind of tough and I would like to get child support."

"Retroactive?" he asked, as if he had been afraid this day would come. Carol-Anne had not considered that. Eight years times four hundred dollars a month. Quick math told her that eight times twelve was ninety-six months, times four hundred. Thirty-something thousand dollars.

Carol-Anne's mouth got dry. "Well, now, I'm en-titled."

Jeff shook his head. "I don't have that kind of money, Carol-Anne. I'm already paying child support to Adrienne for the boys. Got a mortgage on this brownstone. Car note."

She believed him. "A hundred dollars a week is acceptable."

"What about the other part?" Jeff's fear was show-ing. "You're not going to take me to court on that, are you?"

"Can you throw in an extra fifty a month till it's paid?"

"Four-fifty?" He seemed relieved and Carol-Anne wondered how much his ex-wife and kids were get-ting.

"Yeah. Four-fifty."

"Starting?" he asked.

"Now, if you got it."

"Give you a check?"

Carol-Anne nodded, her palms sweaty.

"Be right back." Jeff disappeared upstairs. Nadia looked around her.

"This his house?"

"Yes, honey."

"Can we live here?" Nadia asked.

God forbid. "No, honey."

Nadia thought a minute. Eyed her mother sideways. "Can we go back to Uncle Max?" Carol-Anne was about to answer when Jeff reappeared.

"So," he began, watching the check disappear into Carol-Anne's bag. "Shall I mail it each month, or what?"

"Be quicker if I just come and pick it up. Get to see Nadia that way, too." Carol-Anne heard him sigh.

"Got to admit I thought you were really gonna press me."

"For?"

"That thirty-eight thousand dollars."

Carol-Anne's eyes grew wide. "That much?"

"And some change." He wiped his brow. "You were always good people."

"Yes, I was."

Jeff looked around him. "I ordered pizza. You guys hungry?"

Nadia looked at Carol-Anne for her reply. "Sure, we'll stay for a slice." With the money from Jeff, she would have exactly one hundred dollars left at the end of the month.

Not enough, but it was a start.

Carol-Anne stood beneath the limed shower head and let the warm water rush over her. It was six weeks since she had left Max and she'd not heard a word from him. She refused to call him. Work kept her occupied, while thoughts of him came and went at random.

But nighttime brought on her I-want-Max-back Jones. A maddening Jones, an unreachable itch, like when she masturbated in the shower, feeling empty in the aftermath of coming. *My fingers aren't enough. I need the touch of a flesh-and-blood man. I need to be held. Loved. Wanted.*

But she was *cheap* and *old*. Not up to par. *You got to come up to speed . . . with me,* his exact words. *Like you're on welfare,* wasn't that what he'd said? She got out the tub, wrapped herself in a rough towel. If she had been lacking when she was with Max, she was lacking even more since she left him.

She would be embarrassed if Max saw her now. Living in a cramped studio with Nadia. How much longer could she go on sleeping with her daughter?

In the blink of an eye Nadia would be a preteen and then a teen. Nadia wouldn't even invite CeCe over because there was no place to go, no place to play. Most of her toys were still in storage. If Pleasant Avenue had been a dump, they were living in a real slum now.

Somebody knocked on her door.

Carol-Anne grabbed her robe and checked the clock. A little after eleven. She didn't know who it could be and did not even have the safety of a peephole to find out.

The door would have to be cracked. Hopefully the chain would hold. Carol-Anne held her breath, unlocked the door, finding a man barely out of his teens looking back at her. "Yes?" she said carefully.

"Where's Marcus?"

"Marcus?"

"Where the fuck is Marcus?" he hissed, raising his hand, a large silver gun coming into view. Carol-Anne screamed, drew back. Tried to close the door, but his Timberland boot was wedged too firmly in the door opening.

"You better open this door, bitch, or I'm gonna blow you and the motherfucking door off."

"Please, there's no Marcus here," Carol-Anne begged.

There was a distinct click. Carol-Anne had seen enough movies to know that he had just cocked his gun. "Please," she pleaded.

The gun slid along the tiny opening of the door until it was aimed at her temple. "Marcus got five seconds to get to this door, bitch."

"No," Carol-Anne moaned, slamming against the door with her shoulder, her will, everything she owned, but it was not enough. The door quivered but that was all. Tears streamed down her face. "Please, there's no Marcus here. Just me and my baby . . . me and my baby," she moaned without hope.

"Yo!" another voice shouted. "Yo, motherfucker? What you doing? Marcus don't live there, you crazy fuck. Put that damn gun away."

The man eyed Carol-Anne carefully. Slowly lowered the gun. His smirk, like a hot wire across her cheek, seared her. Without warning, the face vanished and the door slammed violently into its frame.

She willed her body to stop its trembling, face sweaty, ear pressed against the door listening for more terror, for the return of a real-life boogie man, but she heard nothing but the sound of her heart drumming.

Carol-Anne locked the door quickly. Her eyes sought out her sleeping daughter, the terror fresh within.

With everything she owned, she knew. *We can't stay here.*

Max closed the book he had been reading and turned off his reading light. He fixed the covers around his shoulders and closed his eyes. He wasn't sleepy.

Max didn't know how he got to be here, to the loneliness that had been keeping him company since Carol-Anne walked out. Max didn't know how she had done it, had left him and a better way of life behind, only that she had.

Must not have loved me, was his reasoning as he stretched his legs, searching for the edge of the king-sized bed and not finding it.

Because if she really loved me, we would have worked out our problems. We would have sat in my living room till dawn if we had to, speaking words till we found the right ones. Till we found the words that would make it all right, make it better. Heal the rift that had come between us.

What had it been all about, then? Max wanted to know. What had their year together really been about if she didn't love him? Because he certainly loved her. Not a Samone love, but a love real enough and deep enough to touch.

His body rolled, spread like a big X with room to spare. He missed her. It was the type of pain no man should suffer. Yes, Max had spoken ugly, biting words to Carol-Anne, but it was his love for her that had driven his tongue. She had to know that much.

He had expected her to return weeks ago, sorry-faced, full of regret. Missing him, hurting like he was hurting. But Carol-Anne had stayed away and that was what his pain was about. Carol-Anne had left and not come back and he still loved her. Loved her so much, he ached.

Max loved Carol-Anne. Loved Nadia. They were a family and she had torn it asunder. Didn't she know what she had done to him when she left him? Didn't she know how she had taken his heart still beating from his chest and tossed it into the meat shredder?

For a year they had been a family—him, Carol-Anne, Nadia. A real family. Nadia wasn't his flesh and blood, but he loved her as if she were. For the first time in his life Max had felt complete. Felt like the man he always wanted to be, and Carol-Anne had stolen that from him without looking back.

He missed her, missed her beside him, like now, in his big king-sized empty bed. It was more than sex, more than passion. Loving her, missing the feel of her warm brown hands over his body. Her voice in the late night, a faint, deep-timbred whisper that found him in the darkness as she called his name, her body close to his.

Max inhaled the pillow, Carol-Anne's memory swarming him.

Where are you now? he wondered dimly as his breath caught a rhythm all its own. *Where?* he needed to know as his body worked against the mattress. *Do you know I'm missing you?* his mind said as his buttocks humped padding, coils, and springs, his body moving against the soft pale gray sheet beneath him.

Max strained—*oh, God*—as white-hot lightning struck him. Semen shooting against the gray sheets; a milky white puddle that · smeared his belly and brought tears to his eyes. That made him want to weep out loud.

That made him want to stop breathing as sweat dappled his temples with salty urgency. As he found himself coated in spilled seed, seduced by memory.

Max rolled onto his back. Searched the ceiling in the darkness, struggling for air, for reason. Struggling for absolution, but mostly, for Carol-Anne's return.

Carol-Anne and Nadia journeyed to Brooklyn the following month late one Saturday afternoon. Darkness was nearly upon them by the time they reached Jeff's brownstone. Carol-Anne was relieved as she latched the wrought-iron gate behind her and ascended the burnt-orange steps. Relaxed as she rang the bell, hearing its soft buzz from somewhere inside seconds before Jeff appeared in suit and tie.

"Just got in," he told them. He'd had a seminar earlier, the reason for their late visit.

He greeted Nadia as he had the last time, with a

smile, a hug, and a gift. A teddy bear this time.

"I ordered pizza," Jeff told them, ushering them into the foyer. "Should be here soon."

Carol-Anne paused to looked out into the darkening night. She was wary of the street lamps, the shadows, the borough she didn't know.

"I was hoping to make this visit brief. It's dark and I don't like having Nadia on the subway too late."

She felt Jeff staring, at the hair she had had done and the bit of makeup she had put on. His eyes saying he noticed her improvements. Jeff closed the door behind them. Locked it with a click. Pointed toward the mahogany balustrade and stairs. "I got three bedrooms upstairs. You're more than welcome to stay."

A year ago Carol-Anne would have refused the offer. But she could not resist the idea of sleeping without Nadia's little hot knees wedged into her back. Of waking up in a three-story brownstone instead of a tiny studio.

"Okay, but we're leaving first thing."

"Not until you've had my Belgian waffles with Canadian bacon," Jeff offered.

"Nadia, what do you think?"

"I get a bed of my own?" she wanted to know.

"Sure. Everyone gets their own bed," Jeff assured her. "I got Sega Genesis upstairs. Why don't you go check it out? First bedroom to your left."

Nadia raced up the stairs, leaving them alone in the foyer. Jeff looked at her with tender eyes. "Thanks for saying yes."

Carol-Anne dismissed him with quick words— "No problem"—and headed toward the kitchen before he could touch her. Kiss her. Hold her. She hurried off, moving fast. It was a dangerous time for her. The touch of a man. Carol-Anne was ripe for it.

Jeff came to her as she knew he would. After Nadia had fallen asleep, after Carol-Anne had had a shower and slipped into a pair of his pajamas. After she had turned off the light and settled into the soft queen-size bed alone.

He came softly, saying her name, a warning of his intent; giving her the chance to stop him. "Carol-Anne?"

"Yeah," she responded, already wet with desire. Already feeling him inside of her. Seemingly a place left untouched too long.

"Sleeping?" he asked from the hallway, the ceiling light defining shoulders, the narrow waist, the thick full thighs beneath his pajamas.

"No," she answered, throwing back the covers and scooting over. He came on tempered feet. Slow steps toward the bed. Paused again. "You sure?" he asked.

"I'm sure." She was dry-mouthed as he got in, her body responding, drawn to him. He took her into his arms, a quick heat starting when they embraced. His penis pressing against her belly.

He held her. Kissed her. His hunger for her thick, clouding her senses. They kissed, hugged, ran finger-tips over each other's flesh, removing clothes quick, fast, and clumsy. Hugging again, hot skin to hot skin. Rubbing, arching like cats against a sofa. A hot hunger clouding the air with sighs and whimpers. Carol-Anne not caring, reaching for him, guiding him into her parted thighs. Jeff pulling away, getting out of the bed. Disappearing down the hall and coming back, condoms in hand.

"No more babies," he piped. But that was Carol-Anne's least concern in the moment of her need.

Her breast ached for the feel of his chest against them. She pulled him to her, sighing long and pain-fully slow as his mouth found her nipple, a toy for his teeth.

She was hungry for him in a way she could never recall pulling him on top of her and he rolling off, moving to the side to put the condoms on. Not one but two. "Sometimes they break," he offered.

But Carol-Anne was not concerned about pregnancies, AIDS, or other STDs. Her passion made her foolish and silly and dangerous. All that mattered was that Jeff get in her. He pushed, she arched and it hurt. But it was a good hurt, the best hurt. She moved against him quick, the head of his penis touching a new spot. A different kind of sensation came through the pleasure. Her G spot, something she had read about, but never felt. She thought it ironic that Jeff would be the one to find it.

Carol-Anne came. The moment she did, she wanted him off her. Wanted him gone, out and away from her. She could not stand the touch of him, the smell of heavy sex in the air.

She was grateful when he returned to his bed, leaving her alone. The Loud Thoughts were back. They kept her awake for a long time. Asking her questions she did not want to answer.

Asking her how she had fallen so far from grace.

Carol-Anne was awakened with a pounce on her bed, and a shaking of her shoulders.

"Come on, Mommy. Daddy's made breakfast and it's ready."

Carol-Anne opened her eye, saw Nadia leaning into her face, her eyes just like Jeff's, happy and filled with joy.

She gathered up the sheet and comforter, shielding her nakedness from her daughter. Jeff's borrowed pajama top lay discarded somewhere in the bedding.

"I'm coming, you go down and tell him I'll be there in a minute." Nadia scooted off, her father's T-shirt fitting her like a long loose gown. Her voice reached the rafters as she bounced down the hardwood steps, yelling her message.

"Daddy! Mommy's coming in a minute."

Carol-Anne lay there, her eyes picking out the details of the guest room, racked with guilt and shame. She hoped that Jeff understood that last night meant nothing. That last night was about sex, not love.

She hoped that Jeff would not hold her moment of need against her.

Her mind was so overrun with Loud Thoughts by the time she emerged into the breakfast nook that Carol-Anne couldn't think. Couldn't concentrate. She felt the first throb of a headache on its way. She allowed her eyes to glance at him briefly, saying a quick hello and settling down to a place setting.

She had no appetite for the made-from-scratch waffles or the crisp bacon piled high on a server. Waved them off in favor of orange juice and a cup of hot black coffee.

As Jeff moved around his kitchen, wiping counters, pouring more syrup on Nadia's waffles, Carol-Anne found herself repelled by the sight of him. She only wanted one thing now. To leave and never come back.

But Jeff had things she needed, and with much grief Carol-Anne knew that next month, she'd be back.

Chapter 14

Carol-Anne stood at the Lord and Taylor register listening to the blips and beeps the machine was making. Sweat trickled down her back, a fine dampness covered her brow.

Nadia needed a new winter coat, bad-weather boots, underwear. Clothes for school. She had sprouted like a weed in the last few months. Her jeans were high around her ankles, and her tops were so tight they clung to her little frame like cellophane. Nadia was beginning to look like a throwaway child.

Carol-Anne didn't know if Max had canceled the Lord and Taylor charge card. So she stood there, sweating, tense. Afraid the salesperson would tell her that her card had been canceled. That she'd be arrested for trying to use something that wasn't hers.

Carol-Anne had tried to dress the part; tried to wear things she had seen white women wear to high-priced stores. White leather sneakers, blue jeans. Turtleneck and her trench coat.

Carol-Anne had taken a curling iron to her head, using hair spray to keep the style in place. She had scrubbed her face and applied foundation, lipstick, eyeliner, and blush. Worn her real gold earrings.

Carol-Anne had stared in the mirror, checking for flaws, signs of her poverty. With dismay she saw the tips of her sneakers worn down to the grain. That the collar of her trench coat was greasy and darkened from her hair. But she had gone to Lord and Taylor because she had no choice.

The register went on with its clicks and beeps. Spewing data, sending information. Carol-Anne resisted the urge to wipe the sweat off her brow, avoiding the eyes of the sales clerk.

There was a long beep and then the register did nothing. The sales clerk looked at her and Carol-Anne forced herself to smile. "First time I'm using it," she offered.

The silence seemed infinite. She became aware of people moving around her. Carol-Anne studied the ceiling. The register beeped one final time and released the receipt. Ten items in all.

With a flick of her wrist, the sales clerk whisked out the receipt and placed it on the counter for Carol-Anne to sign. Her hand shook as she took the pen. A bead of sweat ran for freedom down the side of her face.

With care, the sales clerk began removing the electronic tags. With the same care, she folded the clothes and eased them into the shopping bag. Handed it to Carol-Anne and said, "Thank you for shopping at Lord and Taylor."

Carol-Anne resisted the urge to run. Made herself turn slowly and head toward the elevators. Looked down into the shopping bag and saw that the bag had not been stapled. Held her receipt aloft in her hand as she headed toward the exit door.

She was stopped by the security guard anyway. Stopped by a black man with no pity or alliance, bent on doing his job.

"Mind if I check your bag?" he asked.

"No . . ." She lifted the bag. "Here."

"Receipt?" he asked.

She handed that over, too. Other people exited the store. Their white faces were set as they moved toward the door. Nobody was stopping them. Trench coats, wispy tendrils of blond hair peeking out of scrungies and bobby pins. Leather sneakers, coral lips, all going by her freely.

His search was thorough. Every item was checked against the receipt. He appeared in no rush, Carol-Anne sensed his condemnation of her, that she was a thief. She watched, dismayed, embarrassed, as the last of Nadia's items were put back into the bag. He returned it to her without benefit of a smile, a thank-you, or even an apology.

His demeanor, this black man, this *brother,* telling her that was what she got for coming here to shop. His masked eyes giving her warning about the next time.

Carol-Anne moved out into the cool brisk day, trembling, sweaty. Scared.

At the end of the month Max would get his statement. He would see that four hundred and ninety-three dollars had been charged in the children's department.

Maybe he would call her and demand she pay it back. Maybe he wouldn't. Carol-Anne would not worry about it now. Her mission was accomplished. Nadia had clothes.

Carol-Anne watched the lights twinkle. She felt like Scrooge. No, she *was* Scrooge. Christmas was three weeks away and Carol-Anne was feeling very "bah, humbug." She said nothing as Tina strung the red, green, blue, yellow, and white blinking lights. Sat there mute and lost in her own thoughts as Nadia and Cecelia found places to hang the peacock-blue and angel-white satin bulbs. Ignored the glass of egg nog with just a dash of rum placed twenty minutes ago on the coffee table just for her.

Carol-Anne wanted to go home. She would have been home except her place was too tiny for a tree and Tina had invited Nadia to help decorate hers.

She studied Tina's back, the wide gave-birth-to-a-child hips. She studied the white mock turtleneck, the black shiny hair cut straight across the shoulders. Carol-Anne listened to the jingle of real fourteen-karat-gold bangles on Tina's arms and felt a cruel vicious victory because none of that had bought her friend a man.

"Okay, guys, it's break time. I'm gonna make you all some hot chocolate and you two take in CeCe's room." CeCe, what a dumb nickname. Who did Tina think her daughter was, a Winans? Did she think her daughter would grow up to be as rich and famous as her namesake, CeCe Winans? Tina was irking her without even trying.

Carol-Anne looked around her. God, she wanted out of this apartment. Out of Tina's fancy-ass one-bedroom on Pleasant. She wanted to get up and leave and get into her pull-out and never step foot on solid ground again.

Carol-Anne wanted to knock the seven-foot Christmas tree from its base.

". . . Carol-Anne."

She had slept with Jeff, again. It wasn't even the end of the month. She had gone all the way to Brooklyn and slept with Jeff for no money. She had gone on a promise. The promise that Jeff would give her money for Christmas shopping. A day later she still didn't know when she was going to get it or even how much. All she had was a promise.

". . . Carol-Anne?"

He never said it, but she knew that Jeff knew she was selling her body; selling her soul for the sake of her daughter. For the sake of Rent. For the sake of Christmas Gifts for Nadia. Just lying back and opening her thighs. *Here Jeff, come and get it. All yours now. Nobody else but yours. You own me. I'm the slave, you the master, and Fort Greene is the Plan-*

tation. She wanted to cry right there sitting on Tina's sofa.

"Carol-Anne!"

How many times had she done it with Jeff since that first time? Too many to count. Liking it still. Coming all the time like a bitch in eternal heat. Wanting to throw up the minute she did. *How many times you porked me, Jeff? How many times more will I let you?*

Something had her by the shoulder. Nails dug into the mohair sweater, shaking her silly.

"Carol-Anne! Answer me."

She blinked. Tears began falling. Through wet lashes she saw Tina looking at her, scared.

"I'm sorry," Carol-Anne said.

Tina took her into her arms. "You go right ahead and cry. You go right ahead. It's been coming for months now, so you go right ahead and cry. Let it all out. Every hurting thing."

"I don't know me anymore, Tina. I don't know who the hell I am."

"You're Carol-Anne. Carol-Anne McClementine" —Tina pushed her away, finding her eyes—"that's who you are. And today is the first day of the rest of your life. Now you go ahead and finish those tears. I'll get you some aspirin and a pillow . . . rest a while."

Tina went to make dinner. When she got back Carol-Anne was asleep.

Tina let her be.

It was late. Past midnight. Nadia and Cecelia fast asleep in Cecelia's bedroom, the mothers keeping company in the living room, the Christmas lights the only illumination.

The fifth of rum was half gone. An empty greasy platter gave testimony to the fried chicken wings eaten hot and fast with Tabasco sauce and Wonder bread.

Carol-Anne told Tina everything. Held back nothing. And when she was done, she felt relieved.

"A mad dance, sweetie. That's what these past months have been for you." Carol-Anne smiled. She hated being called *sweetie* and Tina knew it.

Tina threw her arms up. "You've been twirling and twisting and looking everywhere but straight ahead . . . determined to do your thing. Proud. Knowing it all. Knowing everything . . . about nothing much." Tina shook her head. "Too proud, Carol-Anne."

". . . when I think of the things I've done."

Tina stopped her. "You slept with your child's father a couple times too many. So what? That was yesterday. This is today."

"What about the credit card thing? It's like I stole from Max."

"Stole? What stole? He gave you that card. He knew you still had it. Now if he didn't want you to use it, he would have canceled it long ago. That was a gift. You don't ever feel bad about taking a gift." Tina paused, gave Carol-Anne a careful look. "You have to call him. Talk to him."

Carol-Anne shook her head. "I don't want to."

"Ah, but you *have* to. Common courtesy. You call him and tell him that you used the card *before* he gets the bill. If he's agreeable, ask him how he's been. Tell him how *you've* been. No details but a general summation . . . then you tell him what you realized. Not apologize, 'cause the choices you made were yours to make and nobody can make you apologize for that. But just let him know that he was right, *not* that you were wrong."

"You don't know Max," Carol-Anne offered.

Tina laughed. "You're right. I met him twice, I believe. But I know how you were when you were with him. I know that you left him." Tina took her left hand. "Despite all your hardships you never once even thought about selling that ring on your finger."

The ring. Carol-Anne had forgot about it. She had worn it so long it had become just another part of her. Appraised at sixteen hundred dollars, not once had she thought about selling it.

"You remember what you told me, what he said when he gave it to you?"

"Yeah. It wasn't an engagement ring, but something to let me know he was there for me . . . seems so long ago."

Carol-Anne opened her studio door and let Nadia ahead of her. Her eyes roved the room, looking for space. Looking for air, light. Signs of life. But the cramped room offered nothing more than what it was.

Not even enough room for a damn Christmas tree.

"Hang up your coat, Nadia, then go run a bath."

Carol-Anne needed privacy. She had a phone call to make.

Max tossed his keys onto the coffee table and hit the button on his answering machine.

"Hey, it's me. Michele. Just checking to see if we're still on for tonight. Call me when you get in." *Beep!*

"Max? It's Julie. Haven't heard from you in a while . . . give me a call. I'm home." *Beep!*

"Max. You there, man? You there? Pick up. It's me, Trim. Look, your ass there and you ain't answering then it's gonna be me and you. If you ain't there, then give me a call." *Beep!*

Max hung up his coat. The machine beeped one last time. Whoever it was hadn't left a message, which was fine with him. Max wasn't in the mood for talk.

His phone rang. He let his answering machine pick up.

"Hey, this is Max . . . sorry I'm not in right now, but I certainly want to know who's calling. So at the beep, give me the lowdown." Max cringed. Time to change the message.

"Max? It's me, Carol-Anne."

His heart skipped a beat.

"I was calling to let you know . . . I, er, I, um, damn, this is so hard . . ."

Max turned, debating. Pick up? Or not pick up?

Carol-Anne's voice came out in a rush. "Okay. I charged some things for Nadia on the Lord and Taylor card . . . I can pay you back. Will pay you back. Just things are tight now and she's sprouting like a weed."

Nadia. His stomach churned.

"So, um." A tight laugh. "Well, I . . . let me know what you want me to do. My number is—" The machine beeped, cutting her off.

The phone rang again. Max did not pick up.

"Yeah, me again. My number is two-one-two, two-nine . . ."

She was doing bad. Must have been doing real bad to use the credit card. Max did not care about the Lord and Taylor charge. If he did, she would never have left his apartment with it in her wallet.

But even that didn't move him much; his mind was decided. He wasn't calling to tell her anything. If she wanted to pay him back, she knew his address.

Michele may have had the clothes, but she lacked el egance. She may have had the beauty, but it was only skin deep. She may have had the style, but she had no real class.

Knock on her door and you got the feeling that there was nobody inside. Hollow.

She held Max's arm, negotiating Broadway on teetering high heels. She brushed real hair from her face when the wind blew it against her matte lips. She smelled real good and the feel of her hips meeting his was a sweet kind of tango as they crossed the expanse of Broadway and 54th, but there was no magic there. Not for him.

"Penny?" she asked, irritating him because Max did not feel like talking. About anything. He wanted to take her to his place and do the *nasty* till he got sleepy. Wake up in the morning to find her gone.

Penny for my thoughts? "Nothing. Thinking about nothing," Max said, annoyed.

"Ah, come on. Something going on inside your head."

"Yeah, me and you in my bed." Which shocked him but made Michele giggle.

"Reading my mind again?" Michele asked, her light eyes dazzling with that look Max knew too well. The look that said she was falling in love. Max had seen it on her face often enough but it gave him no joy.

Her falling in love with him was the last thing Max wanted. Loving someone back was the only thing he needed.

Chapter 15

For weeks Carol-Anne had known this moment was coming. She had tried to imagine dealing with it. But nothing she'd considered prepared her.

"Was I bad, Mommy?"

Nadia sat surrounded by ripped and discarded wrapping paper on her grandmother's living-room floor. The little pink Barbie Doll Corvette was empty of its namesake. The three board games were stacked to the side. The sweater, slacks, and leather shoes, forgotten. The new cotton panties and cotton socks half in, half out of the gift box.

"No, baby, you were good."

"So how come Santa didn't get me the stuff I asked for?"

Carol-Anne looked at her daughter. All she had was the truth. "Because Mommy didn't have the money."

Nadia's face clouded. She was confused; her mother's words made no sense. She shook her head. "No, Santa brings me stuff."

Carol-Anne inhaled. *I should have told her sooner, before today. Before now. I could have told her last week or two days ago, softening the meager Christmas she'd have.*

But I didn't. Too busy hoping for a miracle. Hoping that Max would forget the last few months and just pop up with all the things Nadia wanted for

Christmas. That he would come to me, chiding me for my stubbornness, but loving me still. Running out to buy what Nadia wanted for Christmas. Coming back into our lives with undying love.

She released her breath. "Mommy buys you stuff. There is no Santa Claus."

Nadia blinked. Blinked again. "No, Mommy. Santa brings the toys. Santa always brings the toys."

Carol-Anne's hackles raised. "Nadia, there ain't no Santa and there's never been no Santa." Carol-Anne pointed to her chest. "I buy your toys, understand? No Santa. Period, the end."

Nadia looked at her. A salty tear splashed her cheek. She began to cry, and soon her crying turned to sobs. Her shoulders jerked up and down, up and down, as if she were hiccupping.

She's entitled, Carol-Anne thought, *entitled to her sadness. Aren't we all?* A part of her wanted to get up off the couch. Wanted to scoot down on the floor and hold her daughter. But Carol-Anne couldn't move. Didn't want to and hated herself for it. Today Nadia would have to tend to her own sadness.

"Well, now," Miss McClementine said, walking into the living room, "breakfast almost rea—" Nadia's sobs snatched her head. She saw her grandbaby sitting on the floor, full of tears. "What happened?"

Carol-Anne shrugged and turned her back. Held her face in her hands. She did not want to cry. Did not want to moan. Did not want to show her pain, her misery, to her mother.

"Carol-Anne? Nadia? What's going on?" But Carol-Anne was mute and Nadia continued to cry. There was panic in Miss McClementine's voice. "Somebody tell me what's going on 'round here?"

Nadia looked up, her voice desperate and bewildered. "Granny? Mommy says there's no Santa." She looked at her grandmother with wide wet eyes, imploring her granny to change it. Fix it. Tell her something better. "She said she's Santa. That she had no money to buy me stuff."

Carol-Anne sighed. Nadia's twist on her words would bring her mother's wrath. The tears Carol-Anne had been holding on to escaped.

"What you do that for?" Carol-Anne's mother asked.

Carol-Anne turned, her face ugly and flowing with tears. "Because it's the truth. The whole awful truth. She's old enough to know. There ain't no Santa and I ain't got no money." With that, Carol-Anne turned back around.

Even with her back turned, Carol-Anne could feel her mother glaring. Knew her mother's words were going to come, bringing with them more pain. There would be no mercy for her, no understanding.

"Your child down here crying, and all you can do is talk about what you don't have? You know how many Christmases I ain't had no money, but neither you nor your sisters went without . . . She's a baby, Carol-Anne, she deserves better."

Carol-Anne was standing before she realized it. Her voice tumbled out of her like a locomotive. "I'm not you, Mom. I'm not you!" She moved past her mother and went to her old bedroom that was now her mother's den. Slammed the door. It was past noon when she came out again.

She had tried. *I really did try. I went to Jeff's house begging and pleading for some money for Christmas, hoping he'd come through.*

I will never forget the look on his face when I kissed him. A kiss my lips or my heart wanted no part of. I'll never forget the way he pulled back, calling me horrible names. Accusing me of being nothing more than a whore after his money.

Jeff screaming at me like he had never screamed at me before, ranting and raving about how everybody thought he was made of money. How he was expected to give and give and how he got nothing in return.

"It's fucking three days to Christmas, Carol, and what do I have? Who do I have to share with? And here you come, like you always do, hands out and legs open." He had looked at her in disgust. "Like some whore from across town."

Carol-Anne raised her hand and smacked him, the print of it angry upon his cheek. She trembled, screaming with a fury she'd never known before.

"Whore?" Her fist rammed the top of his head. "Whore?" she howled and battered again. Jeff jumped back and Carol-Anne stopped her attack, breathing hard, eyes wild with rage. "I carried your daughter for nine months and have been feeding and clothing her for the past nine years." Tears streamed down her face. "And I've sacrificed and gone without and struggled every day of her life making a home for your daughter."

"Yeah? Nobody told you to get pregnant. Nobody told you to have her."

She stared at him, trembling. "You bastard . . . she's your daughter, goddamn you," she shouted. "Your daughter."

"Well, you never acted like she was until I started handing you over those checks. I've been giving you money for the last few months. Now if you don't have for Christmas, well, tough, sister. 'Cause I don't have none for you."

"What kind of father are you?" Carol-Anne hissed.

"No, Carol-Anne, the question is what kind of *mother* are you?"

"You don't give a damn about her."

"I love my daughter very much, but like I said, you got money from me this month. Not another dime will you get till next. Now if you will excuse me, I got work to get to."

"But you promised me! Money for Nadia's Christmas."

"Did I? You asked and I said I had to see. Don't sound like a promise to me."

"But I—" She couldn't finish. Could not speak out loud about what she'd done.

"You what?" Jeff demanded.

She stared at him, her face crumbling. Silently she implored him not to make her say what her last visit had yielded. The memory of it, Jeff hurting her like he never had before, was branded upon her soul. He had used his body as a weapon that tore into her relentlessly without tenderness or mercy.

"Yeah, weren't you something? Coming up here, middle of the month. All I said was I had to see and there you were, legs open." His expression changed, anger turning his brown eyes dark. "Not because you loved me and wanted me but because you needed money . . ." His lip curled in disgust. "You are so pitiful, you know that? So fucking pitiful . . . get out of my house."

Carol-Anne stood there, unable to protest or deny the charges Jeff had made. All she knew was what she needed and she needed money for Christmas.

"Jeff, please. I'm begging you. Nadia . . . it's Christmas. She's done nothing to you. I'm not asking for me . . . for Nadia." But her words fell on deaf ears.

Jeff grabbed her by her shoulders and scurried her to the front door. He whipped it open and forced her down the stairs. She turned to protest but the heavy door slammed in her face and the fight left her.

It had been a long ride back to Spanish Harlem.

Now as she lay on the daybed, the musings of an embittered Christmas drifting around her, Carol-Anne knew in her heart that she had tried to make it better, to change it. Had tried but not succeeded.

I tried, Momma. I tried, Nadia. Was willing to do

*whatever it took to make it right. But you weren't
there. Didn't see what happened, the things Jeff said,
what I went through. You have no idea and there's
no way I could ever tell you.*

She sat at the holiday table, mute, not talking, her
sisters and their husbands around her, ignoring her
state, pressing on with their holiday cheer. *Yeah, why
wouldn't they? They got husbands. They got nice
places to live and have never struggled the way I do.
Their children got a nice Christmas and I got shit. I
can just hear them thinking, poor, stupid ass Carol-
Anne. She got what she deserved . . . messing around
with a married man.* Carol-Anne pushed yams
around her plate. She had no appetite.

Nadia played with her cousins, clutching their electronic games and expensive dolls as if they were hers,
or would be hers by the night's end. Every now and
then she would look at Carol-Anne, confused and
scared.

Carol-Anne excused herself and went and lay
down on the daybed in the sewing room. *My room,*
she thought, looking around, trying to find fragments
of the life she had lived there.

But nothing that had been hers remained. The
room had been wiped clean. *Did I ever matter, Mom,
as much as my sisters? Or was I always the final insult? You have no right to judge me. I ain't done
nothing different than you, now have I?*

*Max says I'm poor and stuck and scared. Jeff says
I'm a whore. Who am I? Who the fuck am I? Am I
all of those things or none? Somebody please come
and tell me who I am.*

She stared up at the ceiling, feeling tiny and small.

She had never been there, but Carol-Anne knew
exactly where she was. She had hit rock bottom. As
she lay there, darkness all around her, she couldn't
help but wonder if she'd ever see light again.

*   *   *

Black people didn't see therapists. They didn't go to head doctors. Whatever was eating them up inside they either banished through self-will or went mad. The banishment hadn't worked and Carol-Anne didn't have the luxury of going mad.

It helped that she didn't have to pay one red cent for the twice-a-week visits with Sherlyn Jones, who was a big dark-skinned dread-haired Sister from Harlem. Her medical insurance covered all the expenses.

Sherlyn made Carol-Anne feel comfortable from the moment she walked into her office. There was no sign over the door that said Crazy Enter Here. No indication of what went on inside. A simple name-plate was the only indication of an office inside.

Christmas had been the clincher. Christmas had been the get-your-ass-some-help-and-get-it-quick incident. Sitting around, hating everybody and everything. Hating her daughter. Hating herself. So low, so blue, she felt as if she were immersed in a bottle of ink, a feeling that forced her to seek help.

Carol-Anne had no right telling Nadia that there was no Santa Claus. A child was entitled to fantasy; the world got real soon enough. Her mother was right. The same way she schemed and got clothes at Lord and Taylor, Carol-Anne could have detoured to the toy department and charged another hundred on things Nadia wanted for Christmas.

That, or demanded Jeff keep his promise. Fought him tooth and nail, camped out on his doorstep if she had to. But she hadn't.

"Too easy, Carol-Anne. You made it too easy for him. He smelled your desperation all the way from Brooklyn," Sherlyn told her. "And those things he said? He was just angry and took it out on you."

"But I did sleep with him for money."

"No, you did what you thought you had to do; there's a difference."

"Really?" Carol-Anne said with hard eyes.

"Yes, really."

"If it quacks like a duck . . ." Carol-Anne's voice drifted off.

"Beating up on yourself doesn't help. You tried and didn't succeed. Give yourself credit for trying."

"How can I? Christmas was the worst day of my life."

Sherlyn studied her. "Know what I think? I think you did exactly what you did because you were looking for help. And the only way you could get it was by going nuclear. Blasting everything to smithereens and then . . ." Sherlyn paused, showed her pearly white teeth, her voice dropping to a soothing octave. "And then, you could start making your life right again."

"I love my daughter with all my heart."

"Yes, we know that. Every decision you've made in the last months, in the last eight years, has revolved around your daughter. Right or wrong, she was the reason for everything you did. So now you've got to change that approach. You got to do for *you,* so you can do for Nadia." Sherlyn paused. "Tell me about your mother."

Carol-Anne tensed. "What about her?"

Sherlyn shrugged. "I get a sense of rage there."

Carol-Anne laughed. "To say the least."

"Tell me what it's like for you."

"I love her, she's my mother, but it seems nothing I ever did was right. Not washing the dishes, the way I scrubbed the toilet. Even the color panty hose I wore."

"How long?"

"Huh?"

Sherlyn smiled, shrugged. "How long have you been doing things wrong, in your mother's eyes?"

"Wow." Carol-Anne frowned. "Since I can remember."

"Your father? Where's he?"

"Dead."

"When?"

"When did he die?" Carol-Anne asked.

"Yeah."

"In 1979."

"You were, what, twenty-three?"

"Yeah. Twenty-three."

"How would you describe their marriage?"

"They were never married."

"Common law?"

"Never lived together. He stayed one place, we stayed another."

"Until the time he died, did you see him much?"

"Nearly every weekend. He'd take me and my sisters out. Movies, ice skating. Stuff like that. When we got older we'd go to dinner and the movies."

"Would your mother come along?"

Carol-Anne frowned. "No. Never."

Sherlyn jotted on her pad. "Why?"

"Said she wouldn't be seen with another woman's husband."

"He was married to someone else?"

"Yes. Linda. Real nice person."

"But he had how many children with your mother?"

"Four. Me and my three sisters."

"Before or after."

"Before or after what?"

"He married somebody else."

"Before *and* after."

"You were born when?"

"Nineteen fifty-six."

Sherlyn's pen moved fast on the page. "Were you born before he married, or after he married?"

"After. I was the only after child. My sisters were all the before children. They use to tease me and call me *After*-Anne."

"So they knew?"

"Oh, yeah. We knew our father was married to somebody else."

"Do you know why they never married?"

"Who?"

"Your parents."

Carol-Anne paused. Looked away. "My mother said because he couldn't be faithful. Ran around."

"But she had four of his children."

"She loved kids."

"She loved your father?"

It was the first tear of the session. "I don't know."

Sherlyn handed her a tissue. "Did your father and Linda have any children?"

"No, she couldn't have kids." Carol-Anne looked at Sherlyn expectantly, waiting for her comment on a man married to a woman who was barren and having children with a woman who wasn't. Carol-Anne had her own theories and wanted some of them confirmed. She expected Sherlyn to, but the teakettle whistled and that signaled the end of the session. Still the thought hung in the air between them. *Momma was used.*

"Would you like Tetley or peppermint tea?"

"Peppermint."

"Sugar or honey?"

"Honey."

Sheryln's brow rose. "Peppermint tea with honey? Most of my clients take Tetley and sugar."

"Max." Carol-Anne offered.

"What he drank?"

Carol-Anne nodded.

"What does Carol-Anne drink?"

She was forced to smile.

"I'd like to see Nadia," Sherlyn said.

"I don't want to bring her into this."

"She's been in this since before she was born . . . no real rush, but within the month, okay?"

*   *   *

Carol-Anne looked at the closed wooden door. She had been staring at it for half an hour. She tried to hear, but no sounds came from inside.

She could only imagine the horrors that Sherlyn had wormed from Nadia's subconscious. Blamed herself for every single one of them.

Carol-Anne was helping herself to a fifth cup of water when the door swung open. Sherlyn beckoned her with her hands.

"You can come in now. And Nadia, why don't you wait outside for a few minutes? I want to talk to Mommy."

Her baby was smiling. *Thank God,* Carol-Anne thought. *Thank God she can still smile through all the madness. All my madness.*

"Have a seat," Sherlyn said, picking up her legal pad. "Nadia has given me permission to tell you what we talked about . . . The good news is that she loves you. On a conscious level you are the best mommy anyone can have."

"The bad news?"

"Not so bad. She does not like where she lives. She doesn't like to see you cry. And the idea that there is no Santa Claus took her for a real loop. She has a tendency to mix up her father figures. Max and Jeff. She loves Max. Max is the ultimate in her book. And she misses him."

Sherlyn looked at her. "Now she's broken-hearted. Feels it's something she's done. I told her that she's not responsible and you must reinforce that. Also you have to emphasize that Jeff is her biological father and Max was just a good family friend. So you have two hearts to mend. Yours and hers."

"Great," Carol-Anne said.

"She feels abandoned. Emotionally abandoned by Jeff and spiritually and physically abandoned by Max. I got the sense that Max hugged and kissed and did things with her. Played board games, which hand has the nickel, that kind of thing. Physical contact"— Sherlyn raised her hand—"not sexual, but the good kind of physical. Kids need that attention. Pats, hugs, kisses. Hands-on interaction."

Carol-Anne nodded. "Yep, that was Max."

"So you have to take up the slack. Hug her, kiss her. Make clay together. Bake cookies. Those board games she got for Christmas, pull them out and use them."

"And what about me?"

"We still have some way to go on that." The tea kettle whistled.

"How do you do that?" Carol-Anne asked.

"Do what?"

"Time the teakettle to whistle when the session's up?"

Sherlyn stood, moved over to her countertop. "A timer. Impressive, ain't it?"

"Tetley with two sugars and milk, please."

Sherlyn looked over her shoulder. "Good for you."

"I got a check from Jeff."

Sherlyn raised her brow. "Without asking?"

"Without asking, without trudging to Brooklyn. No begging and definitely no sex."

"How much?"

"Four thousand fifty dollars."

"Tax time," Sherlyn offered.

"What has that got to do with anything?"

"Any child support paid can be claimed on his tax return. Four grand is a nice deduction, dontcha think? Men do it all the time. Won't send a dime all year, but right before tax time they send a big check."

"Well, I know what I'm going to do with it."

"What's that?"

"Find a bigger place for me and Nadia."

"So you figured that out, huh?"

"What's that?"

"That you and your daughter need your own space."

"Yeah, just a matter of finding the *right* place."

"You'll find it."

"How do you know?"

Sherlyn handed her her tea. "Because you are ready to receive it, that's why."

"Mommy?"

"Yeah?"

"I like Miz Jones."

"You do?"

"Uh-huh. She let me color and everything."

Carol-Anne raised her brow. Sherlyn didn't say anything about Nadia coloring. "Really? What did you color?"

"Pictures."

"Of?"

"Me and you and Uncle Max."

"No pictures of your father?"

Nadia shook her head.

"Tell me about the picture of you and me and Uncle Max."

"We was in a big house. You was on the first floor, I was on the second and Uncle Max was on the third."

"Must have been a big house," Carol-Anne said, holding her daughter's hand tight as they crossed over to the park.

"Uh-huh. Big enough for everybody."

They entered Central Park and Carol-Anne released her daughter at the entrance to the playground. She took a seat on the bench and pulled her coat up around her neck. It wasn't as warm as she thought, but Nadia didn't mind the cold. She climbed the monkey bars, took a couple of rides on the swing, and slid down the slide.

"Mommy, come seesaw with me." Carol-Anne got

up from the bench, saddled the shiny green slab of wood and held it steady as Nadia slid on.

"Ready?" she asked Nadia.

"Ready!"

"Okay, here we go." Up into the air her daughter went; the blue sky and empty trees framing her smile, picture perfect.

Carol-Anne stood outside the brownstone on Convent Avenue, checking the address on the piece of paper against the brass numbers over the entry doors. She studied the white flower boxes beneath the first-floor windows, the stained-glass side panels, and the shiny black wrought-iron fencing.

She gazed up to the second-floor windows that were massive and bare. Wanted to pinch herself. Wanted to cry. How many times had she passed this very same building, in awe of its elegance and upkeep? How many times had she wondered who lived there and what it felt like to walk the inner halls, live in its sheltered rooms?

She could not believe her luck when Sherlyn called her talking about an aunt who had an apartment to rent. Talking about her Aunt Corinthia who was retired and was looking for a decent tenant to rent her second-floor apartment on Convent Avenue, and how Sherlyn had recommended Carol-Anne to her.

"How many rooms?" Carol-Anne asked.

"More than you will ever need. Two bedrooms, a kitchen, a bathroom, and a living room."

"How much?" had been Carol-Anne's next question.

"Just six hundred. She's not in it for the money. Likes to feel like she's helping somebody who needs help."

"Six, did you say six?"

"Six hundred. Plus your own utilities. I told her all about you and she says she wants to meet you, talk with you. See if things could work out."

A week later Carol-Anne found herself outside the brownstone. She was standing there a while, taking in the building's beauty, disbelieving her good fortune, when the front door swung open and an elderly woman, not quite five feet tall, appeared. She had a head of snow-white hair, cut low and stylish around her face. The satin off-white jogging suit was not the least bit expected but went well with the sneakers just the same.

There was no doubt that Corinthia Mason Jones was the queen of her castle.

"I was watching from my window. Was waiting for you to ring the bell but you were just standing out here staring. Thought maybe you weren't sure of the address."

"Mrs. Jones?" Carol-Anne asked.

"Nobody but. You must be Carol-Anne. Come on in."

The parlor was as it had been forty years ago. Full of well-kept, frequently polished antiques and a fireplace that worked. Tasseled lamp shades, brocade drapes, and a Persian rug finished off the ensemble.

"I like the old stuff," Mrs. Jones said, watching Carol-Anne gaze around the room. "Bought it all when I first moved here. Refused to get rid of a single piece." She indicated the roaring fire in the fireplace. "I like to use it every now and then, especially on days like today. So, tell me a little something about yourself."

Carol-Anne could feel the woman's eyes everywhere upon her. As she formulated what she wanted to say and how she wanted to say it, she realized that Mrs. Jones knew everything about her, was certain that Sherlyn had told her.

"I used to pass your home all the time on the way to City College. Marveling at how well it was kept, wondering who lived inside . . . You have a beautiful home."

"Thank you."

"That's why I stood outside so long. I couldn't believe that this house was where Sherlyn's aunt lived. That maybe I could live here, too."

"Sherlyn told me about your situation. I'm not looking for nothing but a good tenant who pays their rent on time, keeps the noise down, not into anything illegal, and who will respect my home." Corinthia Mason Jones was done. It was Carol-Anne's turn to talk.

Carol-Anne laughed, nervous and caught. Eager. "Well, that's me. I love this house. Absolutely adore it. And believe me, I would treat it just like it was my own." She paused, chancing direct eye contact. Wanting to be sure. Needing to be sure. "Sherlyn said you were only asking six hundred. Is that so?"

"If we agree, it's six hundred for you. It's not what I was asking and when you see the apartment you'll know why, but Sherlyn said you needed help and that's something I like to do in my old age."

"Six hundred dollars a month would be perfect."

Mrs. Jones stood. "Well, I guess we need to go up and see it, then."

Soft light spilled into the entryway. A huge L-shaped room with four windows was in the front. "This is your living room."

Off the hall were the two bedrooms and the bathroom, which had a claw-foot tub big enough to soak in. The shower head looked new, as did the sink and the toilet. The kitchen was the last room and it ran wall to wall, allowing enough space for a dining room table and then some. The appliances were modern, as were the cabinets and the flooring.

Mrs. Jones touched the countertop. "I renovated this five years ago. Called in Sears."

The original wood had never been painted over.

Every window, door, doorway, and baseboard was shellacked cherrywood and the walls were off-white. "Now you'll have to keep up with all the woodwork. I use Murphy's, which is good for wood."

Such beauty, such elegance. Tears filled Carol-Anne's eyes. A real home. A baby-sitter for Nadia. She could start her classes at City College. Take her things out of storage.

Carol-Anne turned. "Can I see the front room again?"

"Go right ahead."

Carol-Anne moved down the hall. Stepped into the front room bathed in the soft light. Her wing chair would go in the corner. Right by the fireplace.

No more bad men at her door, no more Nadia in her bed. She would sit in her chair, draw her brown feet up underneath her, play comfort music, and have her Quiet Time.

Alone, but content.

❈

Chapter 16

Max tossed his tie, took a seat on his sofa, and began sorting his mail. His *Black Enterprise* and *Men's Health* had arrived and Max was glad to see them. He flipped through the stack, saw junk mail, a VISA application—to be tossed for sure—his bank statement, and a *TV Guide*.

At the bottom was a legal-sized envelope with his name penned in ink. The upper right-hand corner said "Carol-Anne McClementine."

His mouth got dry.

Max held it up to the light and saw a sheet of folded paper inside. Visualized her sitting at her kitchen table, taking up her pen. Imagined what she had written.

Max had never wanted her gone. She had made the decision to leave. Yes, he had told her "*You do what you want to do*," but he'd only meant it in that moment.

Looking back, Max saw himself desperately trying to make her at ease, comfortable; feel loved. He had bent over backward, going to that shabby-ass apartment, preparing meals for her in that ancient kitchen. Sleeping in the living room for lack of a bedroom of her own. Showering in that rusted old bathtub stained so deep not even Zud could make it white again.

Walking down Pleasant, passing the junkies and the drug dealers. Abandoned buildings. The roaches, the mice. Living like that because it was how *she* wanted to live. *Not me. Never me. I wanted to pull you up from the slums but you liked it just fine.*

Max tore open the envelope. Pulled out a blank piece of paper. It was just wrapping for a five-hundred-dollar check and the Lord and Taylor charge card cut in half.

He tossed the card pieces in the garbage. Addressed an envelope and put the check inside. Tomorrow he'd mail it.

He didn't want her money.

Carol-Anne looked at her wish list. The fact that she was making one was a sign of trouble. The money from Jeff had disappeared lightning fast. She gazed out her kitchen window, seeing the back of the brownstones on the next street.

For the past two weeks she had been walking around her apartment feeling watched. Most of the windows were still bare and she was too dignified to drape bed sheets.

She needed curtains, a bath mat. Carol-Anne needed lamps for the living room and both bedrooms. She needed a vacuum cleaner for the hallway runner. She needed a real bed. Her pull-out couch was in the living room, and that's where she slept.

Carol-Anne needed a bureau for her clothes, she was living out of garbage bags. She needed end tables and chairs. Her kitchen table was an embarrassment.

She needed towels, washcloths. A hamper for the dirty clothes. She wanted to get Nadia the Aladdin bed set. Carol-Anne wanted plants, carpeting, torch lamps. She wanted new pots, dishes that matched. A microwave.

Everywhere she looked she saw a need. Walking into her apartment depressed her. The beauty of the apartment was lost by her impoverished furnishings. *Looked better empty*, Carol-Anne mused.

Everyone who came to visit—her mother, Tina, even Selma—had marveled at the beauty of the outside and the entry hall. They marveled as they continued upstairs. But when they stepped inside the apartment, the compliments changed. They said things like, *Oh, what a big place. Look at that wood. Kitchen's big enough to eat in. You could give a party in the living room alone.*

She tried to make it pretty. Make it nice. But nothing worked.

Her favorite wing chair sat in the corner like a menace. With its worn brocade seat and chipped wooden legs with the split seams oozing strands of brittle horsehair, there was nothing elegant about the chair at all. Carol-Anne hadn't sat in it once since she moved in.

Start small, Tina had told her. But there were no small things on her list.

She got up from the table, turned off the kitchen light, and moved down the hall. Stopped at the first door and peeked in on a sleeping Nadia.

Carol-Anne glanced at her bedroom, full of plastic bags and boxes, and closed the door. She headed for her living room. Flipped the ceiling light and blinked against the glare. Her eyes drifted to her wing chair. Under the harsh light it looked ready for the junk yard. *And I wanted to put that in Max's living room? I must have been out my mind.*

Carol-Anne refocused. Envisioned what her living room could look like. A love seat against the farthest wall, a new Queen Anne chair by the fireplace. Two end tables, a floor lamp and a table lamp. Persian rug. A ficus tree; the northern exposure was perfect for it. *A living room full of class.*

Carol-Anne laughed. *All Max ever wanted to give me and now I want it for myself.*

As she took the pillows off her couch and unfolded the bed, she wondered if Max had received the check.

She could have used that five hundred dollars. Ten miniblinds, towels, curtains, lamps, and a set of dishes. A bed. It hadn't been easy sending the money, especially since he gave no indication he wanted it.

She thought about calling to find out if he had received it. Thought about calling to say hello. To hear his voice. Listen to his words.

Try to decipher if he still cared.

Luck. Coincidence. Fate. Destiny. Max wasn't sure which one it was. All he knew was one minute he was sitting by himself at the counter at Sylvia's Restaurant waiting for his takeout and the next minute she was standing there.

It had been so long since he'd seen her face. For a second all he could do was stare at her.

"What are you doing here?" Samone asked.

"Takeout."

She laughed and the sound was the best medicine. "Yeah, me too . . . long time." She touched his arm. "How has things been going?"

Max looked away. "All right." Looked back. "And you?"

"Can't complain." She took the seat next to him. Got the attention of the waiter and ordered ribs, potato salad, and collard greens. Corn bread on the side.

Max looked her over, searching for signs of her status. Searching for an indication that she still was in love with someone else. Surrounding noises filtered past them as Samone asked about their mutual friend.

"You talked to Pat lately?"

"No, not recently."

Her face changed. "Then you didn't hear."

"Hear what?"

Samone frowned. "She's moving."

"Moving? Where to?"

"*Hot* lanta. Black capital of the world."

"You're kidding?"

She shook her head. "Wish I was. Ray got transferred. They'll be out of here by summer."

Max was stunned. "I don't believe Pat's leaving."

"Me, either . . . she's been my best friend since forever. Now I'm gonna have to get with MCI or something just so I can keep in contact with her black ass."

"You and her were always tight," Max said, sensing her sadness.

She looked at him, her eyes watery. "Since ninth grade. That's a long time."

Max took her hand, gave it a gentle squeeze. "You'll be okay, Samone."

"I guess. Just hard. Pat not being here."

Max turned back toward the counter. "That's life, babe."

The double doors swung open again. The waiter approached, a brown paper bag in hand. He placed it in front of Max. "Six fifty."

Max reached into his pocket, took out his wallet.

"How you getting home from here?" she asked, not wanting to leave him just yet.

"Way I always do, cabbing it."

"Can you drop me?"

"Sure."

They stood on Lenox Avenue watching traffic, looking for the gypsy cabs that ran in that part of town. Max whistled one down and they scooted into the back.

Samone studied him as they pulled from the curb. "So what's really going on, Max?"

He looked at her, caught off guard. Offered a tight laugh. "Going on? Nothing much."

"No, baby, this here is Samone you talking to. Something's going on."

Max laughed, looked out the window. "Nothing, Samone."

"You lying. I know you, Maxwell Aaron Scutter.

Something is bothering the hell out of you, now what is it?"

"Nothing you need to be concerned with."

She leaned into his face, so close he could smell her perfume. Felt a deep need to kiss her lips. Touch her soft brown hair. "You gonna tell me?"

"Why should I?" he offered with a pleasing smile.

" 'Cause you need to talk to somebody."

He did need to talk to someone. He couldn't talk to Maurice because Maurice didn't like Carol-Anne. He couldn't talk to Ken because all Ken would say was get over it. After that there was no one else.

"You got a few hours?" Max wanted to know.

"That bad?"

He nodded, closing his eyes. "That bad."

When the cab pulled up to Samone's apartment house, they got out together. It felt strange being inside her building, even stranger being inside her apartment.

Pictures of Jon were everywhere. His white face smiled at Max from the wall unit, the side table. From the south wall. Everywhere he looked Max saw the man who had been able to do for Samone what he never could. Make her happy.

Max took the TV tray she handed him— "Thanks"—and opened his bag of food.

"You need anything? Hot sauce?"

"Yeah, that'd be great."

She looked good. Samone always looked good. Her black slacks and white cashmere sweater fit her like nothing else could. The pearls around her neck and the black patent-leather pumps so classic. So Samone. She had always been a fashion horse.

Size seven, eight at the most, Samone wore her clothes like they were tailor-made. She enjoyed looking good. Dressing up was an everyday part of her life.

Max watched her come back with the Tabasco

sauce. Watched amused as she kicked off her pumps and unzipped her tight pants, opened her bag of food and pulled up her sweater sleeves. Looked down at herself. "I really ought to take this off. All I need is some barbecue sauce getting on it." She stood. "Be right back."

Max picked up the remote and clicked on the TV. Turned to catch the stock market report. He was so intent on the numbers scrolling along the bottom of the screen that he did not hear her return.

"Same old Max. Don't you ever let work go?" She stood there in sweats and bare feet. Even in the heart of winter her toenails were painted.

"Just checking a few things."

They ate, stock market on the television, and when the meal was through, Samone clicked the TV off, put on the radio, and got them some wine.

"So," she began. "What happened?"

Max scrunched his shoulders. "She left me."

"Carol-Anne?"

"One and only."

"Why?"

"I'm too high-class."

Samone smiled. "Too high-class? Max, you are one of the most laid-back brothers I know."

"It's different for her. Single mother. Not a lot of money. Whole different way of doing things."

Samone looked surprised. "This was about money?"

"Yeah."

"But you got money."

"I know. That's the problem. I got and she ain't."

She shook her head. "I'm confused."

Max turned toward her, hands open. "Like I said, her world is different. Struggle is a way of life for her. Cutting corners, buying cheap . . . how can I explain?"

"But you were helping her out?"

"I tried, but she never really let me. I'd buy her things, her daughter things. Paid for her daughter's dance lessons, some new carpeting, stuff like that."

"And she didn't like that?"

Max shook his head. "No. She didn't."

"That's a new one. Nowadays most women want men to help them out."

"Not Carol-Anne."

"But you guys were together for over a year."

"I know."

"So what did it?"

"We went out to Maurice and Babette's new house."

"Yeah, and . . ."

"Michele made some remarks to Babette about how Carol-Anne looked. How she was dressed. Carol-Anne overheard it."

"Well, how was she dressed?"

Max looked away. "Like I said, she lives differently. Shops differently. Dresses differently."

"Markdowns?"

"Not even that good. Conway, Kmart . . . plastic earrings."

Samone couldn't help but snicker. "Plastic? Not even imitation gold?"

Max shook his head.

"I see."

"I tried to buy better for her. Gave her a Lord and Taylor charge card and everything. She didn't use it till *after* we broke up. The thing about that night at Maurice's was that Michele was absolutely right . . . I was embarrassed. I ended up telling Carol-Anne off."

"Oh, Lord."

"Yeah. I was sorry, but wasn't. I kept trying to tell her and tell her. I mean, she wasn't sloppy, but just cheap-looking."

"I know that must have been hard."

"Real hard, but I tried not to make it matter 'cause I loved her."

"Do you still love her?"

"I don't know."

"You want her back?"

"Sometimes I do and sometimes I don't . . . you know me, Samone. I don't ask for a lot, but when I step out, you got to be looking as good as I do. No reason in the world for her to dress like that. Not when she was with me."

"Sister had a charge card that you was paying for from Lord and Taylor and she never used it? In all the years we were together you ain't never given me no charge at Lord and Taylor. You must have loved her."

"I just wanted to make things better. She was living in a real rundown place and I was trying to get her to move in with me. Was thinking about going over to the Waterside Apartments."

"And she said no?"

"Well, she did move in with me after she had a bad problem with rats. She was only there a few weeks. Then the thing at Maurice's happened and she left."

"How long's she been gone?"

"Going on nine months."

"That long? You been walking around with this inside of you for that long?"

"Yeah."

She touched his arm. "Poor baby."

He shrugged it away. "Don't pity me, all right?"

"Didn't mean nothing by it." She reached for his glass. "Want some more wine?"

Samone poured, handed Max a glass.

"Max, if somebody doesn't want to be with you, that's their choice. You got to respect that. There are a thousand women out there who would love you for who you are and what you got to offer. Almost a year, that's a long time. I think you should get on with your life."

"That's what my mind says, but my heart's saying something different."

"Listen to your head."

He looked at her with a weary smile. "So how you and Jon doing?"

"We're doing okay."

"Any wedding bells?"

Samone looked away. "Haven't talked about it."

"I thought that was your main agenda."

"Things change, Max."

"Would you?"

She looked at him, suspicious. "Would I what?"

"Marry him?"

"Yeah . . . I would."

Max drained his wine glass. "Well, I better be going."

Samone wiped barbecue sauce from her fingers. "Let me get your coat."

She held it as he slipped into it. Released the soft wool as his fingers closed the buttons, as his eyes found other places to look; the newscaster's voice droned on behind them.

"You be good," was his final decree.

Samone nodded with promise. At the last minute she called out to him. "Max?" Her voice was gentle and . . . afraid. "Anytime you want to talk, number hasn't changed."

"Okay," was all Max could manage as he stepped out the door.

Chapter 17

Max didn't want her money. Carol-Anne knew he didn't need it, but to return it to her the same way it was sent was like a slap in her face.

No note. No nothing. Just her check looking as crisp and as clean as when she first tore it from her checkbook. Had he handled it at all? Had he even considered keeping it?

My little white flag. Reaching out but covering my butt. My peace pipe. You didn't want it. Didn't want me . . . fine. I know exactly what I can do with it. It couldn't have come at a better time.

Carol-Anne went shopping.

And when that money ran out, she got a Fingerhut catalogue. It was Tina's suggestion. "Cheap, Carol-Anne. What you do is you figure out what you can afford to pay them a month and then you order the stuff. You can furnish your whole place. Furniture, kitchen. Clothes."

There was no credit check, no application to fill out. All Carol-Anne had to do was fill out the order form and mail it in. Two weeks later a truck pulled up with her queen-sized brass-plated bed, frame, mattress, and box spring. A Queen Anne chair, a dinette set, complete with four chairs. A vacuum cleaner. Two small dresser drawers. A winter coat, a pair of shoes, and a pair of bad-weather boots, all for one hundred and twelve dollars a month for the next two years.

Now when Carol-Anne came home, slipping her key into her door and stepping inside her apartment, she felt better.

Her home was coming along.

Carol-Anne dropped the blind back in place. There was nothing out there except a cold gray dismal day. The rain had begun day before yesterday and hadn't stopped since.

"I know we normally wait until after, but can I have some tea now?" Carol-Anne asked.

"Sure. I'll put the water on. So, how goes things?"

"Not too bad."

"Glad to hear that. Did you do what I suggested?"

Carol-Anne opened her bag. Pulled out a two-page letter.

"You want me to read it?" Sherlyn asked, putting a tea bag in the cup.

"No, I'll do it . . . 'Dear Max.'" Carol-Anne paused.

Sherlyn nodded her on. "Go ahead."

" 'I'm writing you this letter because someone suggested I do so.'" She looked at Sherlyn, back at the paper. " 'I don't think it matters, or will make a difference to you one way or the other. You proved that when you gave me back my money. By the way, I used it well.

" 'You know I have a new address, which means I got a new place to stay. Gorgeous brownstone; I have the whole second floor. Just me and Nadia. For a long time she talked about you. Lately she hardly mentions you at all. Someone suggested her heart was broken when I left you. True or not, I'm working to make things okay for her again.

" 'I screwed up when I left you. Screwed up before I left you. I can't apologize for that, but realize that

I was wrong. I know you were trying to show us both a better life, but I had lived this old one so long I didn't think I could change. I have.

" 'It was rough for a long time. Real rough, real bad times. I hurt myself, hurt Nadia. But it's gotten better. And part of keeping it better is doing things like writing this letter to you.

" 'I was afraid. Afraid one day you were just going to leave me. Walk away forever. That one day I'd wake up and you'd be gone or changed your mind. The more you tried to do for me, the less I trusted what you did. The thing at Maurice's house—plastic earrings and all. I knew better. In the bottom of my heart I knew better, but I didn't care.

" 'Now I do care. Care about all those things. How I look, where I live, all those things. I never allowed myself to feel your absence in my life. Not really feel it. Bits and pieces, but that was all. It was suggested that I do that now, feel your absence completely and let you know what I feel.

" 'I was always too scared to really love you, held back from you on purpose. I realize now there was nothing to be afraid of. But it's too late. Truth is, I did love you, Max, but not enough, not the right way, and now that you're gone, I love you more.

" 'Well, got to go. Carol-Anne.' "

Carol-Anne extended the letter to Sherlyn, but she wouldn't take it. "That's not for me, that's for you, unless you want to mail it."

"Mail it? You said I didn't have to."

"No, you don't. But you have the option. I think there was a whole lot of truth in it and there's only one person who needs to hear it."

Sherlyn picked up her pen. "Think about it." She made a note on her legal pad.

Chapter 18

Carol-Anne turned the fire down beneath the turkey burgers, then leaned into the hallway. Dinner was almost ready. She called out to Nadia, "Go and wash your hands."

She pulled away from the doorway, the soft polished wood pleasing her fingertips. She took a minute to admire the washed oak kitchen cabinets that gave the room airiness and serenity. Her spider plant, sea-green with white centers, made her feel good.

A real kitchen. A place Carol-Anne loved to be in. To prepare meals, do her budget. Have morning coffee as she stared out upon the sun dancing on the windows of the brownstones behind her; reflecting like a beautiful jewel, perfect and too brilliant to ever possess.

Her kitchen. The new place to have quiet times, to let her Loud Thoughts run free. But the Loud Thoughts weren't so loud anymore. They no longer condemned her. They approached her as a friend. The Loud Thoughts had become just thoughts, full of insight and suggestion, not rage and belittlement.

Carol-Anne took a sponge to the stove, dabbing spilled grease, splattered meat juices. She wiped, watching for the miracle of rebirth as the shiny whiteness returned time and again to her stove top.

Little things gave her pleasure these days.

She eyed the clock, saw it was quarter to seven.

Dinner was late tonight because she was now working overtime. She could no longer depend on Jeff's checks. Sometimes they came, sometimes they did not. Sherlyn promised to talk about forced child support during their next session if Carol-Anne wanted to go that route.

Carol-Anne did. Nadia deserved it.

Things were tight again, but that no longer scared her. Tight, but manageable if she watched things closely. She took the half pound of American cheese out of the refrigerator. Putting it on the counter, she looked over at her purse hanging on the back of the chair.

Nine days.

For nine days Carol-Anne had been toting around the letter in the bottom of her bag. No envelope to protect it from pens with no caps, lipsticks that came undone. General bottom-of-the-bag lint, dust, and debris.

She had looked at the letter today; at its tattered, worn edges and the fuzzy creased lines. Carol-Anne had studied the ink stains as if they were a secret language that would speak only to her. Too worn to mail, too sooty to be given. It left her with two choices, write it over or throw it away.

But Carol-Anne found a third choice. It would stay in the bottom of her bag until it faded, rotted, and crumbled to dust.

There was nothing about Clifford Wagner that appealed to Carol-Anne. He'd been a co-worker for over a year, Carol-Anne considered him just that. Tall enough, but there was no meat to his bones. His nose was way too big for his thin face but matched the size of his wide, wide lips.

He was the wrong color—light-skinned brown, the wrong astrological sign—a Gemini. You never knew which Clifford was coming to work that day. And he was the wrong age—he had just turned twenty-nine, ten years Carol-Anne's junior.

Despite all his deficiencies, he did convince Carol-Anne to join him for an evening of jazz at the Village Vanguard. Carol-Anne went because she couldn't remember the last time she'd gone out. She went because she loved both the Village and jazz and it had been too long since she had indulged herself.

Carol-Anne went, leaving behind the phone number of the club, the time of the show, and the estimated time of her arrival home. Carol-Anne left behind a dark apartment, an unhappy Nadia with Mrs. Corinthia Mason Jones, and two Disney videos because Mrs. Jones didn't have cable but she did have a VCR.

Carol-Anne left the first-floor apartment with the smell of cinnamon and vanilla lingering in the hall as Nadia helped Mrs. Jones bake Toll House cookies. She had refused Clifford's offer to pick her up and called a cab.

Carol-Anne enjoyed the ride from uptown all the way to Lower Manhattan. She peered out the backseat window like a tourist, New Yorkers catching her eye everywhere she looked.

Clifford was waiting for her when she arrived.

He ushered her into the club, pulling out her chair and buying her drinks. He kept his distance, talked shop until the show started, and then became engrossed in the music.

Carol-Anne didn't mind because she wanted to be private with the music, too. After the show, he took her to a restaurant for a late-night snack, and flagged a cab for both of them.

He insisted that she be dropped off first to make sure she got in okay. He didn't try to kiss her, didn't try to hold her hand. Had no come-on lines. He told her he'd had a good time, hoped she had, too, and he would see her on Monday.

It was not the worst date of her life and it wasn't the best, but at least she'd had one. Her first night out since Max.

Since Max.

That thought nudged her up the stairs to her apartment and helped her slip out of her dress and pumps. That thought watched her from her bathroom mirror as she removed makeup and brushed her teeth free of brandy.

That thought, "*since Max*," was there when she pulled back the covers to her bed and crawled into its cold sheets. That thought kept her wide awake for a long time. A very long time.

"Good for you," Sherlyn said, drawing the blinds of her office.

"Yeah, it was kind of nice. He's definitely not my type."

"That's okay. He doesn't have to be. Not every man you date will be your type. Sometimes you go just for the simple act of going. Of getting dressed up, and putting on makeup."

Carol-Anne smiled. "Yeah, it did feel good."

"So." Sherlyn picked up her pen. "Last time you were here we started talking about Jeff and child support. You still want to do that?"

"It's only fair to Nadia."

Sherlyn handed her some papers. "I've got some information on how it's done. Now it won't be quick. It can take months to get anything, but seeing as you're not really getting anything now, I don't think that's an issue."

Carol-Anne took the papers, scanned them quickly. Looked at Sherlyn. "A part of me doesn't want his money. A big part. But this is not about me, is it?" Carol-Anne smiled whimsically. "It's about Nadia, right?"

"This time around, you bet."

"Been thinking about Max, a lot."

"And?"

Carol-Anne shrugged, self-conscious. "No *and*. Just thinking."

"I assumed you didn't mail that letter."

"You assumed right."

"You know, you're going to have to do something. No, let me rephrase that; you don't *have* to do anything. It's definitely your choice. But you got to know that this thing between you and him is still unresolved. You need closure, Carol-Anne."

"We had closure."

"No, you had attitude and disagreement. That's not the same thing. I can't make you, I can only suggest. My experience is you will continue to think about Max for all the wrong reasons, in all the wrong ways, at all the wrong times, until you close that chapter"—she had a twinkle in her eye—"or open a new one."

"You talking about starting again?"

Sherlyn raised her brow. "You seem surprised."

"I am."

"Why?"

"It's been over so long. He's never called me."

"Because it's not on him. It's on you. You left him. Not vice-versa."

Carol-Anne's mind was going now. She felt safe to talk about what she hadn't discussed with anyone. Was looking for someone to lead the way. To tell her it was okay. "I don't see how I can, after all this time. What, ten months?"

"If he loved you, then time is just a way to measure how long you've been apart, that's all."

"But that's it. I don't know if he does."

Sherlyn clucked her teeth. "Carol-Anne Mc-Clementine, how you gonna sit there and tell that lie? You know he does. It was all in your letter. What you don't know is if his love is strong enough, big enough, to forgive you. And right now, you're too scared to find out."

Carol-Anne shook her head. "Not scared."

"Not scared? Then what?"

Carol-Anne's eyes sought Sherlyn's. "Petrified."

Carol-Anne waited.

Waited until dinner was over. Waited until Nadia was bathed, in bed and asleep. Carol-Anne waited for the quiet and silence.

She wanted no interruptions.

Carol-Anne picked up the phone and called Max.

"Hello?" The female voice on the other end was the most shocking thing Carol-Anne had experienced in a long time. It cut off her vocal cords and made her mouth fall open.

"Hello?" That voice again. That female voice knowing Carol-Anne without even realizing that it did. That voice coming back like a specter from a bad past to haunt her, mock her. Michele answering Max's phone.

"Somebody there?" And then Carol-Anne heard him, heard him asking who was it and heard Michele say nobody. "Hang up."

Click. Buzz.

Carol-Anne had waited. Had waited for quiet, peace of mind, for Nadia to fall asleep. She had waited for her sanity to return, a better way of living and signs that everything was going to be okay again.

But maybe, came the brittle thought, this time she had waited too long.

District Council 37 had its offices in Lower Manhattan. With New York City workers as its benefactor, the union had more than enough funds to build the magnificent structure on Barclay Street off West Broadway. With its state-of-the-art design, lush carpeting, and impressive offices, DC 37, as it was called, looked better than most of the places its union workers toiled away in.

Carol-Anne had been there before for training sessions, but this day she arrived a little past one in the afternoon for different reasons. This day she was seeking out legal services to help her with her child-support case.

As she sat in the office of soft mauve walls and matching carpeting, as she sat before Jennifer Laiken, Paralegal, she foresaw the uphill battle ahead of her.

"Can I ask why?" Ms. Laiken wanted to know, her eyes scanning Nadia's birth certificate with quick, darting eyes.

"Because at the time I wanted to forget the fact that he was Nadia's father. I didn't want her coming to me years later asking questions about a man named Jeffrey Gadson. So I left it blank."

Ms. Laiken shook her head and Carol-Anne knew she did not like this woman. "Makes it harder now. If he fights you, and his history of scattered child-support payments indicates he will, we will have to pull him in for paternity testing, which is not easy to do. A judge can order it, but that means more time in court."

Carol-Anne looked at Ms. Laiken, with her butch black choppy hair, her pale white skin, and her beady black eyes, and wanted every single dime her union ever took from her paycheck.

"I know it's not going to be easy, or simple. But I'm willing to do whatever I have to to get this for my child."

"Okay." But Ms. Laiken did not seemed convinced. Ms. Laiken seemed annoyed. Ms. Laiken wasn't even an attorney, just a paralegal. Where were the attorneys? Carol-Anne wanted to know. She didn't want a paralegal, she wanted an *esquire*. She wanted the person who goes into the courtroom and fights for your rights, not the clerk who did research and handled initial investigations.

"I will be getting an attorney?" Carol-Anne asked.

Ms. Laiken's eyes flew up, shocked and stunned. Carol-Anne returned her gaze, keeping it steady; letting her know that she didn't think much of Ms. Laiken's skills, personable or otherwise.

"When you go to court you will have an attorney representing you. Until such time I will be handling your case."

But that wasn't how it went on *Perry Mason* or even *Matlock*. Matlock got down into the trenches with you, held your hand, guided you from beginning to end. Knew you, met with you before you even entered the courthouse. He didn't show up on the court date, introducing himself for the first time.

Carol-Anne wanted Matlock. She did not want Ms. Laiken.

"How could an attorney I've never met do a good job for me?"

"Ms. McClementine, I assure you that you will get the best legal services your money can buy." Which told Carol-Anne right there that maybe she should seek another lawyer. Because as it stood now, her union dues were only ten dollars a month. How much legal help could that buy?

"So what happens next?"

"I need you to fill out some forms and we'll get the ball rolling."

Carol-Anne went into her bag. Got out her pen. Began.

Carol-Anne slipped on her leather gloves and pulled her tam over her head. Exited the building. The sun was high in the sky, but a bitter wind disregarded its importance.

She walked.

She wondered if the child-support issue would get

funky. If this business about getting Nadia money from her daddy would get nasty. Wondered if Jeff would take the stand and tell the courtroom how Carol-Anne had slept with him. Wondered if it would be forever written in court documents that Carol-Anne had sold her body for her child.

Would her grandchilden and great-grandchildren be able to go down to Family Court and pull the records and learn about their family scandals?

Thirty-nine thousand dollars. It would be worth the fight.

Carol-Anne headed for the train, but at the last minute she changed her mind. J & R Music World was only a couple blocks away. She had heard Nancy Wilson's latest CD on the radio and decided to go pick it up.

Carol-Anne hadn't paid much attention to Nancy until Max had come into her life. Max loved Nancy and Carol-Anne came to love her, too. She found herself, more often than not, listening to the few Nancy Wilson CDs she owned. Listening lost and caught in a past that did not touch her future. With Nancy, Carol-Anne could be with Max anytime she wanted.

Carol-Anne knew how much she had in her pocketbook. Six tokens, twenty-two dollars, and twelve cents. There were some groceries she had to pick up and she didn't get paid until Thursday. Today was only Tuesday. Even as Carol-Anne entered J & R Music World, she knew she was spending money she didn't have. That by tomorrow she would regret it.

She stopped a clerk. "Can you tell me where Nancy Wilson's new CD is?" And followed the finger pointed toward the back.

Max.

Tall, handsome. Sporting a fedora, the wool coat fitting him well. Max. Holding a CD, looking down, unaware that Carol-Anne was ten feet away. Max.

The sloping forehead, Chinese eyes, mustache clipped neat over round brown lips. Max. Ten feet away, absorbed, in love with Nancy.

Looking up he turned his head slowly. His eyes widened. No smiles for her appearance. Looking at her unkindly, surprised. Hurt. Wounded. Still suffering.

"Max." His pain found her, her escape fresh inside of him, tender and throbbing with every breath he took. His eyelids slid downward, hiding half his pupils, shielding her from his secret misery. But Carol-Anne knew and the knowledge moved her forward.

"Oh, Max." Her hand reached out to touch his face. To settle the pain that found its way to his brow. Her eyes, liquid and wet, found his, her own heart breaking and torn asunder. "I'm sorry."

Time stood still. Him and her and Nancy. The way it was. The way it used to be. The way it should have stayed. Her hand moved slowly, reluctant to leave his face. Reluctant to leave the warm brown skin, abrasive with a needed shave.

His silence zapped her courage, took away her strength to say more. Carol-Anne turned automatic. Her hand lifted, carefully taking the Nancy Wilson CD from the rack. She turned and headed toward the register, an eternal war within her.

Should she leave the CD unbought and walk out or turn back around and go to him? Should she throw her aching arms around him and nestle in the Max smell of warmth and Aramis, wallowing in the heaviness of his absence?

Debating, blinking back tears. Wet, shiny eyes wide, seeing nothing. Carol-Anne turned, bumping into a woman, startling her. Carol-Anne mumbled "Excuse me," stumbling over her own feet to get to him. Her feet skimmed the hardwood floor like stones, setting sparks, lighting fires in her wake.

She rounded the aisle, searching out the fedora, the

eyes of Chinese descent. She searched for the brown-
ness of his skin, the love he'd once had. But the rack
in front of Nancy was empty.

Max had vanished, taking her soul with him.

Carol-Anne moved, head whipping, searching
aisles, rounding racks of music. She moved, her high
heels making her journey awkward, missing custom-
ers with her shoulders, her bag, her hips. She spotted
the stairs and forced herself not to make a run for
them. Eyes up, she moved. Found herself on the second floor, more rows of music, no sign of the fedora.

Carol-Anne moved to the rail, looking down. Spotted him at the register. She turned, tip-tapped quickly
down the stairs. Did a quick tango with a couple
coming up. Her heart beating as her foot touched the
first floor.

Flying toward the register, watching as Max
slipped his wallet into his coat and headed for the
door. She dashed ahead, reached for the door that
had just swung closed. Listened to the alarm sound
as the unpaid-for CD set off the system.

"Miss?"

Carol-Anne turned, embarrassed. Nancy forgotten
in her sticky palm. She thrust the CD at the clerk and
left the store. But the streets of Manhattan had swallowed Max whole.

Michele turned away, lying back flat on the bed.
"What is wrong with you?"

Max's brow rose, a simple summation coming off
his lips. "Nothing."

Michele shook her head. Brown curls bouncing
with the motion. "No, Max. Something's wrong . . .
it's like I ain't even here."

"It's nothing."

Michele turned, looked at him. Her eyes reflecting
all she felt, all she sensed. "Something's wrong, Max,

and I wish to God you'd tell me because I can't take your moods anymore."

Max smiled, a small laugh escaping before he could hold it back. He did not look at her, but continued to stare at the ceiling. "You want to know what's wrong? You and me, that's what's wrong."

"What's that supposed to mean?"

"Never should have been, that's all."

"What you mean, never should have been? We've been seeing each other since last year."

Max shook his head, a half-smile on his face. "A week, a month, a year. Don't matter the time. I should have just let it alone."

"Oh, I'm an *it* now." Michele threw back the covers, the strap of her nightgown hastily grabbed and adjusted with quick, agitated fingers. "Well, fuck you, okay? Just fuck you."

Max gave her room for her drama, as Michele whirled around the room, getting dressed, cursing him, breathing hard. As she stood staring at him with hateful fire, Max gave her all the room she needed because he knew that when she was gone, she'd be gone.

And that was all Max wanted. He wanted Michele gone.

Chapter 19

Nadia stood at the living room doorway not daring to enter. She knew her mother didn't want to be disturbed. The music was loud, her mother's eyes were closed, and Nadia knew she was taking time out. *Away from people and things,* was how Carol-Anne explained it to her. Her mother wanted to be alone, but she had a phone call.

"Mommy?"

Carol-Anne looked up, pulled away from the music, from the sound of Nancy Wilson singing. The look in Nadia's eye said there was something to be asked, affairs Carol-Anne didn't want to consider. This was her time. Her moment of solitude. Carol-Anne's eyes drifted.

"I'll fix you something in a few minutes."

"No." A frown creased Nadia's brow. "The phone. For you."

Carol-Anne had not heard it ring, but she had been expecting a call from Mrs. Jones telling her to turn down that music. Loud tonight, louder than she ever played her stereo. Carol-Anne needed Nancy, singing and moaning and gleaning around her like a hurricane.

"Mrs. Jones," Carol-Anne decided, rising slowly as if her bones ached.

"No, Mommy . . . Uncle Max."

Time stood still making the world seem rigid and

unyielding. One second, holding itself, waiting for Carol-Anne to decide if it were good or bad.

Carol-Anne got up and turned off the stereo. Nadia vanished up the hall as she picked up the phone.

"Hello?"

"Hi. It's me, Max."

"Hi, Max."

Silence. Carol-Anne was looking for the right words. But there were none, only what her heart wanted to speak. "I miss you," she told him.

"Miss you, too."

Tell him, Carol-Anne. "Gotta tell you something, Max."

"I'm listening."

"I'm sorry. For leaving you the way I did. I was afraid you'd leave me."

"That was never my plan."

"Yeah, but I didn't know that." She paused again. Gathering the courage to ask all that she wanted to know. "You still love me, Max?"

It was so unexpected, what she asked, how she asked. Like she was seven again and didn't have a clue. Her voice, tiny and unimportant, out there swaying on a limb.

"Yeah."

Carol-Anne smiled, laughed into the receiver. "I knew you did. I want to see you. Really see you."

Her urgency surprised him. That wasn't her style. Carol-Anne would sooner hide in a corner with her wants and needs than speak them out loud.

"Tonight?"

"Yeah, like now."

"Kinda sudden, don't you think?"

She could hear the hesitancy in his voice. "Kinda sudden? I haven't seen you in nearly a year. There's nothing sudden about wanting to see you."

"I was just calling to see how you were doing."

"If you don't want to come, just say so . . . it's okay."

But he did want to see her. "What's the address?"

She threw her arms around him.

Loose, wide, limbs over him like new vines. Carol-Anne, happy, pleased. Laughing, smiling, easy and free. Hugging him tightly in the downstairs foyer; studying him closely with joyous eyes.

"God, you look good," she relinquished. Carol-Anne. Bolder, out there, unafraid. Even the way she looked was different. A new hairstyle that was so sleek and smooth Max was certain Good Ole Tina hadn't had a thing to do with it. Her eyebrows were plucked, the navy blue sweatpants and top fairly new, and her white Reeboks were sparkling white. No more cutoffs, stained T-shirts, those flip-flops she used as slippers. She was looking real good.

She grabbed his hand. "Come on, Nadia's half asleep."

His eyes took in everything, the thickly carpeted steps, the wood trim and balustrade, shiny and as gleamy as the hallway in his parents' home.

Max took in the Queen Anne chair in a pastel blend of mint, peach, sienna, and green, the new cherrywood end tables with the seductively curved legs. The brass torchère and table lamp. The area rug over the hardwood floor. The fireplace, unlit, was surrounded by creamy marble bordered with intricate carved wood. And there to his delight was Nadia, leaned into the corner of the sofa, eyes drooping and half asleep.

"Nadia?"

Her eyes struggled to open, growing wide when she realized who it was. He heard the joy in her voice as she sat up, getting to her feet. "Uncle Max."

Her feet carried her fast toward him and Max did what he always had, bent down low to receive her.

But she had grown, and Max stumbled to keep his balance.

"How's my favorite girl?" he asked, hugging Nadia tight, one dooky braid stabbing him in his left eye.

"Fine," she sang, happy and excited. She pulled back and looked him squarely in the eyes. "You gonna stay with us?" It was all Nadia wanted to know.

"Stay? I just came to visit."

"But there's lots of room now."

Max looked up at Carol-Anne, expecting her to look away, as usual, but her eyes mirrored Nadia's. Max stood, eased off his coat.

"Put this away for me, okay?"

Nadia grabbed the bulky wool and raced off to find a place for it.

"Good night, baby." Carol-Anne closed the door, turning toward Max. "Let me give you a tour."

She showed off her kitchen, opened the freezer to show it was frost-free, pointing to the two trays of ice. "A real freezer."

Carol-Anne showed him the bathroom with the shiny white tub and sparkling shower head. She showed him all the closet space and her brass-framed bed. She made him sit in her new chair and pointed out the fireplace. "Next Christmas I'll have garlands and Christmas stockings hanging from that bad boy."

Max was impressed. "This is a great apartment. With some real nice touches."

"I love it here. God was definitely looking out for me."

Max studied her, shaking his head. "You're looking as good as I always knew you could."

"Thank you. Been paying real close attention. Real close. A full three hundred and sixty, that's what I've been through . . . bad apartments, scary nights. Being mean to my kid." Carol-Anne shook her head. "A real nightmare, you know?"

But he didn't. "How's Nadia doing?"

"Better, thank God. I was so busy trying to protect her that I ended up hurting her, real bad. I'm in therapy." She hadn't meant to let that slip. Hadn't meant to share how deep her descent had been. Carol-Anne laughed, a little. "Me, in therapy. A lot of issues I had to deal with. Am dealing with. It's helping me."

"To?"

"To live my life better. Not be so afraid. So scared. Do better for me and Nadia, that kind of stuff. Black people have this idea that you have to be stark raving mad to get professional help. I wasn't insane, wasn't crazy, just kind of lost. Off track."

"You sound better."

"Oh, from the last time, when I went screaming out of your apartment, snatching up things like your place was on fire." Her eyes sparkled. "Yes, I'm much better than that . . . but it was all part of the process, of getting to a point where I had no choice but to seek help, which was always a hard thing for me to do."

Carol-Anne shook her head. "Our worlds are so different. I couldn't get with your life without losing a big part of mine. But it's different now. I mean I actually threw out that lousy-ass chair and you know how much I loved that chair."

Max looked around him. "You threw out the chair?"

"Gone, in the garbage."

"This is a new Carol-Anne."

She nodded. "Absolutely. For the better. I look around me and like my life." She studied him, saw that he was leery. "I'm not the person I was. I'm almost brand spanking new. I like me. For once in my life I really can get with who I am. So if it's the old Carol-Anne you're interested in, sorry, but she's gone."

"Don't be."

"Don't be what?" she wanted to know.

"Be sorry. If you like you, then that's all that matters."

Carol-Anne laughed. "I'm just trying to make my life better. And it's working. Six months ago, two months ago, I could have never been this honest and this straightforward with you. The secrets are out of my life now. Everything is up front. My life is working, for me, not against me. The key word is *working*. And you know the saying, 'if it ain't broke, don't fix it.' "

"Haven't given up meat yet, have you?"

"Meat?"

"Yeah, become a vegetarian."

"No, 'course not."

"Then there's still hope."

"For?"

"For some of the old Carol-Anne. I don't mind you being brand spanking new, but there were things about the old Carol-Anne I loved."

She didn't miss the emphasis.

He didn't stay the night. Kept a respectable distance.

Carol-Anne didn't press him. Didn't press him about a few moments in the sheets; gave no protest when he glanced at his watch and decided it was time to go.

She hugged him once, hard and tight, at the front door. Let him slip easy out of her arms, no formal plans made. No discussions about getting back together.

Carol-Anne let him go, not knowing if he would return. Was not afraid that he wouldn't, allowing herself the hope that he would. Her cards had been laid on the table tonight. Whatever happened next, would be on Max.

*   *   *

"All rise."

Carol-Anne stood, smoothing the navy skirt, forcing her hands at her sides. She took a quick look around the courtroom, didn't see Jeff. A part of her expected Jeff to be a no-show.

The judge surveyed her courtroom before sitting down. Her eyes wandered to the defense table and saw that it was empty.

"Will Counsel approach the bench?"

Martin Kisco released his pen and it clattered to the top of the hardwood desk. He took measured steps to the bench and leaned his head in close to the judge, whose breath smelled of peppermint. He remained there for a few seconds, his head nodding at the judge's words, and then turned around, coming back to the table.

"She's gonna adjourn. A summons will be sent to Jeff—"

Carol-Anne cut him off mid-sentence. "A summons? He's already been summoned and he still hasn't shown. This is our second trip down here."

"This will be his last chance. If he doesn't appear to answer the summons, then you will be awarded judgment. Only problem is, you'll have a piece of paper saying he owes you, but then you have to find out on your own where his assets are. Where he works, bank accounts, things like that."

"Well, I know where he banks."

Martin smiled crooked teeth toward her. There was a stain on the lapel of his suit jacket and the collar of his shirt was dirty. "Chances are that account's been closed. Jeff is obviously no dummy. I'm sure he has obtained legal counsel in this matter. He knows he has to pay you eventually, but right now he's buying time. So that by the time you do track down his assets, you won't be able to get them, with the exception of maybe current child support. All that back pay will have to wait. And if there are other liens, then you have to wait in line."

"Shit."

Martin nodded, no longer smiling. "Exactly."

A new court date was given. Three weeks later. Jeff showed up with two lawyers. Carol-Anne's worst fears were realized as her life with Jeff before and after Nadia was entered into court records. The judge convened at lunch and came back with her decision.

Jeffrey Gadson was indeed the father of Nadia Clarice McClementine, and he was ordered to pay Carol-Anne Phyllis McClementine thirty-nine thousand eight hundred fifty dollars in back child support and four hundred dollars a month commencing the first day of May, nineteen hundred and ninety-five.

The lawyers converged. A settlement was offered. Jeff was willing to pay a one-time back payment of twenty-five thousand dollars. *Take this lump sum now or try and get all that money in dribs and drabs later,* her attorney told her.

"You'll have to find all his banks, pay marshal fees to execute the liens. There may be other liens ahead of yours. Nadia may have kids of her own by the time you see all that money . . . Twenty-five thousand isn't a lot of money, and yes he's getting away with over thirteen grand, but if I were you, I'd take that offer. He has a cashier's check ready to hand over."

Pay off all her bills. Have a little nest egg. Carol-Anne agreed.

Carol-Anne unbuttoned her trench, letting the chill spring air inside, cooling her. She walked down the court steps, the check snug inside her bag.

Her mind was busy thinking of her next stop. Thinking of her life forever inscribed in the records of the Family Court of the County of New York. Thinking of the time Jeffrey had spent on the stand talking about their life to the judge.

But mostly Carol-Anne's mind was on how the truth had set her free.

Chapter 20

Carol-Anne walked down Fifth Avenue, eyes blank, thoughts scattered, Sherlyn's office one block away. She walked with just enough self-awareness to keep a grip on her Coach bag and to feel the soft cushion of her new Avia sneakers. Carol-Anne was aware of how stiff her new denim jeans were and heard the faint crinkly sound of her new leather jacket.

She walked, head forward, unseeing, rehearsing words in her head. Today, she would tell Sherlyn she would not be coming back.

Carol-Anne dropped the blind back in place and took a seat. She had been pacing since she arrived.

She did not want to be here. She wanted to be home, with her stereo on low and curled up on her love seat. Starting the book she had picked up at Barnes and Noble.

"I know you don't want to be here, Carol-Anne. I know you have a million and one things to do and can't wait to get home, but we've only got twenty-five minutes more, okay?"

"Okay."

"We were talking about your mother and father."

"Don't know why. He's dead and they never married. End of that story." God, she felt well. She felt whole and at peace. Carol-Anne felt so good she hadn't wanted to come today. Had called to cancel but Sherlyn insisted that she come.

She felt alive and filled with purpose. Back on track. She would finish school, get her degree, and then find a higher-paying job. There were no more reasons to see Sherlyn.

"When they were together did you sense any intimacy or kindness?"

That was easy to answer. "No."

"So when he came and picked you and your sisters up, there was no physical contact between them? A peck on the cheek? A handshake? A smile?"

"No. My mother would disappear into her room until we left."

"Your father ever mention her, talk about her?"

"Only to ask how she was treating us. Can we talk about something else?"

"Like?" Sherlyn asked.

"Like how much longer do I have to come here?"

Sherlyn smiled. "It's only been a few weeks, Carol-Anne."

"Thirteen to be exact."

"So you think you're ready to abandon therapy?"

"I feel I've come around."

"To?"

"To my old self. The old Carol-Anne is back." But she felt uncomfortable saying it.

"The idea is to move forward, not go back," Sherlyn said with a slight smile.

"But I am moving forward. I'm working on my relationship with Nadia. I'll be going back to school. Got a wonderful apartment. I think I'm doing great."

"Well, it's good you feel better. But weren't your concerns a little more than school, and a new place?"

"No, not much."

"Let me ask you this. If you had gone from your first apartment to Convent Avenue, would it have changed anything about what happened Christmas morning?"

"Well, yeah."

"Such as?"

"Well, I'd have had space for a Christmas tree."

"But if you didn't have money for gifts, would that have made much of a difference?"

"I wouldn't have felt the way I felt."

Sherlyn laughed. "That must be some apartment. I must remember to come upstairs and look at it again next time I'm at Aunt Corinthia's."

Sherlyn was being sarcastic and Carol-Anne did not appreciate it. She had been feeling so good; why was Sherlyn trying to take her off her natural high?

"It's not just the apartment."

Sherlyn nodded. "Go on."

"The space would have given me room to think more clearly."

"So you're saying that having a bigger place would have allowed you time to think things through."

"Yes."

"Okay, so let's say you had the bigger place and you thought things through and you realized you could have charged some Christmas gifts for Nadia to make her Christmas better. And you did all that and Christmas went off without a hitch. Could you honestly say there was nothing else that needed attention?"

Carol-Anne paused. She knew there was a right answer and a wrong answer. Knew she had to give the right answer even if it wasn't the truth. "Yes, that's what I'm saying."

Sherlyn threw up her hands. "Okay . . . Look, nobody's holding a gun to your head to be here. And I never see somebody who doesn't want to see me. If you want to stop coming, then stop coming."

She did not expect that from Sherlyn. It caught her by surprise. "Kinda feel it's like a condition to keep the apartment. Like your aunt don't want any crazy people in her house."

"Number one, you're not crazy, Carol-Anne, and number two, my aunt doesn't think you are. You are under no obligation whatsoever to come back after today. If my aunt asks, I will tell her. More than likely she won't."

"So I can leave today and never turn back?"

Sherlyn nodded. "Absolutely. I will mark your file closed and that will be that."

It was what she wanted, wasn't it? Her life was fine now. But Carol-Anne felt uneasy. The parent thing had her going, Sherlyn was steering her toward something important and a big part of Carol-Anne wanted to find out what.

She looked at her. "You think I should come back."

"Wonderful thing about therapy is the client decides when enough is enough, so it don't matter what *I* think."

Carol-Anne looked at her watch. There were still twenty minutes left to the session. "I always knew my father loved me," Carol-Anne began, settling back into the chair. Sherlyn nodded, picking up her pen.

Twenty minutes later the teakettle blew, signaling the end of the session. Carol-Anne's last session. They stood at the office door, pensive and hesitant.

"Thank you for everything, Sherlyn." Carol-Anne hugged her, hard. Harder than either of them expected. She pulled back, her eyes wide and wounded. This was what she wanted, right?

"You take care of yourself," Sherlyn told her, opening the door for Carol-Anne's exit.

It wasn't a new thought. It was not something that had popped into her mind at the last minute. Carol-Anne had been thinking about it for a while. Wanting to, but unable to actually do it.

Saturday. Early afternoon. Maybe he was home. Maybe he wasn't. Maybe he'd let her in, maybe he wouldn't. No matter. At least she'd stop thinking about it; free her mind through the act of doing. Of going to see Max.

Max's lobby.

Carol-Anne found it hard to believe that she had once called this home. That she had fled the world of doormen and chandeliers, polished shiny floors, and live plants lining the mirrored walls.

She watched the doorman hang up the receiver.

"Go right up."

Carol-Anne stepped into the lobby. The elevator was empty. Her reflection bounced off the brass-paneled walls. She did not check herself. Did not fiddle with her hair, adjust her jacket; run a finger over her eyebrows to smooth them. Carol-Anne was not concerned about her looks.

Ping! The doors slid open. Carol-Anne stepped out onto the hard shiny floor, looking up the hallway. Max was waiting, concern all over his face.

"What's wrong?" he asked.

Her smile dimmed a watt. "Nothing. I just came by to see you."

"Oh," was the only word he could find.

Carol-Anne looked at the closed door behind him. "Can I come in?" But she knew the answer.

"Company."

"*Oh,*" It was her time to be stunned. She looked away. Tried to find what else she could get out of her impromptu visit. Tried to find the questions she would need answered late in the night as she sat in her living room with its pretty furnishings in her new silk pajamas. Carol-Anne tried to find the questions she would ask herself after the fact. After this fiasco.

I got them, she wanted to tell him. *I got all those things you wanted me to have. Look at me, don't I look different, better? Aren't I stylish and pretty and*

*polished and refined? Aren't I a sophisticate? Can't
you tell that woman in your bed that I'm back and
she has to go? That I'm standing right before you the
way you've always wanted me to?*

*Can't you love me again? Love me the way I never
wanted you to love me back then?*

"Serious?" she asked, affected.

Max looked away.

Carol-Anne kept talking because silence would
bring her tears. "Have no right asking that, do I?"

She considered the day, considered how bright and
sunny the world was outside the hallway in which she
now found herself. Carol-Anne considered how the
birds were still chirping in the early afternoon and
how the whole city seemed alive with life and spring-
time. She could not see herself going back out there
into its beauty. Could not see herself leaving here, but
knew she had to.

Max shook his head. "It's different now, Carol-
Anne. You got to know it's different now."

"Different, yes. But I guess what I really need to
know is if there's a chance it will ever be the way it
was."

"It can't be the way it was. We're different people
now." Max would not look at her.

How different? was what Carol-Anne wanted to
know. Her difference was a good difference, a better
difference. She didn't know about his difference.

Max had a new life now. Love was no longer a
requirement. Companions were his thing and Max
had quite a few. They came when he called and stayed
away when he didn't. Carol-Anne's departure had al-
tered his perspective.

He wasn't willing to risk Carol-Anne doing another turnabout on him. Yes, she had changed, and
on the surface the changes looked real good from
where he was standing. But there was more to this
than where she shopped and how her apartment was

decorated. It went deeper than that and Max wasn't sure those issues had been resolved. A big part of him didn't want to invest the time to find out.

Max touched her shoulder, wanting her to understand.

"I've tried that route, Carol-Anne. Not what I'm about anymore."

She eyed him sideways. There was a hostility in her voice that surprised neither of them. "Oh, what, you a player now?"

His eyes slid away. "Let's just say I'm living my life."

Carol-Anne took a moment to study him. To remember the tall handsome sweet chocolate man who had loved her once. And when she'd had her fill, she turned and walked away.

She didn't expect the funk to descend. Thought her months of therapy would shield her from the depression that had claimed her by the time she got home. Without fanfare Carol-Anne collected her daughter from Mrs. Jones's apartment and took her upstairs. Made Nadia a lunch of peanut butter and jelly on Wonder bread. A glass of cold milk on the side and apples cut into chunks.

Without words she moved around the kitchen, wishing Tina was up the hall. Carol-Anne needed to talk.

Nadia was watching her mother with wide eyes.

Carol-Anne closed the cabinet door. Went to the fridge, jar in hand. Was about to place it on the shelf when the label caught her eye. Peanut butter. That didn't go in the fridge, the milk did. Where had she put the milk?

Carol-Anne felt Nadia's stare. Looked at her and laughed. A brittle sound that shattered her soul.

"Silly me, right?" Carol-Anne asked, going to the

cabinet and retrieving the jug of milk. Searching but not finding peace in the midst of her chaos.

Carol-Anne drew her feet up under her. Her body was wedged against the back of her Queen Anne chair. The music on her stereo was so low it was barely a garble of noise coming through her speaker.

For most of her life Carol-Anne had wanted money. Money was always her biggest problem. Not love, not a career. Not raising a child. Money, her main concern. She had always felt that if she had enough of it, all her problems would be solved. Life would be a piece of cake. But she had money now, over twenty grand sitting in Citibank, and life was no more perfect or fixed than it had been before.

There were improvements. She was financially freed up. She had a nice apartment. Nadia had what she needed. But that was as far as the Money Brick Road took Carol-Anne, and there was more out there, so much more.

More than nice clothes and bills paid on time. More than lobster and steak dinners and new shoes. More than the big color TV in her living room and the white silk robe she put on after her baths.

More than three new trench coats in black, oat-meal, and taupe. More than the cab she took home from work once a week. More, so much more.

Where was the love?

Couldn't buy that. Couldn't go to court and have a judge decree it for you. Couldn't make a man you love love you back. Couldn't unchange his heart. Money couldn't fix that.

Carol-Anne used to hear rich people say money couldn't buy you happiness. Now that she had a little bit, she knew they were absolutely right.

And that's what she wanted. All she wanted. Not money, but happiness. Not money, but love.

She picked up the phone. Dialed Max's number.

Listened to the first ring, scared of the second one. Heard a click on the third, his recorded voice coming at her, *"leave a message at the beep,"* and opened her mouth.

"I love you." It was all she could say, all that she wanted him to know.

Across town, Max kept his eyes on the television screen.

Julie sat up, looked at him. "Who was that?"

"Nobody."

"Must be somebody," Julie supposed, curious about this woman who had confessed her love. "I mean, she did say she loved you, Max."

Max was mute. Julie settled back next to him. Found herself feeling sorry for the woman, whoever she was. Julie herself had once told Max that she loved him. She didn't see him for a whole month after that.

Nowadays Julie kept her feelings to herself, content with the times Max saw her and made do when he was not around, her emotions locked in a box to which Max had the key.

Chapter 21

Carol-Anne removed the two tacks from her cork board, the photo of herself, Nadia, and Max falling into her electronic typewriter.

Forty years old. Nadia would be ten soon. Time moving swiftly around them both. A smooth kind of fear crept up into Carol-Anne's heart. She was afraid of being alone.

Change. Life was full of it. Nadia had spent a weekend at Jeff's and enjoyed it. She came home excited, laden with gifts, talking nonstop about what her and her daddy did; in love with him in a way all little girls should be.

Except Nadia was no longer little. Nadia was going on ten and that thought scared Carol-Anne. She found herself worrying about the life skills she had shown her daughter. Of being so afraid of love that she ran it straight out her front door. Carol-Anne found herself wondering if Nadia would repeat her mistakes.

All too soon her baby would be a teenager and dating. Already there were love notes from boys in school. Simple questions, asking Nadia if she liked them or not, asking her to check yes or no. The one Carol-Anne had found had not been answered yet and that had been a relief.

More times than not she found herself talking with Nadia, introducing the birds and bees in a language she hoped Nadia would understand. Using words like *vagina* and *penis* and *sperm* and *eggs.* Words like *periods, menstruation. Pubic hair,* which Nadia had already begun to sprout.

Her daughter. Growing every day, it seemed. Nadia was nearly to her shoulder. Her chest was forming round little orbs, five minutes from a training bra. Nadia had legs like a young colt. Her face was elongating, her chin thinning, her cheeks sharpening.

Nearly ten, Nadia had a long waist and narrow hips. Her derriere was high and round. Every time Carol-Anne looked at her she tasted fear in her mouth. Boys would want Nadia. Would Nadia want them back? Had Carol-Anne given her daughter enough sense of self-worth and self-love to overcome that tricky, risky period of fourteen through seventeen, when a boy's love could outwit every single *don't* a mother ever told you? When words like *keep your pants on and your dress down* fly out the window because your body wants to solve the mystery of sex, wants to go all the way.

A beauty Nadia never possessed as a toddler was coming into her like a fire. Every time Carol-Anne looked at Nadia she saw more and more perfection, from the color of Nadia's velvet dark skin to the watermelon-pink of her lips.

A natural beauty.

Boys would want her daughter. Would want her Nadia. Soon Carol-Anne would have to sit her daughter down and open her mouth and speak words. Speak words her mother never spoke to her. Carol-Anne would have to talk to Nadia about sex. About pleasure and what the touch of a man could do. She would have to open the world up to her daughter as she never had before.

"Morning."

Carol-Anne jumped. She did not hear him coming. Did not see him peek into her cubicle.

"Oh, Cliff, you scared me." She smiled. Glad for the intrusion.

"Thinking hard, huh?"

Carol-Anne pulled back from her desk. "Yeah, a little too hard."

" 'Bout?"

Carol-Anne saw his wide wide nose, his thick brown lips. Tried to find the beauty there. Could not. Her hands could circle his waist and nearly touch, she was certain. Clifford would never look sexy in shorts, or a Speedo. His yellowish light brown skin would never entice her tongue, her hands. Carol-Anne looked up at Clifford, feeling a brief sadness. Too bad, it was obvious he liked her.

"Kids," she offered.

"Kids?"

"Well, kid. One . . . Nadia."

"Problems?"

"No."

"Oh."

Carol-Anne waved him off. She didn't want to discuss it. "Never mind, Clifford. Never mind."

"You like Joe?" he asked, switching channels.

"Joe?"

He smiled, lips spreading, nostrils flaring so wide the tip drew down. "Yeah, Williams. Joe Williams."

"Sings jazz, right?"

"Traditional, yeah."

Carol-Anne shook her head. "Not really," and wished him gone.

"He's gonna be at S.O.B.'s."

Carol-Anne didn't respond.

"Tomorrow night," Clifford went on to say. "Interested?"

Carol-Anne shook her head no.

Telling Tina about Cliff was easy. Now as the tale faded, Carol-Anne reeled back, laughing. "No, I don't think so."

Tina gave her a skeptical look. "Carol-Anne. I've never known you to be hung up on somebody's looks."

"Never dated an ugly man. In my whole life, never."

"Beauty's in the eye of the beholder."

"Yeah, well behold this. Clifford is ugh-leee."

"Can't be that bad. You went out with him in public."

" 'Cause it didn't mean anything to me."

"And it does now?"

"I don't want him getting the wrong idea. If I say yes, he'll think I want to get with him or something."

"Going to a jazz club ain't getting with nobody . . . I think you should go."

"Why's that?"

" 'Cause you ain't been nowhere or done anything since the last time you went out with Cliff. And ain't nobody else knocking on your door."

"Maybe I don't want nobody to knock on my door."

"Carol-Anne McClementine, this is Tina you talking to . . . Max is gone, sweetie. Time you moved on." Tina's advice, painful, was the type Carol-Anne was in no mood to take.

Carol-Anne waved her hand. "Ain't about Max."

Tina nodded. "First right answer you gave all night. No, it's not about Max and never was about Max. It's about you. About Carol-Anne and what she gonna do with the rest of her life."

Carol-Anne grew tense. "Not in the mood for your sermons tonight."

Tina heard the warning in her voice. Did not care. "Truth is truth."

Carol-Anne stood up. She didn't have to sit there and listen to Tina preach. This was her place. She picked up her glass and headed up the hall, dismissing her. "Gotta do the dishes; you staying?"

Tina rose from the love seat. "Better be on my way . . . CeCe, come on. Time to go."

Carol-Anne did not walk her friend to the front door. Did not issue a goodbye. Carol-Anne put the stopper in her sink, squirted dish detergent, and turned on the faucet. She slid her hands into the hot sudsy water, listening for the sound of her front door closing.

For all her knowledge, for all her optimism, what did Tina have to show for it? Tina hadn't had a real man in years. A few dates here and there that had gone nowhere fast was all. Carol-Anne resented Tina telling her how to run her life.

She looked up toward the ceiling, seeking a God she could not see in a world that didn't seem to understand her. *Give me credit. Somebody, somewhere, give me credit for what I've done, not for what I need to do.*

Validation. For a long time Carol-Anne had given it to herself when nobody else would. But the load was getting too heavy to bear. She was trying harder than ever but it seemed nobody could see that. All they did was pick at her faults.

Carol-Anne wanted kudos. Acknowledgment for her struggles, for how far she had come. Needed it to take her life to the next step. The next step where her life would be full and complete and she would be loved.

Changes. Carol-Anne's life seemed full of them, like Tina finding a man at a time when Carol-Anne couldn't.

The phone call came weeks after. Weeks after Carol-Anne wanted her best friend gone. Tina's voice was bursting, excited, rushed. Eager to share her find.

"Met this guy today." Four words, simple words, detouring their friendship. The end of their togetherness. A man coming into their midst, putting the brakes on their relationship.

Carol-Anne sat, phone pressed to her ear, listening to Tina gush about the man she'd met. Carol-Anne listened to infinite details. *Taller than me, pretty brown skin, cute smile.* Dimples! *Teeth like Denzel. Dressed real, real nice. Sweet. Oh, God, but is he sweet. Gave me his number*—the ultimate test of a man's intent—*and he called meeeee . . .* Serious enough. Calling the same day they met.

Wants to take me out this weekend. Memorial Day weekend and sister friend's got a date! Major holiday and he wanted to spend it with Tina, a sure sign of something real there. A real potential.

Sister friend's got a date! All too soon her best friend, her run-around-town buddy, her confidante, would be falling in love and wouldn't have any time for her. Carol-Anne would be called on to hold back her envy, hold back her jealousy, and bide her time. Waiting, holding her breath for when Mr. Wonderful was no longer so wonderful and Tina's magic world would vanish.

When he would break dates, promises, and eventually break her heart. Carol-Anne would have to wait, would have to suffer alone. There would be no time for her. No time for Carol-Anne in Tina's life.

Changes.

Life never stayed the same for long.

Carol-Anne closed the foyer door, the smell of Red still heavy in the air. She watched through the frosted pane as the black Legend peeled away from in front of her brownstone. Watched until the red lights vanished from sight.

Above her she could hear Nadia squealing with delight at Cecelia's arrival. Dimly considered whether to do the microwave popcorn and the movie now, or wait until later. Wondered if Tina would be back first thing in the morning as she promised or would pick up her child way past noon.

That's what friends are for, or so the song went. But this was not a Gladys Knight/Elton John/Dionne Warwick/Stevie Wonder lyric. This was her life. The one she had been living since Tina met Carl. Her life, watching Cecelia nearly every weekend. Tina dropping her off Friday nights, coming back on Saturday, full of energy and a man's attraction. Trying to hide her happiness for Carol-Anne's sake.

It was easy enough to pick at Tina, to dissect her new lifestyle. "What about Cecelia? Does Carl ever do things with her, the three of you? You spending all your weekends with him, what about Cecelia?" Carol-Anne asked.

"Carl and Max are two different people, Carol-Anne. Just 'cause Max was willing to play surrogate daddy don't mean Carl has to."

Carl. All that and a bag of chips, as they say. He had eyes like diamonds. They sparkled at you all the time. The first time Carol-Anne had met him, she was afraid to look him in the face because his eyes made her feel as if he were in love with her.

Carl. Forty-two and single. No kids, no ex-wife, and treating her friend Tina royally. Taking Tina places the way Max used to take her. Few flaws except his lack of interest in Cecelia, which was the way Tina preferred it. "I don't want what happened to Nadia to happen to CeCe. I don't want her brokenhearted if me and him break up. My life is my life," Tina reasoned.

Cecelia didn't seem to mind being with Carol-Anne and Nadia most weekends. *Mommy's more fun now. We do a lot of stuff during the week,* Cecelia had told her.

Cecelia didn't have a problem with it, Nadia didn't have a problem with it, and certainly Tina and Carl didn't have a problem with it. The only person who had a problem with it was Carol-Anne.

End of May. One year, one month, since she had left Max.

For thirteen months Carol-Anne had carried his memory like a token in her pocket. Twelve months, beyond full term. It was time to give birth to the memory and expel it from her soul.

On Saturday night Carol-Anne went to Carnegie Hall to see Cassandra Wilson all by herself. She felt self-conscious and totally uncomfortable until the show started. She wandered the lobby, a white wine in hand, no one to talk with and no real place to rest her eyes. It seemed forever before the house lights dimmed and she took her seat.

Carol-Anne felt as if everyone in Carnegie Hall was watching her. Felt as if every sad song Cassandra sang was for her benefit only. Still, she congratulated herself on doing it. On going out alone on a Saturday night. Of getting up the courage to come and sit next to an empty seat, holding her head high.

Afterward she walked Fifty-seventh Street in white palazzo pants and a matching jacket with sheer sleeves. Her white-heeled sandals comfortable for her trek. Her white sequined purse secure in her palm.

Carol-Anne strolled down Fifty-seventh, passing the various cafes—the Russian Tea Room, the Hardrock, and the Motown, which at the last minute she decided to enter.

Standing room only, there were no seats. Carol-Anne managed a seat at the bar, ordered another wine, and spent time studying the huge spinning forty-five hoisted from the ceiling. She sat surprised and awed when Whitney Houston whisked by with her entourage as she exited, leaving a private party up on the third floor.

When her drink was finished, Carol-Anne gathered

her nerve and walked the first floor, eyeing with interest the bluish-green sharkskin suits worn by the Four Tops, the sequined gowns the Supremes once wore.

Nobody was paying her much mind.

She headed for the steps to the second floor, her feet hitting the carpet to the rhythm of "Psychedelic Shack," an old Temptations hit.

Head down, moving to the beat, Carol-Anne wasn't looking where she was going. It wasn't until she bumped someone's arm that she realized her mistake.

Her head jerked around, ready to apologize, but the words got stuck in her throat.

"Carol-Anne?"

"Max." The last person she expected to see.

Awkward silence. She was three steps from the top, he thirteen from the bottom, their pause causing a slight traffic jam as people navigated around them.

They stayed there seemingly for a long time. Mute, staring, unmoving.

"I'm sorry, sir, ma'am, you have to clear the stairs," ordered a waitress.

Carol-Anne didn't know which way to go.

"Going up," she offered to him apologetically.

Max pointed down. "Men's room."

They both moved in the same direction twice. To the right. A quick dance on the carpeted steps. Max laughed nervously. Carol-Anne smiled at the stupidity, as well.

"Look, I'll go left, you go left," Carol-Anne offered and soon the way was clear. Carol-Anne continued up the steps, smitten, afraid. Consumed.

She felt foolish about everything. From her white-on-white ensemble right down to trying to go out alone on a Saturday night. She felt the urge to snatch the fake diamond clusters from her ears, to snap off the costume jewelry from her wrist. Carol-Anne felt like ripping the sheer white sleeves off the shoulders of her jacket. Felt like kicking her white kidskin sandals off her feet. For a second she felt a need to muss her perfect hair and swipe the red lipstick from her lips.

Carol-Anne felt like a true fraud.

Is this really who I am? I don't even know anymore. This isn't me. This is the me Max wanted me to be. But for what? Have my clothes or new lifestyle brought him one second closer to me? Here I am, out in the middle of a Saturday night, dressed like some ghetto princess, and for what? For whom?

Who the hell am I?

A tear gathered in her eye before she could stop it. Carol-Anne realized she had been rooted to her spot at the top of the steps. She felt people pushing past her and knew she'd have to move. But she didn't want to.

Carol-Anne wanted to strip off her clothes and break down and cry. Wanted to disown the fraud in her. Was giving it serious thought when the waitress told her what she already knew.

"You have to move."

Max splashed cold water on his face and took the paper towel offered. Upstairs Julie waited, seated at their table by the open balcony.

Carol-Anne, alone on a Saturday night.

Carol-Anne looking so radiant and so pretty in her summer white. So perfect, so unflawed. So loving. Loving him still.

Max swallowed.

A year and he still missed her. Still could find the love for her so easily. No woman able to undo what Carol-Anne had done to him, for him. No woman bringing forth a love fire.

He missed her. Sometimes so much he ached.

It had been fun for a while. Being a player again. His new life drawing kudos from his friends. All his women pretty, attractive, matching his lifestyle. Exciting, like being in his twenties again when love didn't figure in his equation.

But Max was tired of the game.

He was getting too old for it. Even Samone was tying the knot. He had gotten the invitation in the mail. Her dream coming true.

But what about mine?

Max was tired of running around. Tired of sleeping with a bunch of women. It wasn't what he wanted anymore. He wanted love. Carol-Anne still loved him. He hadn't been sure before. Hadn't trusted that message on his answering machine those weeks back.

But tonight he had seen it for himself.

Carol-Anne loved him, maybe like she never had before. His absence had not killed her love fire, it had only made it stronger.

Max looked at himself in the mirror again, wondering what he was going to do.

Move.

Carol-Anne moved. She circled the veranda as if her soles were on fire. A need to finish what she had started forcing her around the walkway with agitation.

Yes, she would tour the upstairs quick and then go down and out the front door. She would finish this night she had started. And when she got home, she'd never have to do it again.

Carol-Anne reached the first floor and realized she had to make one more stop. The two drinks had filled her bladder. She didn't want to go downstairs. Didn't want to give Max a chance to see her in her fraud attire, but nature was calling and it left her no choice.

Carol-Anne hurried down the stairs.

Max came out of the bathroom.

They came face-to-face.

Carol-Anne wanted to give a simple smile and

move out of his way. Didn't want her need to show any longer than it had done already. Had convinced herself she would do just that, smile, say "excuse me," and move past him.

Move beyond him.

Get over him. Forget him.

"You still love me?" The words out of his mouth stunned her. But how could she, the urban fairy princess all dressed for a ball, possibly tell him anything but the truth?

"Oh, yes," she half sighed, glad to say it. They started off hugging, which soon became squeezing. Kissing rounded off their act. People passed them, the handsome gent, the pretty lady locked in their passionate embrace. Strangers eyeing them in typical New York style, with all of five seconds of their attention before they were looking elsewhere, moving on.

Max wanted to leave Julie. Wanted to leave her sitting upstairs waiting for his return. Carol-Anne talked him out of it, prodding him up to the second floor of the Motown Cafe.

"What do I tell her?" Max had asked as Carol-Anne rubbed lipstick off his lips with her fingers.

"The truth."

"The truth?"

Carol-Anne had smiled. "Yeah. Tell her that I love you."

Max went back upstairs, taking a seat. He didn't say it right away, instead nursing the remnants of his Remy, which was now mostly ice water. Max sat back, waiting for Julie's eyes to meet his. His face lost its smile as he leaned in close, taking her cool hands between his.

"I have to go now, Julie. I'm sorry but I can't see you home. I'll give you cab fare, but I can't stay."

Of course she frowned, concern coming out of her

in waves. The love she had tried to hide now all over her face.

"What's the matter?"

"Nothing bad, just that I have to go—now."

"Why?"

Max paused, wondering if he could say it, if he could manage the words without hurting Julie too badly, without risking her having a scene right there on the second-floor promenade of the Motown Cafe.

His eyebrow raised, his eyes drifted to the side. "I have to go because Carol-Anne still loves me . . . I'm sorry." Max stood, took a fifty from his wallet. Eased it under the platter of fried sweet potato chips. Walked away.

Max kept walking even as the crumpled bill bounced off the back of his head. His pace was even. He refused to run, ready for a fist in his back, a spiked heel in his shin. Soon enough he was down the stairs and outside, the cab door wide open and Carol-Anne in the back.

He got into the yellow pumpkin, he and Carol-Anne racing uptown lightning quick.

Max leaned Carol-Anne against the foyer wall. Kissed her easy and soft. Carol-Anne held onto her moan, not wanting to wake Mrs. Jones.

Her whole body throbbed.

With much effort, Carol-Anne took his hand and on tiptoes headed up the stairs. Quietly she slipped her key into her door and took off her shoes. Max, following suit, did the same.

"Shhh . . ." she whispered as they moved down the hall.

A floorboard creaked and Max chuckled, soft and low against her neck. One body they moved toward her bedroom. She didn't turn on lights, liking the shadow and the warm, breezy darkness.

She closed her bedroom door.

Max pulled her close to him. Her heat matched his fire as their bodies met, rubbed, enticed. His fingers eased the buttons of her jacket through the eyelet. The lace bra was luminescent in the darkness. With care Max took off her jacket, unzipped her pants, was gentle with her, like the first time.

She stood before him, Urban Fairy Princess Carol-Anne, her prince arriving unexpectedly. She stood still, picture perfect in lace bra, wispy panties. Her soft belly no longer firm but seductive enough above the satin to entice his tongue.

His tongue. On her flesh.

His nose, against her groin.

Her body moist, opening, throbbing for life, for him. For the man she could love again. Large warm brown hands moved onto her waist, up toward her breast. A breast that ached for his touch.

Lips on her quivering stomach, thumbs against her lace-covered nipples. Max on his knees before her. Had she died and gone to heaven?

"Mommy?"

Carol-Anne trembled, not wanting to stop what had begun. Not wanting to move away from Max's hands, his tongue of fire.

Raps on the closed door. "Mommy?"

Nadia, not asleep. Awakened by the sounds of her moans? Max's laughter? They both froze as the knob turned one way and then the other. Carol-Anne let go of her breath. Yes, she had locked it. Locked it in case Nadia awoke.

Nadia had.

Carol-Anne pulled away from Max, reached for her white silk robe, gathered it around her, tying it tight, calling out to say, "Just a minute, Nadia. One sec."

Max stood, making a half-circle as he tried to ease back from the passion, his need of Carol-Anne now halted by her daughter's arrival.

Carol-Anne turned quickly, gathered her discarded clothes off the floor, forced them into her closet. She eyed Max with critical inspection, wished away his erection making a tent of his loose soft slacks. Went to the door and opened it.

"Hi, baby, what's wrong?"

Nadia eyed her mother with caution, studied the darkness of her room, the man standing behind her. Knew without knowing. Those talks coming back to her filtering through the darkness. Something in the air, a kind of fuzzy energy seeping from the room.

"Just Uncle Max," Carol-Anne offered.

His voice came out of the darkness tight and strained. "Hi, Nadia."

There was a long pause before Nadia responded. "Hi, Uncle Max." Nadia turned around and went back to her room. It was a while before Carol-Anne closed the door.

They lay there in her bed, side by side. Carol-Anne's voice was coated in concern.

"Not like her," Carol-Anne said, resigned.

"She's growing up, Carol-Anne. She knows that when Uncle Max stays over it's not like a sleep-over, that other things go on."

Carol-Anne shook her head. "Didn't think she'd make the connection between our talks and what we do."

Max took her hand, kissed her knuckles, laid it aside, all she would let him do. She couldn't make love, not now. Not with Nadia no doubt still awake and listening for the slightest squeak of her bed, the softest moan from her lips. Carol-Anne lay next to Max feeling as unsexual as she had ever felt.

"Her and Jeff are getting along wonderfully these days."

"Oh."

Carol-Anne nodded. "Yeah. That's a part of it, I'm

sure. Probably a bunch of stuff. Puberty, reconnecting with her father. You not being around and then appearing one night in my bedroom and me half-dressed . . . sex. I guess it's about sex."

"You want me to go?" Max asked.

Carol-Anne sighed. "Do you mind?"

Max sat up, reached for his socks. "Mind, sure I do. But I understand." He stood and grabbed his pants. "Not gonna get any rest now anyway, not with you lying next to me in white lace. I'll call you tomorrow. In the meantime, maybe you should talk with Nadia."

"Yeah, maybe I should."

Carol-Anne moved around her kitchen, the peach cotton robe untied over her long nightgown. Nadia sat at the breakfast table studying the back of the Froot Loops box.

Tension so thick it could be cut with a knife.

Sex. The word made Carol-Anne's stomach tremble.

"One or two, Nadia?" Carol-Anne stood at the counter, the bread bag open and her hand inside.

"One, please."

Carol-Anne eased the bread into the toaster trying to find the right words, the correct way to begin. To talk about sex and love. To talk about the touch of a man.

"Guess you were surprised to see Uncle Max last night, huh?" She hated the sound in her voice, the fear that coated every syllable.

"Yeah."

Carol-Anne laughed a tiny bit. "Yeah, me, too." She turned, walked to the table and sat down. Gently she lifted the cereal box away from Nadia's face. Stared until Nadia looked up.

"What we talked about? About sex, it's what two people do when they love each other. And it's what me and Uncle Max do, as well." Carol-Anne swallowed. "Nothing to be ashamed of and I don't ever want you to feel shamed about it."

Nadia's cheeks puffed once, twice. Difficult words trying to make their way out. "What about Daddy?"

Carol-Anne shook her head. "He's your father, Nadia, not the man I love. I love Max. Max loves me."

"Daddy loves you. He tells me all the time."

Carol-Anne's lips pulled down a little bit. "That may be so, but I don't love him. I haven't for a long time."

"He says you do. He says you do but you don't know it."

Carol-Anne wanted to laugh, but held her tongue. "He might think that, Nadia, but that doesn't make it so. I love Max. I have sex with Max."

Nadia eyed her, weighing her next words. "You had sex with Daddy."

Carol-Anne forced herself to move ahead. "Yeah, I did. When I had you, when I loved him. Long time ago."

"No, not then. After. When we all stayed over that time and he . . . and he made waffles." There were tears in Nadia's eyes.

How could she explain it? Carol-Anne wasn't sure, but knew she had to try. She could not look at her daughter as the words came.

"Sex is a funny animal, Nadia. The best and right times are when you love somebody. But sex can get like a need, just like eating. Sometimes you're so hungry, you'll eat the first thing you see. Sex can be like that. That time with your father was like that. It was a need and I sort of ate the first thing I saw."

Carol-Anne risked a look at her daughter. Held her eyes steady. "But you got to remember, the best sex is when you love somebody and they love you back. You should always try to hold out for that kind of sex, not the other kind. Not the hungry-and-take-the-first-thing-you-see kind."

"Why?" Nadia asked her.

An excellent question. *What's my answer? What can I say now?* Sex with Jeff, for the most part, was still good, up until the moment it was over.

"Because love is always best."

"He coming back here?"

"Who?"

"Max."

"Uncle Max."

Nadia pulled her eyes away. "He's not my uncle."

That threw Carol-Anne for a loop. Once Nadia had loved Max with all her heart. Now she didn't like him at all. Maybe Tina had a point. Keep the boyfriend and your daughter separate.

"You're right. He's not. But he loved you like you were his daughter. When you wanted dance lessons, he paid for them. When you needed clothes, he bought them. When you wanted to go to the movies and dance concerts, he took you.

"When we needed a place to stay, he let you stay with him. Max has been more of a father to you than Jeff ever was . . . You don't want to call him uncle, so be it, Nadia. It is your choice. But don't ever forget what that man did for you, you hear me?" Carol-Anne's voice was fever-pitched but nothing in her could tame it. "You hear me, little girl?" She felt an urge to raise her hand, to slap that face wide-eyed before her. Carol-Anne felt a rage at her daughter she had never felt before.

She jumped up from the table before she did her daughter real harm. Nadia sat, tears spattering her bowl of Froot Loops.

The toast popped up. Carol-Anne took it out and laid it on the plate. Sucked her burned fingers, her back turned.

Chapter 22

"*Relax.*"

Carol-Anne wanted to. Wanted to give in to the warmth of Max's hands on her bare back, wanted to let the aromatic body oil being kneaded into her flesh take her away. She wanted to let go of the tension that had been racking her spine since morning when she and Nadia had had their little talk.

But she couldn't.

Not even in the sanctity of Max's bedroom, with Nadia miles away.

Carol-Anne wanted Max's hands to do their magic, to take away the madness and bring back the fire that had been there last night right before Nadia knocked on her bedroom door. She wanted to be hot and wet and wanting. Wanted to pant and moan and groan against him, but couldn't.

The hot bath hadn't relaxed her. The champagne, seeing Max naked for the first time in almost a year, hadn't. All Carol-Anne could think about was reading Nadia the riot act about how she was to think of Max.

His hands moved over her lower back, thick fingers massaging the base of her spine, nudging bones, soothing muscles. Carol-Anne closed her eyes, sighed a little.

"Yeah, that's it."

His voice fell upon her like rain, soothing, refreshing. Carol-Anne laughed. "Say that again," she murmured.

"What?" Max wanted to know.

"Anything. Shakespeare, the *Daily News*, the Holy Koran. Don't matter, just as long as it's your voice."

"Two. Four. Six. Eight. Ten. Twelve."

Carol-Anne shook her head. "No, don't stop."

"Fourteen . . ."

"Ooh."

"Sixteen, eighteen, twenty."

She peered at him from over her shoulder. "Your voice. It's something, you know that?"

"I've been told."

"No, I mean it. Right up there with Isaac and Barry."

"Don't forget Vaughn."

"Ah, yeah, Harper. WBLS. 'The Quiet Storm' . . . I used to lay awake at night listening to his program, thinking serious time about you."

"Missed me?"

"Oh, Max, more than you'd ever know. Didn't think I'd ever see the day."

He eased onto her back, his mouth close to her ear. Holding his weight, giving her a gentle pressure.

"What?"

Carol-Anne sighed. Feeling him hard and warm against her spine. "This. Me and you, here like this."

He laughed against her neck, the sound vibrating into her soul. "Love's a funny thing." He eased off her, turning her onto her back; staring down at her with soft eyes.

Max kissed her eyes, the space on the top of her nose. He moved his fingers through her short hair, leaving her scalp tingling.

"Better?" he asked.

Carol-Anne closed her eyes and nodded.

"Good."

Max took a breast into his hand, cupping it, palming it. Working the nipple to a head. Carol-Anne reached down and touched him, her hands engulfing his balls, massaging them gently, one against the other. Max moaned.

She licked his chest, teased his nipple with her teeth. A spasm went through him that made her smile. She did it again, parting her thighs as his drifting hands found her wetness. Slippery wet. Sticky wet. Wanting wet.

He rubbed the head of her clitoris with his thumb. Carol-Anne arched against his hands, eager and anxious. He slid one warm finger deep inside of her and her uterus contracted around it hard. Deep.

She wanted him.

Carol-Anne pulled him on top of her, but he paused. Reached to the nightstand and retrieved a condom. Seconds ticking as he slipped it on. Carol-Anne thought of Jeff and his double condoms. Wondered if Max had taken the same precautions.

On her. His hairy chest against her breast the best medicine. Lifting up, poised. The tip of his penis nestled a quarter inch between her lips. They fluttered around him like butterfly wings.

Carol-Anne resisted the need to push against him. She wanted to savor the moment, the pause as her juices flowed over the head of his latex-covered penis.

Loving him. Him loving her, the best sex.

She moaned, whispered the word *now*. With a gentle push, he dipped an inch. Hurting her, but it was a good pain. Her hands found the arch of his behind, held on and forced him deeper. Another inch he went. Carol-Anne felt faint. As though she couldn't breathe. As though she would die. Didn't mind.

Another inch. She could feel his heat, the weight of him inside of her. She licked her lips and moved against him. This wondrous thing called love sex. Her daughter wanted to deny her this, this ultimate pleasure?

"More," she begged, driven mad, beyond reason. One hard push, one long slow hard push, and he was home. Her vagina contracted around him, fierce and brisk. Like machine-gun fire they moved through her, about him.

Her voice was a harsh whisper. *"Don't move."* He felt too good right where he was, too good to risk losing the spot he was in. "No, *don't*," Carol-Anne asked as she felt his buttocks twitch beneath her fingers.

A searing flash of pleasure ripped through her like lightning. Carol-Anne's eyes squeezed shut as the pleasure hit its plateau and she came in a searing flash. Came in the arms of the man who loved her.

Carol-Anne's arms hung over the edge of Max's bed. Her naked body cooling in the afterglow. Max was in the kitchen making them a snack. She looked around her, seeking out the familiar, closing her eyes to the reality of being here.

Nadia. Her thoughts drifted.

Carol-Anne didn't want to go that route. The pre-adolescent daughter at odds with her momma's boyfriend. Not with Max, the man who had treated her better than any man ever had. The daddy she had known when there was no Jeff.

The nerve of him to fill her daughter's head with false hope. Carol-Anne could just imagine the tales coming off his lips. Make-believe stories of when they would be a family again.

Carol-Anne knew why Nadia had bought into it so easily. For a long time there had been no Uncle Max. There had been no surrogate daddy. The good times had vanished like he did.

Nadia didn't know that her mother had left Max. Nadia only knew that Max was gone from their life and life got rotten after that. It was easy for Jeff to fill the void. What little girl didn't want a daddy?

Carol-Anne rolled on her back, eyed the clock. She would be going home soon. And when she did, Max would be right beside her. Nadia would have to get over it.

Nobody was going to deny Carol-Anne Max. Not even her daughter.

"Nadia?" Carol-Anne peered around her front door. "You dressed?"

"No," came her daughter's voice.

"Well, go put something on. Max is here." Carol-Anne dropped the *Uncle*. Nadia didn't have to call him Uncle if she didn't want to.

"Hi, Nadia," Max called out.

There was no response. Carol-Anne gave him a pensive look as the sound of Nadia's closing door reached them. "I'm sorry."

"It's okay."

She pointed across the hall. "Go ahead into the living room. I'll be back."

Carol-Anne did not want to do this. Did not want to play bad cop now. She had enjoyed being with Max and did not want to take anything from the memory. But she couldn't let it slide. She wasn't sure what she would say as she tried Nadia's door, surprised that it was locked.

"Nadia, open up, it's me."

Carol-Anne wasn't sure how she would lay out her words, what her tone would be while she waited for the lock to be turned. She didn't want to yell or scream or threaten. She wanted Nadia to understand.

"Nadia," she said as evenly as she could.

"Justa men-net." That tone. That intolerable annoying tone was a new flavor in her daughter's voice. A new tone Nadia was using more and more with her. Full of preteen annoyance and the insinuation that mothers didn't know anything and didn't have a clue about how *they* felt. Nadia, no longer her little girl. Nadia moving all too fast toward the great divide where mothers and daughters clashed and collided and hardly saw eye-to-eye.

It would be years before they would come together. Years down the road before they accepted and respected each other for who they were. Those good moments, special times of being mother and daughter, already vanishing in the thickness of adolescent emotions and hormones surely on their way.

She hadn't even gotten into her daughter's room and already things were sour. Carol-Anne twisted the knob again, her voice less patient. "Now, Nadia."

Carol-Anne pictured Max in the living room. Imagined him sitting feeling like an intruder. It wasn't how she wanted Max to feel ever again. She blamed her daughter for it.

The door swung open; Nadia's back was turned as she picked up a red Converse sneaker. Her daughter, her little muffin, was standing, jeans two sizes too big dripping off her hips, barely clinging to the wide elastic band of her Calvin Klein boxer shorts. The yellow T-shirt just as large, just as droopy, falling off one arm.

Grungy homeboy.

Nadia's father had bought her these clothes. These hoodlum-run-around-the-streets-Gangsta-rap-wannabe attire. Jeff bought her these because Carol-Anne would not. Nadia was a little girl, not some roughneck boy from around the way.

Carol-Anne hated that outfit and Nadia knew it.

She took a deep breath. "I want to talk to you." Nadia didn't look up, but continued the business of tying one red Converse sneaker.

"Nadia, I said I want to talk to you."

"I'm listening." That tone again. Carol-Anne's hands clenched. When had she lost her? When had Nadia slipped away and been replaced by this evil little monster?

But Nadia wasn't a monster. Nadia was her daughter.

Her voice hissed like a snake. "Stand up and look at me." It brought Nadia to attention. Her eyes, hurt and moist, were fully upon her mother.

"Let's get one thing straight." Carol-Anne didn't want to start this way, didn't want to start off defensive and negative. Wanted her words to be a soft buffer between their anger. But it was too late now. "You are nine years old, you understand? Nine. Not fifteen, not twenty-one, but nine. You are a child, in my house, living under my roof. I am your mother. Not your friend, your homie, or your pal. My house, my rules. When you are grown and on your own, then you get to do your thing."

Carol-Anne pointed her finger. "Number one, when an adult speaks to you, you will speak back. Number two, take them big-ass sloppy boyish clothes off your skinny little narrow behind. And number three, you don't have to like anybody I bring in here, but as long as they respect you, you *will* respect them back, you got that? Now you change those clothes and come out here and say hello to Max. You understand me, Nadia Clarice McClementine?"

Carol-Anne took a breath, waiting for an affirmative.

She got it. "Yes, Mommy." Carol-Anne turned and walked out of the room. Feeling like a mother. Feeling in control again.

Five minutes later, Nadia drifted into the room like smoke. Her eyes turned downward, her face long. She glanced at Max beneath half lids, finger to her mouth muffling her greeting.

"Hi, Uncle Max."

"Hi, Nadia."

She looked to her mother, embarrassed and ashamed. Not daring to leave until she was told.

"You can go," Carol-Anne instructed, leaning

back against the sofa, watching her daughter's departure with a careful eye.

Carol-Anne wanted Max to spend the night.

Max didn't think it was a good idea.

He kissed her nose at her front door. "I know you're out to score Brownie points, but I think we should hold off on that for a while . . . let her get used to me being around again."

She held Max easy by the waist. "Gonna miss you."

"I'll plan something for the three of us during the week. See what's doing around town. See how it goes. Take it from there." Max's face was pensive. "Don't want to rush her, y'know?"

Carol-Anne smiled, looking up at him. "You're so good, you know that?"

There was nothing more exhilarating than a summer night at Lincoln Center. No one could resist its allure, its festivity. Banners advertising Mostly Mozart, the Met, and the New York Philharmonic flowed in the warm night breeze. The Metropolitan Opera House, Avery Fisher Hall, and the New York State Theatre sat fixed and majestic around the open plaza. People strolled around and about the large fountain, recessed lighting coloring the spray that sparkled into the night air.

There was an open-air theatre nestled in the back toward the northwest. In the summer free concerts were given there. This was Max, Carol-Anne, and Nadia's destination. The three of them moved up the Lincoln Center Plaza steps. Nadia's eyes were everywhere at once. So many people, milling about, sipping drinks, lounging around the edge of the fountain. Elegantly dressed men and women entered the halls of the Metropolitan for a night of opera. The lobby of Avery Fisher hall was dim, its doors locked.

Across the street the huge glass windows of

WABC-TV displayed their logo, a circle with the number seven inside.

They made their way past the fountain, the breeze surrounding them in a fine mist as they went by. They moved through the tree-lined walkway, the folding chairs already half-filled with people. They let Nadia choose the seats, settled in, ate their picnic dinner, and waited for the show to start.

Tonight's program was a dance troupe from West Africa. It was all Nadia could do to stay in her seat.

The dance lessons had stopped. Even after Carol-Anne was financially able to pay, Nadia said she didn't want to dance anymore. A fair talent at best, Carol-Anne still believed Nadia would have done well in dance.

Now as Nadia sat between them, head moving, shoulders shaking, Carol-Anne wondered if she would change her mind, would want to return to the Dance Theatre of Harlem to continue her studies. Carol-Anne wanted to ask her, but there was still tension between them.

Nadia had been moody and sullen on the trip over. Had balked at taking Carol-Anne's hand as they crossed the street. "I'm not a baby. I can walk by myself," she had uttered.

A fact that Carol-Anne was hard-pressed to remember.

Up to her shoulder already, her daughter was a stone's throw from standing eye-to-eye with her. Her little girl was changing so rapidly and swiftly.

The first number ended. Nadia sat back, her two palms meeting, making loud applause. "Man," she said, to no one. Not to Max who was seated on her left or her mother who was on her right. "They are something. Man."

Neither Max nor Carol-Anne responded. They had been walking on eggs around Nadia since Max picked them up. Max not saying any more to Nadia than hello.

"They were so good," Nadia piped, excited, eager for the next number. "Weren't they?" she asked, her eyes looking straight ahead. Max nodded, Carol-Anne murmured, "Ahem." She felt strange sitting next to her daughter, reins handed over, Nadia deciding things.

Nadia bent her head, studying her program. Max looked at Carol-Anne, Carol-Anne looked back, mute. Tense. Max smiled at her, but the joy didn't quite reach her soul.

Max closed the cab door, turned and headed up the brownstone steps. He did not want to go inside. The evening had not turned out the way it was supposed to. Nadia still had few words for him.

Nadia was distant and cold. Looking at him with hooded, sometimes hateful eyes. Max didn't know this Nadia. He only knew the little eight-year-old who had approached him that day long ago in the ice-cream parlor. Who had liked him the minute they met.

Max knew only the movies he had taken her to, the times he had baby-sat her, their hours of playing Monopoly on the living room floor. Max knew only the hugs and kisses she used to give so freely and the brightness of her eyes when she used to look at him. Knew only the joy in his heart at the way she used to say *Uncle Max* as if he were the greatest person in the world.

This Nadia was so different. This Nadia who had taken his gift of a night of dance and not so much as said thank you. This Nadia who sat down and ate cheeseburgers and fries Max bought for her at the diner, but would not even look him in the eye. Who didn't want him there.

Max and Carol-Anne had spoken few words the whole night, cautious and careful of Nadia between them, not wanting to offend by showing their feelings. Playing it smooth, playing it light the whole night.

This Nadia did not need him. This Nadia wanted him gone.

"You coming, Max?" Carol-Anne asked from the top step.

"Yeah." But everything inside of him was telling him he should just go on home.

Nadia went to her room and closed her door. No good night, no thank you, no nothing. Carol-Anne dropped her bag onto her sofa, stood, arms folded.

"We tried it your way. Now we're gonna do it mine," was her final decree as she went to change her clothes.

Carol-Anne moved around her kitchen, her white silk pajama top and bottom swishing. She dumped ice around the bottle of champagne. Cut up chunks of Gouda and wine cheese. She arranged wafer-thin sesame crackers, laid the cheese knife on the linen cloth. Carol-Anne retrieved two tulip glasses and put them in the center of her sterling silver tray. Gathered it into her hands and headed for the living room, perfume drifting behind her.

She entered her living room, set down the tray, asked Max to pop the cork as she went to her CD rack and found Nancy Wilson. She dimmed the torch lamp, took the glass of bubbly from Max's hand, and settled close beside him.

Carol-Anne took a sip, laughed at the bubbles that burst around her nose. Looked at Max. "Good, huh?"

"Yes, very good," he responded, his eyes fastened on the living room doorway.

"She won't come in here."

Max put down his glass gently. Looked perplexed. "Don't even know her anymore."

"Caught me by surprise, too. Never thought that Nadia would change like this. So busy looking after me, I didn't even notice her." Carol-Anne closed her eyes, leaned her head back. "I love this song."

"One of my favorites, too."

"Played it a lot when you were gone," Carol-Anne confessed.

Max slipped his arm around her shoulder. "Did you now?"

"All the time, it seemed. Playing it, feeling sad. Missing you."

"All past now."

Carol-Anne took his hand, kissed the back of it. "Thank God."

"We got a wedding to go to."

"Whose?"

Max swallowed. "Samone's."

Carol-Anne sat up, looking at him, surprised. "Getting married?"

Max nodded. "Yep. September twenty-first."

"First day of fall."

Max nodded again, close-mouthed.

"How you feel about it?" Carol-Anne asked.

"How can I feel about it? What she always wanted."

Carol-Anne shook her head. "Don't think I could ever do that."

"Do what?"

"Marry a white man." Carol-Anne turned, her arms sliding around his waist, smiling up at him. "Like my chocolate too much."

Max moved his hand over her hip. "Satin, nice."

"Bought it with you in mind."

"I like."

"Do you now?"

"Oh, yeah." But his eyes were still fastened on the door.

"Relax, Max," Carol-Anne said, turning his head to kiss him. But he couldn't. Couldn't relax. Couldn't make love.

Wouldn't stay the night.

Chapter 23

Pacification.

Carol-Anne watched her mother gather up the crayons and remove the coloring book from the table, her face clouded with worry.

"Guess my baby is growing up. Ain't never known her not to want to color her granny a picture." The hand landed gently on top of Nadia's head and Carol-Anne watched in horror as Nadia shook away from it.

"Stop, Granny." The tone which Nadia used was an affront to grandmothers everywhere and Carol-Anne just knew the back of her mother's hand was about to meet the softness of Nadia's cheek. But when her mother chuckled, tucking the crayons and coloring books into the kitchen drawer, it was all Carol-Anne could do not to chastise her mother for letting Nadia get away with such behavior.

"Nadia, you don't talk to your grandmother like that. Now you apologize."

"No, no. It's all right, Carol-Anne. She is growing up and coloring is for babies, right, sweetheart?" her mother decided with a wounded smile.

"Yeah, Granny, sure," Nadia said, bored.

"Well, now, I don't have none of them video games you like to play but maybe you'd like to play me a game of checkers. You know your granny loves checkers."

Sullenly Nadia shook her head no. Turned toward her mother. "Can we go now?"

"We will go when I say we can go," Carol-Anne said hotly.

Nadia sucked her teeth, rolled her eyes. Her arms were folding tightly over her chest when Carol-Anne's palm made contact with her face.

"Don't you ever suck your teeth at me, you hear me, Nadia? I will knock you into the next world if you even think about doing it again."

The tears, a mainstay these days, arrived. But Carol-Anne was not impressed or sympathetic. "And you better dry those eyes of yours before I give you something to really wail about."

"Carol-Anne," her mother pleaded.

"No, Momma. You don't know what Nadia's been like these last few weeks. I swear she ain't gonna live to see ten if she keeps it up."

"That true, Nadia?" her grandmother asked, concerned.

"She's mean, Granny. She's mean and hateful and—" Nadia broke off.

"No, baby, your momma may be a lot of things but she ain't mean. She just wants what's best for you . . ." Her grandmother reached for her. "Now you come on. I tell you what, why don't we go in the living room and watch a little TV, what you say? Find something nice for us on the television."

Nadia pulled out of her embrace, getting up from the table. Her body trembled with unspent rage. "I don't want to watch TV. I don't want to be here. I want to go to my daddy's house."

Carol-Anne jumped up but her mother held her by the wrist. "Let her be, Carol-Anne. Just let her be."

Carol-Anne looked into the eyes of the woman who had never allowed her such luxuries and could not believe it was the same person.

How many backhands had she received for simply

laughing at the dinner table or not brushing her teeth fast enough? How many times had her mother beaten her for leaving a sock on the floor or forgetting to put a box of cereal away?

Who was this woman before her now so full of compassion and understanding? Where had she come from?

"I never got away with anything like that, Momma."

"Well now, Carol-Anne, you are not Nadia and Nadia is not you."

"Well now, Carol-Anne, you are not Nadia." Her voice was raw, as were her eyes. She clung to Max hurting with a new pain. "That's what she said to me."

"Your mother didn't mean anything by it, Carol-Anne."

"Oh, but didn't she, though? What the fuck's that supposed to mean? What? Nadia's too good and I'm not good enough?"

Max had no answers for her. Had seen firsthand the way her mother fawned over Nadia and the sometimes cool response she gave her own daughter.

"All my life, all my damn life, I was never good enough for her." She turned in his arms, a finger pointing at her chest. "What I ever do that was so unforgivable? What I ever do but try to love her because she was my mother?"

"People are funny sometimes, Carol-Anne," Max said softly.

"We not talking about people. We're talking about my mother who's supposed to love me and care about me."

"I'm sure she loves you."

"Oh, yeah? Well, I sure can't tell."

Max looked down at her, wishing a hundred things for her. He did not know her pain; his mother had always treated him with love and kindness. It was a while before he spoke.

"Maybe you should talk to her."

"About what? What am I supposed to say? Momma, why you treat me so bad?"

Max sighed. "It's a start."

"She won't answer. She never answers. She just folds herself up in a big old impenetrable ball of self-ishness and you can probe and probe but she never lets you in."

"When was the last time you tried?"

"Tried what?"

"Talking with her."

Max's question threw Carol-Anne for a loop. She searched her brain and could not find a definite answer.

"Long time ago, I'm sure."

"So it's been a while," he said evenly.

"Yeah."

"Maybe it's time you tried again."

"You don't know what she's like, Max. What my life's been like. She'd never do it, talk to me. Not the way I need her to."

"Won't know till you try. You've come a long way, Carol-Anne. A real long way. Can't leave no stone unturned now, you know what I'm saying? Even if she refuses to answer, you owe it to yourself to at least try."

"She won't," Carol-Anne said, resigned, but Max knew that in that moment Carol-Anne was willing to try.

Clarice McClementine's smile faded when she opened her door and saw her youngest daughter minus her grandbaby.

"Where's Nadia?" Miss McClementine asked.

Carol-Anne was slow to answer. "With my friend Tina." Her mother turned away and Carol-Anne closed the door. Dutifully and with a heavy heart, Carol-Anne followed her mother to the kitchen.

"Made her chili. Big pot. Figured she could take some home with her. You know how she loves her granny's chili."

"I'll get some before I go."

It had been nearly a decade since Carol-Anne had come to her mother's apartment without Nadia. It didn't take a genius to figure out what Carol-Anne wanted. After so many years of mutual silence, Carol-Anne wanted to talk.

But Clarice McClementine had spent a lifetime not speaking, decades upon decades of keeping things to herself, hoarding life's incidents like a troll beneath a bridge.

Carol-Anne knew this as she sat at her mother's table, Nadia's absence picking scabs on old wounds that had never quite healed. Nadia had been the buffer, the go-between for a mother and daughter who had never come to terms. Who both held on to their opinions of the other and had come to tolerate each other for the sake of a child. But Nadia was not here now and there was no salve to numb what had always been.

"Momma?"

"Yeah," her mother answered, picking up the dishcloth and wetting it beneath the faucet.

"I saw a therapist."

"Therapist, for what?"

Carol-Anne wished it had been for a bone in need of fixing instead of a spirit in need of healing.

"For my head."

Her mother turned, glaring at her. "A shrink, Carol-Anne?"

Carol-Anne swallowed, nodded. "Yes, Momma, a shrink."

Her mother turned away abruptly, dismissing her. "Don't know why folks always running off to strangers to tell their troubles. I've had troubles all my life and I ain't never looked to nobody to help me fix them."

"But I'm not you, Momma." Carol-Anne said those words so softly and full of pain that she might as well have shouted them, because the effect was the same. The silence of the kitchen solidified; sides were drawn in an emotional war about to begin. Years in the making, like the rains after the dry season, it would be torrential and without mercy.

Carol-Anne shifted, stilled. Opened her mouth and asked the hard question. "How come you never loved me?"

Clarice McClementine paused from her stove-wiping. Tossed the wet cloth into the sink and turned toward the child she had never wanted to know.

She pulled out a chair, sat her bulk down wearily. Took a moment to figure words in her head. Sighed. "It wasn't that I never loved you, Carol-Anne." Her voice was gentle. "Just never wanted you." There was a kindness there that Carol-Anne had never heard, spoken with such bitter words.

"Had every intention of going to see a man up on a Hundred and Thirty-seventh Street. Back in them days there was no clinics a woman could go to. Now, if you were rich and white, you could fly to Mexico. But I wasn't. I was poor and black with three children underfoot."

Her mother sighed, looked away. "Your father insisted you be born. Linda couldn't have no babies and I could. Said it was my duty to let you live . . . for a whole two weeks we argued over it. It was hard enough with your three sisters.

"Couldn't see how I could have a married man's baby. See, that was the thing. When I had your sisters your father hadn't married yet and though it was still frowned upon, it happened. But you . . ." Her mother's eyes accused her, laid the blame upon her shoulders. "You happened after he married Linda." The fire faded. "Didn't see how I could hold my head up and have you, too."

Her mother rose, went to the stove. Opened the lid and picked up the large wooden spoon. Stirred, filling the kitchen with the smell of chili peppers and tomato sauce.

"But your daddy insisted. Said you were a gift from God. Your granny was against it. Called me every name in the book and then some. Said I'd never amount to anything." Her mother chuckled, took her seat. "Some days I think she was right.

"One day I decided to go to the man who could undo what me and your father had done. Put on my coat and everything, headed for the door—but I couldn't turn the knob. Was like my hand wouldn't work. Musta stood there a good twenty minutes trying to leave. Realized I couldn't.

"When your father came by I told him what I had tried to do. He held me for hours. Thanking me, kissing me, praising me for my gift to him." Her mother's eyes were damp. "That was the last time we ever hugged, touched. The last.

"My belly grew and your sisters knew another baby was on the way. You came a little early. Couldn't find your father. Spent seven hours in labor alone. Your daddy nowhere to be found, my own momma disowning me. It was a hard time for me. I was laid up in that hospital moaning and screaming, nobody came. I was alone like I had never been before."

Her mother wiped her eyes. "And when you finally arrived, a-kicking and a-screaming, I hated you. Hated your father. Felt like he took a big chunk of me with no plans of returning it." Her mother shook her head. "Never could feel about you the way I felt about your sisters." Clarice looked down. "I look at your life and know all the whys. I know all your sorrows 'cause I made them so."

Tears streamed down Carol-Anne's face. Her mother got up and got a paper towel for her. "When you got pregnant with Nadia I felt like you were stamped with all my sins. But I came to love Nadia in a way I never came to love you and I'm sorry, baby. Momma is so sorry."

She reached for Carol-Anne but Carol-Anne was stuck to her chair. A lifetime of troubles explained away in less than five minutes. A lifetime of pain and suffering of which she had no design over, but was simply a victim to.

She did not want her mother's arms. Did not want her mother's apology. Fought against it. "No, don't touch me!"

Her mother sat back down. Wiped her eyes some more. "You hate me? That's fair, Carol-Anne. Never gave you much of myself. Can't ask you to forgive what I've done. Life is about the trenches and I've dug mine deep. But your father loved you. Loved you more than he loved anyone. You was his favorite. You was his pride and joy. Not me, not you sisters, not even his wife, Linda. Was you he loved the most. If you don't remember anything else, you remember he was the one who begged for your life."

Carol-Anne sat there a long time. Stone-faced, the tears flowing endlessly down her cheek. She lowered her throbbing head, moaning into the folds of her arms, needing a daddy who was sixteen years in the grave, a mother who could truly love her.

She didn't know how long she sat sprawled against the table, sobbing, before the pain began to lessen, before her heart and mind came together and found the truth that had been missing from both her and her mother's life for so long.

She pulled herself together, raising her head for the

first time in minutes. Wiped her face and blew her nose.

"You're wrong, Momma," Carol-Anne said, soft and dismal. "You're the reason why I'm here. Daddy didn't do that. You did. You can't explain that away 'cause there's nothing to explain. It was your choice and you chose me."

"No, it was your father."

"No, Momma, it was you."

Her mother looked away. Her face caved in and a moan escaped. Clarice McClementine covered her face, ashamed and full of sorrow. She wept intense, strained tears. The simple gift of truth relieving her of the burden she'd carried for too long.

For the first time in a long time Carol-Anne felt the need to hold her. To open her heart to the woman who had given her birth. She stood, moved around the back of her mother's chair. Eased her arms around her shoulders.

"I forgive you, Momma. I forgive you. We make choices, some right, some wrong, and I forgive you the choices you made."

The moment released itself, and Carol-Anne pulled away. She took her seat and faced the person she could never recall hugging.

There was a pleading in her voice, the need to share the burden, pull back the curtain on the sorrows in her life. "Life was hard for me, Momma. Real hard. Days when I didn't know if I was coming or going. You made me feel so guilty about so many things in my life."

"I know and I'm sorry."

"For a long time I felt like nobody and nothing."

"I know you did," her mother said softly.

"I mean, Claudia, Lucy, and Sandra seemed to do everything right and I could only do things wrong."

"It was different for your sisters."

"Yes, it was," Carol-Anne said with conviction.

"I couldn't tell you before. How could a mother tell her child she wasn't wanted? I knew I was harder on you than any of your sisters, but I did love you, Carol-Anne."

"Did you, Momma, did you really?"

"More than I ever told you. More than I ever showed. You was my last child, my baby. The last thing me and your daddy done together. No way I couldn't love you."

Clarice McClementine got up and went to the stove. Stirred the pot of chili and searched her cabinets for a bowl. Took care in spooning the rusty-brown potion into the container. Wrapped it tight in a plastic bag and placed it before Carol-Anne. "Put enough in there for you and Nadia. Think I put in a little too much chili but it'll be fine with some rice."

Carol-Anne rose quickly, her arms going around her mother. "Thank you, Momma."

"For what, baby?" her mother asked, perplexed.

"For opening your heart . . . to me."

Carol-Anne walked down 110th Street, her head full and on the brink of overload. So much to settle, so much to accept. Her mother did love her but could never show it. How do you keep that kind of a love a secret? How do you hoard your emotions so tightly that someone could go for decades without knowing?

Clarice McClementine had loved Carol-Anne like she had loved Carol-Anne's father, unable to show it or tell a soul. Forty years of denying her heart. Forty years of feeling one thing and doing another, building a fortress so thick and wide it was nearly impenetrable.

But Carol-Anne had done it. Had broken through her mother's hostility and brought forth the answers she'd needed all her life. Carol-Anne had gotten to the source of who she was and how she came to be.

Chapter 24

"Hello, Miss McClementine."

Carol-Anne stood, hand on the doorknob, looking down at Jeffrey Gadson, Jr., Alex behind him. Carol-Anne wore gray slacks, a white short-sleeved sweater and gold sandals. She held the door, taking in her ex-lover's sons, her daughter's half-brothers. Was startled to see how much Jeff junior had changed since the last time she saw him.

Taller. Handsome. Looking much like his father. Jeff junior. Thirteen years old now. A teenager with peach fuzz over his lip, civility in his eyes. His tone, respectful, so unlike the first and last time they had met two Thanksgivings ago.

Jeff junior and Alex had not understood the hows and whys of the dark-skinned little girl coming into their midst. Did not comprehend Nadia laying claim to their father. They had perceived Carol-Anne and Nadia as intruders. Thieves of their father's time and attention.

But time had changed their perceptions. Nadia's induction had taken nothing away, but added to their lives. They had come to like the idea of having a little sister, had grown fond of Nadia.

"Hello, guys." She moved back, making room. "Come on in."

It was Nadia's tenth-birthday party.

Carol-Anne spied the gifts piled in Nadia's father's arms. Quickly counted four.

"Go on up, Nadia's waiting."

An understatement. Nadia had been waiting for over a week. Gushing to friends about her party and how her brothers were coming, about how cute Jeff junior was.

Nadia. In stockings, two-inch heels, and a baby-doll dress and curls. Waiting by the top of the stairs, smiling, laughing. Her short dress showing too much thigh as she twisted in anticipation. Nadia hugged Jeff Junior. Swatted Alex on the arm, in love with her big brothers.

"Are we early?" Jeff asked, moving ahead of her up the stairs.

"No. Right on time."

Carol-Anne moved through the cluster of white ribbons tethered to helium balloons that hung from the ceiling like spaghetti. She left Nadia to her guests and went back to the kitchen to check on the few pieces of chicken not quite done.

"He here?" Tina asked from the kitchen table, the spoon moving briskly through the large bowl of potato salad.

"Yeah. Go sneak a peek," Carol-Anne suggested. Tina was back in less than a minute.

"About right," Tina decided, settling in at the table.

"Meaning?"

"Like you said. You ain't never dated no ugly men."

She wasn't sure if he was going to come. Would have understood if he had not. Nadia was treating Max with politeness but not much else. It was only at Carol-Anne's insistence that Nadia invited him at all.

"How's it going?" Max asked, closing the foyer door.

"Nadia's having a grand old time."

"Jeff here?"

"Yeah. Him and his sons."

Max took a deep breath. "Let's go."

Old Dirty Bastard's "Ooh Baby, I Like It Raw" boomed from the living room. Two dozen boys and girls danced on the hardwood floors. Max stood there, watching Nadia dip and swirl, her short dress swishing and twirling as she did. Max watched as Nadia navigated her pelvis and hips as funky as the reggae songstress Patra doing the butterfly. Nadia's face, serious and intense with every dip and every turning in and out of her legs.

Max watched the boy Nadia danced with. Watched the mesmerizing pleasure that dotted his young smooth face as Nadia's little waist snatched him up in the rapture. Carol-Anne shook her head, uncomfortable. Her daughter was dancing like a video whore.

"The culture," Max offered, reading her thoughts.

"Whose?" Carol-Anne asked, her arms folding, face pensive.

"It's her party. Just a dance. Lighten up." Max knew his words were moot. Carol-Anne had been in a fierce war with her daughter for weeks.

"She's excited, Carol-Anne, her first real party. Give her a little slack, please?"

She could not ignore the gentle nudging of his eyes, the way his hand felt upon her arm; let go some of her tension with a sigh. "You're right," she said after a while.

Max's eyes drifted about the room, noticed a brown-skinned man in the corner. Even with a quick glance it was easy to see this was Nadia's father. Max had no idea how this meeting would go, but steeled himself for the worst as Jeff spotted him, came over and extended his hand.

"You must be Max," Jeff said with an easy smile.

Max's brow rose. "Jeff, right?"

"Yeah. Nadia's told me a lot about you."

"I'm sure . . . you have a wonderful daughter."

Jeff took at glance at Nadia. "Yes, I do."

"Auntie Anne?" Carol-Anne turned and saw Cecelia standing excited behind her. Cecelia, a duplicate of her own daughter with the curls, the stockings, and the heels. The short dress.

"Yeah, CeCe?"

She indicated Alex, who was lurking behind her. "He wants another hot dog."

"Well, if Alex wants another hot dog, tell Alex he can help himself. It's in the kitchen."

Cecelia turned, taking his hand. "Come on. I'll fix it."

Carol-Anne watched them leave. Little girls learned early.

Nadia appeared, wiping her forehead, panting for breath. She stood there, a second in time, looking at Max standing next to her father. Her face went through various metamorphoses until it decided on a smile. She stood on tippy-toes, leaned up and kissed Max's face. "Hi, Uncle Max."

"Happy birthday, Nadia."

She surprised Max by taking his hand. "Come, let me introduce you to my big brother." Carol-Anne watched them slip through the crowd. Turned to Jeff senior.

"She has a crush on little Jeff."

Jeff nodded. "Yeah, I've noticed. I laid down the law with little Jeff. He knows that Nadia is his sister."

But as Carol-Anne watched Nadia introduce Jeff junior to Max, her eyes bright and shiny, she only had one question. "Jeff junior knows, but does Nadia?"

Over. Done. Her apartment a disaster zone with cups and plates of uneaten cake. Helium balloons drifting around the ceilings, the dying ones riding invisible breezes like ghosts up to a haunting.

Up the hall and behind a closed door, Nadia, Cecelia, Jeff junior, and Alex were involved in Nadia's brand-new Sega Genesis video game.

"They're fine," Max insisted, but Carol-Anne gave a look that said she knew better.

"I was ten once, Max. That's when it all starts. Curiosity about kissing a boy, one thing leading to another." Carol-Anne folded her arms, head shaking.

"Jeff *and* Alex know better," Jeff senior added as he worked on putting Barbie's Dream House together even though Carol-Anne insisted Nadia was beyond Barbie and would never play with it.

Tina appeared, wiping her damp hands quickly against the sides of her jeans. "Well, your kitchen is done. And so am I." She looked around at the two men in Carol-Anne's life and couldn't hold back her smile. She turned, sending her voice up the hall.

"Cecelia! Time to go." Fifteen seconds was all the time Tina waited before she went down the hall and barged through the door.

Jeff junior was showing Nadia how to work controls, Alex was reading a comic book, and Cecelia was playing a game on Nadia's computer.

"Let's go, young lady," were Tina's last words as she went out, leaving the door wide open.

Jeff said he was leaving, too, but Carol-Anne asked to him stay a few minutes. "Need to talk to you about Nadia."

The air conditioner hummed and dripped onto the window ledge. The sound of children racing up and down Convent Avenue eased through the glass panes. From up the hall Nadia's voice rose, excited over some minor video victory

Carol-Anne studied the man she had loved so long

ago for all the wrong reasons. Felt a deep need to apologize for it.

"Nadia thinks we're getting back together," she said evenly.

Jeff looked away.

"You've been telling her things, Jeff, that just aren't true and you've got to stop it."

"I didn't mean any harm, Carol-Anne." It was strange hearing her full name come off his tongue. From the time they met he had called her Carol. Only recently had he started using her given name.

"But you are causing great harm between me and Nadia. Nadia and Max. It's not right and you've got to stop."

"She wants it as much as I do."

"But I don't want it. And she wants it only because you want it . . . For ten years Nadia had no father. For over a year she's had Max. I've allowed you back in her life because she wanted it, but you don't have any rights beyond that. My life is my life, Jeff, not yours and not Nadia's. You understand?"

"Just that—"

"Just what? What? You and Adrienne didn't work out? Well, tough, Jeff, 'cause that's how life goes. I'm not in love with you, I do not love you, and I am not coming back."

Wounded. Carol-Anne never thought she'd see that look in his eyes. Never thought Jeff could care beyond his own reasoning. Knew better than to be a sucker for his grief.

"You love Max?"

"Yes. With everything I own, I do. He's been good to me. Been good to Nadia. The first man in all my daughter's life who treated her like she was some-body, something special. Yes, I love Max and Max loves me." Carol-Anne paused. "He loves Nadia, too."

Jeff looked away. "I'll talk to her."

"Yes, you do that. And another thing. No more sloppy hip-hop clothes for her, okay? I got enough to deal with without fighting over what she can and can't wear."

"She wanted it," Jeff said, as if that were reason enough. Carol-Anne realized that Jeff didn't have a clue about real parenting.

"That doesn't mean she gets it."

Carol-Anne watched as Nadia gathered up her opened gifts, stacked beneath her chin.

"Got it?" Carol-Anne asked, at the ready to help her move them to her room.

"Got it." Carefully, Nadia navigated the hall, turning into her room. Carol-Anne followed.

"Some party, huh?" Carol-Anne asked.

"The best."

"Got a lot of nice things."

"I sure did."

Carol-Anne paused, scrunched her shoulders. "So, how does it feel being ten?"

Her daughter looked at her, her eyes luminous and delighted. "So much better than being nine."

Carol-Anne laughed. "Think so?"

"Definitely." Nadia put her gifts on her bed, sat on the edge. Looked down. Looked up at her mother. "Mommy?"

The word itself was so sweet it made Carol-Anne teary-eyed. Her voice was a whisper. "Yeah, baby?"

"Can't love two men, can you?"

Carol-Anne took a slow breath. "No, you can't."

"If you had to choose, who would it be? Daddy or Uncle Max?"

Carol-Anne risked a question of her own. "If you could choose for me, who'd you choose?"

"You don't look at Daddy the same way you look at Uncle Max."

"No, I don't."

"When you look at Uncle Max you get this dreamy kinda look."

Carol-Anne nodded, her heart beating hard.

"When you look at Daddy mostly it's like you're annoyed."

"Your father can tick me off."

"So I guess if I were me, I'd pick Daddy. But if I was you, I'd have to say Uncle Max."

Carol-Anne reached down and hugged her daughter. So hard it took the breath out of both of them. She peered down into Nadia's face, into the beautiful Nubian face, stunned by the wisdom there. "You are so smart, you know that?"

✕

Chapter 25

September 21 dawned bright and sunny. The sunlight dappled through the trees, a sweet breeze blew through the air, and the whole world glowed with the fire of the first day of autumn.

The street in front of Ebenezer A.M.E. Church flowed with women in their Sunday finest, men in polished shoes and suits, and children who wove through the gathered masses, agitated with excitement.

Stretch limousines in pearly gray took up a quarter of the street. The century-old church with its peaked roof and large stained-glass windows was a true testament to the Harlem faithful who had come for generations for worship and fellowship.

"Over there." Carol-Anne pointed, spotting a parking spot half a block away. She fidgeted with the edge of her lavender lace glove, checked the lap of her lavender satin dress. Reached in her bag, pulling out her makeup mirror, checking her makeup one more time.

"You look fine, babe," Max offered as he wheeled the rental car into the space. Carol-Anne had known so that morning as she primped in front of her full-length mirror, realizing that her sheer lavender stockings, lavender lace-covered shoes, and matching lace gloves spoke of a great beauty.

She had known it this morning when Max came

and picked her up, his eyes alight and on fire at the sight of her. Carol-Anne had taken extra care in planning her outfit, going to Lord and Taylor, Max at her side, to pick out the dress and the accessories. For a moment or two this morning Carol-Anne had felt like the bride, had felt that special and pretty, but as Max cut the motor and got out on the driver's side, as he rounded the car to get her door, Carol-Anne was no longer sure.

Samone would be a knockout.

All sorts of visions danced through Carol-Anne's head as she tried to fathom what Samone would look like as a bride. Tight white satin with a long detachable train? Would she go for the Cinderella look with the low-cut lace bodice and a wide hoop skirt that emphasized her tiny waist?

Would her hairstyle be long brown tendrils of curls so tender and silky they looked as if they were made of air, or would she gather up her massive strands, letting a few seductive ones fall around her head like ribbons?

Carol-Anne had been cagey and guarded for the last four days as this day, this first day of autumn, arrived. She could not help but reflect back to that New Year's Eve when Samone's presence had knocked her own importance to Max out the window.

Carol-Anne found herself studying Max intently as they made their way to the church. Wondered what his thoughts were, wishing he would at least talk about it, share his feelings about Samone marrying that white man. About Samone marrying any man.

Carol-Anne didn't have a clue, didn't have even an inkling, as he stopped to hug a short older woman dressed in a peach gown and matching shoes.

"Aunti," Max said, wrapping his arms tightly around the woman, her upper body vanishing into the folds of his suit.

"Max, oh, Max. So good to see you," the woman named Aunti said, pulling back to study him at arm's length, her smile still warm and buttery smooth as she saw Carol-Anne.

Carol-Anne did not expect the hand that touched her arm. Did not expect the smile that shone on her like summer to remain so long. Did not expect the older woman to receive her as if she were some long-lost niece.

"Who's this?" Miss Aunti wanted to know.

Carol-Anne felt Max's arm go around her in a kind of daze. "This is my friend, Carol-Anne."

Aunti took up her hand, squeezing it as if to relay a cryptic message. "So nice to meet you."

Still dazed, Carol-Anne returned the salutation. "Nice to meet you, too," she faltered.

"Aunti, call me Aunti. Everyone does," she said with that sweet smile. She turned, pivoting on the two-inch heels, her face set and unsure. "Odell is around here somewhere," she intoned.

"It's okay, Aunti, I'll catch him later. We better get a seat." Max's feet started moving, Carol-Anne drifting along beside him.

It was a madhouse of walking and stopping and greeting and introductions. Max running into more of Samone's family than Carol-Anne had expected. She was introduced to them all, their names forgotten the moment they pressed on. By the time they got inside the historic church, with its fifty-foot arched ceiling and massive hand-hewn support beams, Carol-Anne felt as if she had just run a ten-kilometer race.

Real flowers bordered every single pew in the place. Carol-Anne found herself counting off the rows, and came up with forty. Up ahead at the altar the awning made of petals looked too perfect to be real. Tall white candles in brass holders twinkled and danced like stars.

The church was packed.

Jonathon, Samone's husband-to-be, stood up front, a similar-looking white man beside him. Carol-Anne watched as he looked around nervously, and checked his watch. Carol-Anne saw a handful of white people in the first row and wondered where the rest of Jon's family was.

"Nice," she heard Max say as his eyes took a sweep of the church.

"Yeah," Carol-Anne answered, her heart beating fast as the music changed and a man's voice boomed from the speakers hidden discreetly around the church.

"I am the light and the way," the voice began. The tall dignified pastor in robes as fine as a king's made his way up the red-carpeted aisle.

And so it begins, came the thought. *And so it begins.*

Samone was an angel.

She was Glinda the Good Witch, she was Isis and Mother Mary and every single beatific woman known to mankind. She was perfect and pure and full of light. Everything about her sparkled, glowed, and shimmered.

Her dress was simple in its beauty, her train barely kissing the floor. Her veil was as demure as a Muslim woman's head covering. Her face was so pure it was hard to see any makeup beyond lipstick.

Samone didn't walk, she drifted, as if on a cloud of love and magic, with so much inner peace she caused everyone watching to weep at her beauty.

Carol-Anne included.

Carol-Anne did not expect tears at the sight of Samone walking demurely down the aisle with her father. Did not expect the flood of emotion to catch her up as it caught up others, but it had.

There was no doubt that Samone was in love with the white man who waited at the altar, whose own eyes glistened with unspent tears. Everyone was touched, no one was left unscathed.

It was, in all senses, a wedding heaven-bound.

"Go ahead," Max said, urging Carol-Anne out of the chair.

"No, Max."

"Go ahead, Carol-Anne."

Carol-Anne dropped her purse into his lap, stood, walking toward the huge dance floor. Lined up with the other thirty or so single ladies, hands eager for the feel of the bouquet in their hands.

Carol-Anne half raised her hand, confident and assured that the bouquet would never make it past the first row of women. She parked herself all the way in the back, with three lines of eager females in front of her. She was certain she didn't have a chance, which suited her fine.

She saw Samone raise her hand, watched her lower it. The bouquet rose again, lowered, as disgruntled women aired their impatience and told her to get on with it. Then the bouquet was leaving Samone's fingers, falling high up into the air, tumbling backward, escaping clawing fingers by mere millimeters. The bouquet seemed airborne for a long time even though it was less than three seconds before it plopped against Carol-Anne's breast and instinct drew her hands to it.

She looked down at the floral arrangement of orchids and gardenias as if it were an alien from outer space. She sensed women turning, moving back and away from her, and soon found herself in the middle of the floor, the bouquet in her hand.

Carol-Anne saw Samone smiling at her, genuine and sincere. Turned and saw Max standing, clapping hard. Found herself side by side with Samone as the photographer took a photo op. Still dazed, still disbelieving, not believing in luck, fate, or destiny, but believing in tall dark handsome men who could love her, Carol-Anne took her seat as Max headed toward the floor, ready to snatch the garter that had adorned Samone's thigh since morning.

There were so many men on the floor that Max became lost in the commotion. Only when his low-powered growl reached her did Carol-Anne realize Max had lucked up. That according to legend, they would be the next to marry.

As Carol-Anne made her way to the chair in the middle of the reception hall, Max standing handsome and dignified, the lacy garter between those strong brown fingers, she finally saw the possibility of making the legend come true.

The possibility so potent, so real, so desirable and wanted, Carol-Anne welcomed it with open arms.

She believed.